THE
FESTIVAL
OF
TRIAL
AND
EMBER

LOGAN MIEHL

Published by Touchwood Publishing.
Visit www.loganmiehl.com for more information about the author, updates, or new books.

This is a work of fiction. Names, characters, places, and incidents are either the product of the author's imagination or are used fictitiously. Any resemblance to actual people, living or dead, or to businesses, companies, events, institutions, or locales is completely coincidental.

Cover by Jenny Zemanek at Seedlings Design Studio
Editing by Catherine Jones Payne at Quill Pen Editorial Services
Book Layout ©2017 BookDesignTemplates.com

The Festival of Trial and Ember by Logan Miehl – 2nd ed.
ISBN 978-0-9978547-4-9

To my dad, Brian. You are the bravest creative I know.
This book exists because of you.

Where dips the rocky highland
Of Sleuth Wood in the lake,
There lies a leafy island
Where flapping herons wake
The drowsy water rats;
There we've hid our faery vats,
Full of berrys
And of reddest stolen cherries.
Come away, O human child!
To the waters and the wild
With a faery, hand in hand,
For the world's more full of weeping than you can understand.

Where the wave of moonlight glosses
The dim gray sands with light,
Far off by furthest Rosses
We foot it all the night,
Weaving olden dances
Mingling hands and mingling glances
Till the moon has taken flight;
To and fro we leap
And chase the frothy bubbles,
While the world is full of troubles
And anxious in its sleep.
Come away, O human child!
To the waters and the wild
With a faery, hand in hand,
For the world's more full of weeping than you can understand.

"THE STOLEN CHILD" BY WILLIAM BUTLER YEATS

PRONUNCIATION GUIDE

Róisín	row-*Sheen*
Cináed	kin-*Ay*-juh
Naoise	*Nee*-sha
Aimsir	*I'm*-shur
Lughnasa	*Loo*-ness-ah

{ 1 }

Many poets, and all mystic and occult writers, in all ages and countries, have declared that behind the visible are chains on chains of conscious beings . . . who have no inherent form but change according to their whim, or the mind that sees them. . . . The visible world is merely their skin. In dreams we go amongst them, and play with them, and combat with them.

- *Irish Fairy and Folk Tales* by William Butler Yeats (1918)

I'm not the type of girl who believes in supernatural creatures. But I'd be lying if I said there isn't something *otherworldly* sitting right outside my window.

Faint tapping on the glass woke me up, and as soon as my blurry gaze fixated on two soulless eyes, all remnants of sleep vanished, replaced by a wild, crazed kind of panic.

Those eyes. Even through the grungy window, with nothing more than a clouded moon overhead, I can see those eyes glow and shimmer with an iridescent blend of colors. As if I'm staring at two oils slicks punched into an otherwise faceless demon.

A puff of respiration sticks to the glass. I've been holding my breath this whole time—my chest pinched in agony— which means the creature must have a mouth. Or a nose. Or whatever demons use to exhale.

If a thin sheet of glass didn't stand between us, I would have felt its breath on my face. The thought tugs hard on my stomach and sends an icy trail of sweat down my back.

Somehow that smudge of fog is impossibly intrusive. I want to wipe it away in one swift motion with the corner of my sheet.

The darkness shifts, and as the smudge is sucked from the glass and back into the air, there's nothing sitting on the other side. Whatever was watching me is gone.

If there was ever anything at all.

My inner logic chimes in like an annoying know-it-all. But tonight I cling to that logic, trying to force whatever just happened underneath my bed as I would do with any other nightmare.

I realize I'm still holding my breath, and I heave out a trembling sigh as I hug my knees to my chest with tight shoulders and clammy hands.

What was that thing? And why was it watching me in the middle of the night?

At this point I know sleep will evade me, like a teasing cat that brushes past you but bolts under the couch when you reach to stroke its back. In foster home #4, I lived with a stereotypical forty-something-year-old cat lady, and her cats were as confusing as a middle school relationship.

Speaking of middle school, my roommate Angie just started snoring. Even after we've shared a room for nearly a year, the noise still freaks me out. Especially when I'm already jumpy as all hell.

My heart quiets back down as I turn from the empty window to watch Angie sleep. She's a foster kid like me, but, unlike me, she knows one of her parents. Granted, he's in jail, and her other relatives copped out of taking her in. Sometimes I hear her crying at night. For being in her terrible-tween years, she's a sweet kid. Which makes hearing her snore like a mountain man even more unsettling.

If I lived in a nicer place, like with the Alberts' in foster home #3, I could close the blinds or curtains on the window. Maybe then—but, then again, maybe not—I could get some sleep around here.

I finally convince myself that whoever, or more like *whatever*, was sitting outside the window isn't coming back, and I lean against the wall, folding my pillow around my head to muffle the snoring. Even with the pillow blocking my view of the window, I can't shake the eerie vibes crawling around the darkened room, pricking my skin like thousands of spiders' legs.

Time moves slower than final period with Mr. Openshaw. Thank everything good I scraped by his class with a C. There's no way I could survive two semesters of calculus.

I reach for my phone, and the screen blinds me. It's still early, but not so early that I have to keep pretending to sleep. Sure enough, I can see a faint pink glow lighting up the sky. I give it another ten minutes before inching one foot after the other onto the cold, wooden floor.

Moving with habitual efficiency, I change into a pair of cut-off jeans and a T-shirt. I tie a light sweater around my waist and pull some socks on while making my way to the door. Angie doesn't stir as I pass her bed, grabbing my backpack and shoes.

Right before I ease the door shut, I glance at Angie, snuggled up with an old, ratty stuffed animal, and try to imagine what my life would look like if I'd decided long ago to take her passive approach to life. How different would things be if I simply let them happen, instead of battling my circumstances at every turn?

I'd still be in foster care, that's clear. Probably not passed around to as many homes, though.

And maybe you'd still live with Darren.

The thought bites at me, reminding me once again of my biggest regret. In many ways, it's what drives me every day. I can't right that wrong, but I can do my best to never lose him the way I did the first time.

I sneak into the kitchen and set my pack down, unzipping it to evaluate my inventory. Two granola bars, a water bottle, and a few dehydrated meals I found in Steve's camping gear in the garage. Steve is the foster "dad" here, never home because he drives a truck.

He also never camps, so I didn't feel too bad about snagging some items from his outdoor stash a few months ago. Sure, the sleeping bag and flashlight add what most would call unnecessary weight to my pack. But when the world is out to get you, you learn to plan for the worst.

I grab a few more snacks from the pantry and shove them into the lumpy backpack. After I tug my sneakers on and pull my dishwater-brown hair into a loose ponytail, I look at the time on my phone and decide to take the bus to the library.

Sue often insists on driving Angie and me, and the other foster kid, Garrett, everywhere we need to go. She also packs our lunches and drives us to and from school in a light-blue minivan. It's sad, but I think she lives for moments like that.

I'm really not in the mood for a dysfunctional breakfast gathering or a stuffy car ride to the library afterward, so I write a note for Sue and leave it on the table. That way she won't panic and call the cops like she did the first time I disappeared for the day.

I hop over the notoriously squeaky floorboard in front of the door on my way out into the early morning.

Until recently, I'd never bothered with leaving notes and checking in if I was late. But now that Darren lives closer to me, the last thing I want is to ruin what I've got here. I can't risk being relocated again, putting more miles between us.

After summer break, senior year begins. While most kids my age are applying for colleges and racking up their list of extracurriculars, I'm biding my time until I can move out, get a job closer to Darren, and live life on my own terms for once.

The fresh air clears my jittery, sleep-deprived mind as I walk to the bus stop. Thoughts of the demon creature settle beneath the surface of my conscious mind. I'll need to keep myself busy, probably for several days, or else the memories will send me into a tailspin, and I might not be able to continue telling myself that it was only a hallucination.

I wish I could say that this marks the first time I've seen something . . . unexplainable. There's more than one troubling memory gathering cobwebs in my brain.

But this occurrence felt different. Too personal. I mean, Judas Priest, the thing sat itself directly outside my window and tapped its demon finger on the glass. Whether it actually happened or I somehow imagined it, it doesn't erase the weight sitting in my gut, tightening my shoulders, and making it hard to breathe or do anything more than place one foot in front of the other on the sidewalk.

I round the street corner and hear something moving in the neighbor's willow tree. Its unkempt, drooping branches spill into the sidewalk as always, shifting with a distinct sway.

The boulder in my stomach tells me that this is no innocent summer breeze. I don't want to let last night turn me into a nervous wreck, but I also don't want to be stupid, either.

I jump into the street, giving the tree plenty of space, and continue rounding the corner as the branches settle into a stillness that makes my skin itch with anticipation. Whatever moved those branches doesn't want me to know it's hiding in there. I'm tempted to go tearing through the tree to prove to myself that it's nothing more than some snot-faced kid messing around.

At six in the morning. During summer vacation.

A familiar belch of exhaust signals a bus pulling into the stop. Its markers show it won't take me to the library but to where Darren lives, several hours north of here.

I start jogging toward the bus. As soon as I look away from the tree, I hear a steady rhythm of footfalls behind me. The faster I run, the louder they sound. My hand shoots through the bus doors to stop them from closing, and I pause to glance down the sidewalk at my pursuer.

Nothing. Just a handful of leaves and a plastic bag tumbling around in the wind.

The driver makes a comment about 'picking up the pace.' I brush the bangs from my eyes, taking one last backward look before I climb onto the bus. I find an empty seat and hug my pack to my chest. My pulse pounds in my throat as I lick my dry lips.

I'm totally overreacting.

I watch the dirt particles skitter over the ground, and then another movement catches my eye. A blurry, shifting form caught in the wind, moving down the sidewalk.

The bus pulls away, and I stare at the ghost-like form until I can't crane my neck any further.

For a second, I think I might barf, but I swallow the bile and focus on breathing.

Against my better judgment, I watch out the window for any signs of the ghost, or the demon, reappearing. This distracts me from thinking about the consequences of taking a five-hour bus ride to see Darren without any advance thought. It's not like I haven't done this before, but like I said, I don't want to ruin a good thing right before I'm in the clear.

My eyes start to ache from meticulously watching every passing object. I force myself to stare at the back of the seat in front of me instead, trying to convince myself that nothing happened, that there's no reason to turn into a lunatic.

As I snuggle my shoulder blades into the seat, I rest my head against the window and focus on imagining Darren's expression when I show up out of nowhere to surprise him.

I sigh, deflating my tight chest that feels like it's been constricted by a hundred rubber bands all morning.

My breath fogs the glass. Just a smudge, but it triggers a scene I know will haunt me for a long time. A deep shudder aches in my bones as I try in vain to think about anything other than the creature watching me sleep through the window.

{ 2 }

I believe when I am in the mood that all nature is full of people whom we cannot see, and that some of these are ugly or grotesque, and some wicked or foolish, but very many beautiful beyond any one we have ever seen.

- *Irish Fairy and Folk Tales* by William Butler Yeats (1918)

After about an hour, I finally doze off and vacillate between napping and staring out the window for the rest of the trip.

As the bus glides around the highway curves, my window reveals the familiar Boston skyline. I dig through my pack for a granola bar and chew absentmindedly as my sleepiness fades.

And then my mind plays back every detail of my hellish morning.

I rub a hand over my face and tuck my bangs behind an ear. My mouthful of granola bar slides down my throat like mud, and I shove the other half into my pocket uneaten.

Distracting myself as quickly as possible, I reorganize everything in my pack, untying the jacket from around my waist and placing it on top of the food. Before I zip it closed, I look at my phone, thinking about texting Sue to tell her where I am.

Nope. She's not my babysitter. What does she care if I'm at the library or visiting Darren? I'd be gone for the same amount of time either way.

Knowing Darren's foster parents, Howard and Juliana Roberts, he probably won't have more than a couple hours to spend with me anyway. I picture the three of them eating ice cream cones in the park or building sandcastles at the beach. At least, that's what I've always imagined happens when you take any semblance of a normal family and give them an entire summer of possibilities.

The bus is nearing my stop, and I scoot to the aisle and clutch the straps of my backpack. I'm sure I look like an excited kid on her first day of kindergarten. What can I say? Visiting Darren beats any other activity, on any agenda, ever. He's the only person I care about unconditionally and who loves me the same in return.

I sense someone watching me as I stand up. Taking a quick visual survey of the bus, I look over the rows of benches with feigned casualty. Everyone is busy watching out the window or scrolling on their phones.

A glint of sunlight brings my attention to the mirror above the driver, where the driver's face is staring directly at me. Our eyes meet for a moment too long before I look away. I know it's stupid, but I think I saw tusks growing from his mouth. Like a boar and a man mixed into one being.

The bus jerks to a stop. I swallow hard and keep my head down as I walk up the aisle, determined to maintain a blank expression as I pass the driver and step onto the street.

I have every intention of following through on this plan, but right before I turn to step down the stairs, my curiosity acts with a will of its own.

I lift my head and stare right at the driver. He's been watching me walk toward him this entire time, and his gaze doesn't waver now. His face is round and fleshy with beady eyes and a wide mouth. It's his large mouth that captivates my attention before I race down the steps and onto the sidewalk.

Before I can get a second look, the door closes right on my back, and the bus leaves me standing in a cloud of exhaust. I cough and blink hard, feeling slightly nauseated—in part from the burn of pollution, but mostly, I think, because I'm going into shock.

The bus driver had two faces.

Not two heads, and not two faces squished side by side on one head. But two different faces on top of each other, almost like each one was fighting for the spotlight. The first face is the one that I saw when I got on the bus—a pudgy, middle-aged man with no distinguishable features. The second drained the lifeblood from my body and left me cold and terrified—his skin had a leathered texture, and the whites of his eyes were inked over in black. The most prominent detail was his mouth—wide and lipless with two battered ivory tusks jutting out on each side.

I'm still standing in the same spot on the sidewalk, gripping the straps on my backpack so tightly that when I force my hands to loosen their hold, my whitened knuckles ache.

It's official. I am now a crazy person.

The wave of nausea climbing through me reaches its peak, crashing down to my core. I almost topple over when someone brushes past me to cross the street. Leaning forward, I rest my hands on my knees and force myself to breathe.

I cannot allow my problems to interfere with my precious time with Darren. I can't let anything ruin this. Not even back-to-back hallucinations.

My feet start to move before my mind can fully catch up. Thankfully, I've been in this town several times and can rely on instinct to direct me.

The house Darren lives in is tucked away from the city in a quiet suburb where pristine lawns and driveways decorated with shiny cars encase rows of perfect houses. Every time I come here, I feel like I'm stepping inside a page of *Better Homes and Gardens* magazine.

The Roberts' house looks like the others: classic brick walls, dark roof, and pale shutters hugging every window. Juliana's garden is in full summer bloom. The vivid flowers and foliage blend together into the kind of natural balance that you know isn't natural at all but the result of many hours of labor.

Sue's garden *is* what I would call natural, with weeds and flowers popping up wherever they please, creating chaos that I appreciate. It's not trying to be anything but what it is.

I walk along the garden path, noticing a white sign staked into the grass that reads "Winner of the best lawn award."

Yep. Juliana's garden is the pride of her sophisticated heart. Well, that and her foster "son," of course. To her, my brother can do no wrong.

And to a large degree, she's right.

Biting my lip, I push through an invisible barrier of angst between me and the front door.

My fist meets the white-painted wood with three quick, determined knocks. I step back and wait for one of the Robertses to open, bracing myself for the inevitably awkward encounter.

Needless to say, I am not counted among their adoring fans. From what Darren tells me, they deserve every praise and more. If I didn't burn water, I would bake them a freaking cake for all they've done for him.

But I'm still holding out. Not quite preparing for the worst, but close. It will take a whole lot more than pretty gardens and financial stability for my brother to convince me of their awesomeness. Or at least that it will last.

After a few silent moments, I walk around to the back of the house and peek into Darren's room. His blinds are open, revealing walls covered in random superhero and fantasy posters, along with model airplanes and spaceships hanging from the ceiling. His bed covers are a tangled mess, and several books are scattered across the floor. But it's the unfinished slice of French toast topped with melted whipped cream on his desk that tells me all I need to know.

The Robertses must have surprised him with some sort of summer adventure—the only logical reason Darren would ever leave unfinished food behind. His gangly twelve-year-old body hit its first growth spurt this year, which only increased his need to empty the contents of the fridge whenever possible.

I send Darren a text, and within a few minutes, he replies with a picture of himself standing next to a huge tank of sea lions.

I sigh and lean against the brick wall of the house.

Great.

Of course I decide to surprise Darren on the same day that the Robertses take him to the aquarium. When I text to ask how long they'll be, he replies that they'll hurry back home, but it could be a couple of hours.

I readjust my pack and start toward the waterfront where there are more distractions to pass the time.

Sailboats bob like colorful birds floating on the water, their sails tied down and crusted over with salt spray. Ocean waves lap against the cement wall that prevents the water from flooding the shops and sidewalks behind me.

I listen to a mother talking to her kid. The girl can't be more than five, but she's arguing her case like an attorney. She wants to chase the seagulls scattered across the grass, picking at garbage, but the mom wants the girl to keep holding her hand. The father pushes a stroller where a chubby baby dozes underneath a little hat. They stop in front of a bookstore and step inside.

My biological parents disappeared when I was nearly six years old, and Darren still a small baby. No one knows what happened to them. I like to believe they died in a private airplane crash that was never recorded, or something equally epic. It helps me not hate them so much for abandoning us with no relatives and not a dime to our names.

I look away from the bookstore and face the water, letting my legs swing above the frothing waves. It's been years since Darren and I were found alone and placed in foster care. But sometimes I can't stop the anger from beating against me like the water on this wall.

Being angry doesn't change a thing, but the anger still remains, constantly thrashing out at an immovable force, never explaining why some parents won't let their kids leave their side to chase seagulls while others abandon their kids alone in the middle of the night and never come back.

I pop my headphones in and blare my favorite soundtrack, forcing my mind to shut up. I don't want to think about my parents, or the Robertses, or monster-faced bus drivers. I especially don't want to remember the creature sitting outside my window. I'm tired of thinking about things that can never be explained, things that have no black-or-white answer.

Things that no one but me seems to notice or care about.

Maybe I really am losing my mind.

I clench my teeth, refusing to write myself off as mentally unstable just yet. Who knows what would happen if I admitted these hallucinations to anyone. I cringe at the thought of being locked in a white room. Interrogated by doctors. Labeled with terms I don't understand.

Shaking my head, I turn up the volume and let the steady rhythm drown everything out. My eyes close, and I tip my face toward the sky. The sun warms my skin with a gentle heat that tingles through my clothes. I can smell the ocean breeze as it fills my lungs and eases my nerves that feel like open-ended wires.

The water hits me before I realize I'm falling. Freezing liquid swallows me, and I scramble for the surface, coughing up a lungful of salt water.

Despite my blurred vision, I see a figure standing above me on the wall. Something wrapped around my neck forces me back under as I fight to free myself. I flail my arms, and they catch my earphones, which have snagged on a crack in the wall. I yank the buds from my ears and kick upward again, gasping and retching.

Whoever was standing on the wall is now gone.

Out of nowhere, someone dives over top of me and into the ocean, and the splash pushes me against the cement. A head of golden-blond hair bursts out of the water inches from my face.

I cry out and kick him, and he retreats with a yelp when my foot meets its target.

"What the crap!" I scream, shoving water into his face. "What kind of moron thinks it's okay to push someone into the ocean?"

He splutters for a moment before shoving water right back at me. "Come off it, lass. No one pushed you in."

I peer through the water dripping down my eyelashes. His thick accent and foreign verbiage surprise me. We stop splashing each other, and our eyes meet as we tread water.

"So, you didn't push me in?"

He shakes his head, and the movement flings water off his curls. "I saw you fall in and was trying to save you."

His eyes, a vibrant mixture of blues and greens, seem sincere enough. I realize for the first time how incredibly hot he is.

"How do we get back up?"

He nods in the direction of a group of boats tied together along the nearest dock. "We swim."

For once, I'm grateful for those swimming lessons my third foster mom forced me to take. I nod and follow him as he cuts through the water with experienced strokes. My simple version of a breaststroke barely gets me to the dock, and at an embarrassingly slow rate. My would-be-rescuer hoists himself onto the dock and kneels there, waiting for me as I doggy-paddle the rest of the way, panting and coughing like a half-drowned rat.

He reaches a hand down, and I grasp it. His grip is warm and firm as he pulls me out of the water and onto the dock in a breathless instant. We sit there, me trying to slow my heart rate, acutely aware of his eyes on me.

Unsticking my bangs from my forehead and tucking them behind an ear, I glance over at him and notice his full lips twitching into a dimpled smirk.

"What?" I ask, my own grin threatening to crack open at any second.

The corner of his mouth caves, and his smile illuminates his features and completely stops my fluttering heart.

"That was humorous, was it not?"

Laughter bubbles up from my chest before I can hold it in. He joins me as we sit there, drenched and tired from a long swim in the hot, midday sun.

The laughter dies, and he stands. I follow, noticing the cool wedge arising between us, reminding me we're two strangers and nothing more.

I try not to care that his tight, buttoned shirt clings to his torso, or notice how he shakes his head and runs a hand through his unruly hair in a casual motion, brushing curls off a face that belongs to a Greek god, not some random guy who just dove into the ocean to save me.

His gaze flickers over to me, forcing me to behave.

"Well, thanks," I say, painfully conscious of the way my clothes and hair are plastered to me in the most unflattering way possible. At this point, I'm anxious to get to my pack before someone steals it. And the longer I stand here, the more time he has to think about what a complete weirdo I am.

After all, I did just fall off the barrier. *Who does that?*

His mouth curves into a small frown as he wrings water from the bottom of his khaki shorts. "No thanks are needed. Good day to you."

I swallow and try to hide my disappointment. Of course he has no interest in someone like me. A washed-up teenager who can barely swim and can't hold a candle to his gorgeous-ness.

"K," I mutter, folding my arms over my chest and striding up the dock. And as if the moment isn't mortifying enough, my shoes slosh and squeak with every step.

{ 3 }

By some miracle, my pack is still sitting on the edge of the wall. I find the nearest restroom, soak up some of the water in my clothes with wads of paper towels, and lean over the sink, squeezing out the end of my ponytail.

After school ended, I made a friend bleach the tips of my plain brown hair so I could dye it any color I wanted. Current color: flaming red. Some of the dye drips into the sink, but that's what happens when you buy the cheap stuff.

I make the mistake of glancing at the mirror, confirming my worst fears.

Drowned rat. A stupid, twitterpated rat.

I find the nearest café and order some food before sitting at a corner table and letting the day's events settle around me.

Why does today suck so much?

When I detangled myself from the headphones, my phone sank to the bottom of the pier right along with them. I have no way to contact Darren, or Sue, or anybody.

As I swallow another bite of sandwich, I lean into the chair, letting my mind linger on those golden curls. And those eyes, the color and depth of the ocean.

My mysterious rescuer.

Not mine, I remind myself with a pang of humiliation. He's just a random guy. Probably a foreign exchange student from Ireland. Or a tourist here to pick up the kind of girls who drool over guys with accents.

Which is why he dismissed me the way spoiled kids turn away leftover pizza. He has his pick of girls—I know the type. Pretty, bikini-clad, with plenty of lip gloss to go around.

Heck, I don't even own a swimsuit.

The image of his smirk falling right off his face when I thanked him unsettles me a little. I doubt he pushed me in, but his expression suggested a sense of responsibility that makes me wonder if he knows more than he let on.

I finish the sandwich and decide to try Darren's place again. If he's not back, I think the universe will have made its evil intentions for me clear. I only hope on the return route that the bus driver is a one-face kind of person.

I retrace my steps to the Roberts' home, and as I round the bend into their neighborhood, my heart plummets.

The house is dark and lifeless. They still aren't home.

I run to the door anyway, and when no one answers, I check to see if they left anything open. When even the back door doesn't budge, I curse and kick my sneaker at it. Am I desperate enough to break in? Explaining that would be fun.

Hey, you're home! How did I get in? Well, I climbed through the second-story window. You see, my hallucinations were getting worse, and I didn't want to be outside after dark. No big deal.

Without warning, I feel the temperature drop. The sky is just as clear as it was moments ago, with a hot July sun peering down at me. Looking around the backyard, I get the undeniable sense that I'm not alone. I leap into a dead sprint and don't stop until I've bolted several blocks.

As I slow my pace, my raging pulse quiets enough for me to hear something else. At first I think I'm imagining the sound, but then I stop walking and, sure enough, the faint patter of feet hitting the sidewalk echoes from somewhere behind me. I turn to look back, and that's when I see it.

A being dredged from my worst nightmares stands half a block away. Its skinny, jagged form looks like it's made of smoke and tree branches. Two soulless holes of shimmering, iridescent liquid lock onto me. Without question, they are the same eyes I saw outside my window last night.

My stare seems to piss the demon off. It raises its head and screams. I run, my mind racing along with me. If I knock on the nearest door, I have no way to know if someone is home, or if they'll let me in.

I see a sign ahead that reads "Evergreen Cemetery" and pivot hard. I'm running so fast that I collide with the metal gate before I can stop. I rattle the lock and chain. Nothing.

With wild-hot adrenaline coursing through me, I clamber over the top of the fence and land in a heap on the other side. The cemetery wall shades me, hiding me from view. I hold my breath as I wait for the creature to run past. That is, unless it saw me hop the fence.

The creature slithers up to the gate, its tall shadow etched into the grass beside me. I don't dare peek forward in case it sees me, so I watch in horror as its scraggly, bony fingers wrap themselves through the holes in the gate. Another scream roils from its mouth, and my stomach clenches like an icy fist. I press my back against wall, covering my ears with my hands.

When the noise stops, I hear the creature slither away, hissing and whimpering.

Silence floats around me for several minutes before my constricted throat finally swallows, and I allow myself to really breathe.

Headstones engraved with faceless names appear like a ragtag group of children gathered together to play on the warm grass. Some stones squat low near the earth while others stretch to the sky, their arms forming a cross above them. I swallow again, willing the thick lump blocking my airway to dissolve.

Under any other circumstance, I would be a little creeped out to be trapped in a cemetery. Alone for who knows how long.

But what is a little clichéd fear compared to the real-life haunted-house action that just happened? As messed up as it sounds, I feel a nudge of security the further I walk into the graveyard.

I can still hear the sizzling sound that crackled through the air when the creature touched the gate. I swear I saw its mutilated hand brighten to a dull orange before pulling away. As if the metal burned its demon flesh.

It can't get in here, I tell myself. *Wait it out and then run to the Roberts' house.*

My feet stop somewhere near the center of the grave-
stones. Several tall trees line the main road that cuts through
the grounds. I choose one of the trees and let my pack fall to
the grass. My stiff body follows after, sinking until my backside rests in the space between the lawn and the tree trunk.

Thoughts of Darren and the Robertses getting home, and
Darren calling me and getting no answer, add to my suffocating dread. Sue will probably call the cops if I don't show up
tonight. I should have borrowed someone's phone right after I
clambered out of the water.

But how was I supposed to know the demon creature followed me here to kill me?

My eyes burn with unshed tears as I stare blankly at the
nearest headstone. I can just make out the name engraved on
the rock's face.

Branna of the Harp.

I feel stupid even thinking it, but I whisper a few words
from a simple prayer I've known since forever. Like many
other strange things stored up inside me, Darren thinks the
memory must be from our parents.

I say it to myself over and over again as the smell of sweet
grass and sunshine numb my senses, and I feel a heavy exhaustion blanket me, pulling me almost against my will into a
deep sleep.

My last thought is about the weird name on the gravestone.
If the demon exists as more than a hallucination, maybe the
dead version of Branna can be my guardian angel today.

I wake up with a start, and my head hits the tree with a painful *thwack*. My hand moves to caress the surely-swelling bruise, and my breath catches as I hear footsteps drawing closer.

I lean forward and peek around the tree.

Goldilocks Guy walks toward me. His lithe, beautiful body makes its way through the graves like he's modeling for the next zombie movie. Light shadows crawling across the grass bring me back to reality.

How long have I been asleep? Panic shocks my veins, and I jump to my feet. *And more importantly, where is the demon now?*

Grabbing my pack, I brush the hair from my face and grimace as my fingers run along a crusted line of drool. I must have been out like a light, as cold as the graves around me.

I know I have to ask pretty boy for his help. Calling a cab to come get me will save me from frantically sprinting to reach the Roberts' place before my demon stalker eats me.

Taking a deep breath, I step out from behind the tree. Foreign guy is only a few yards away, facing my direction. I pretend to be looking at the headstones beside me. He'll notice me and think that seeing me here is happenstance.

Which it is.

Instead of stopping to acknowledge me, Goldilocks gives me a startled but curt nod and then continues down the path. He doesn't go far before he kneels on the ground in front of Branna of the Harp's headstone.

A cluster of wildflowers rests against his chest. His blond curls, turned an even brighter hue of gold now that they're dry, flutter around his solemn face. I pause behind the tree, not wanting to interrupt.

He kisses his fingers and touches the small gray stone, and I notice the date engraved below the name.

Unknown – 1983

I curse under my breath. This is his grandmother's—or worse, maybe even his mother's—grave. And I prayed to her to protect me from the boogieman.

He stands up and turns around, raw emotion shimmering in his eyes. All I want to do is melt like a popsicle and disappear into the dirt.

I have the worst timing. Ever.

Clearing my throat, I offer a small wave. "Hey, I don't know if you remember me, but I'm wondering if I can borrow your phone to call a cab?"

"I do not own that kind of device," he says, turning his back to me.

I stand there like an idiot for a few more seconds, and then I continue down the main path. Maybe this cemetery has an office with a phone that I can borrow. As I walk, I try to ignore the hot sting of humiliation that seems to be a trend with Goldilocks.

The pack resting snuggly against my shoulders protects some of my heat from the cool breeze. Clouds are gathering into a promising summer storm. I walk faster.

A small building sits just inside the cemetery walls. I run to the door and knock.

Nothing.

The blinds are closed, and a little jiggle on the handle tells me the door is locked. Panic resurfaces faster than I can stifle it.

Although my original plan was to run to Darren's house, actually putting that plan into action is another story. That demon could very well be waiting for me to come out of my hiding place. And I doubt I can outrun it again.

When I turn around, I'm suddenly face-to-face with the blond stranger. I yelp and fall into the door. He raises his eyebrows.

Did he just watch me try to break into the building?

"Is something the matter?" he asks, his lips twitching.

I glare at him, not in the mood to be teased. Especially after he shunned me. "Yeah, you could say that."

His eyes move from the door and then back to me. "Do you have employment here?"

Employment? Who is this guy? "No. I need a phone. Mine sank when I got pushed in the ocean."

A crease forms between his eyes, and his mouth puckers up like he's confused. "I believe you fell in." He says it with enough deliberation that I almost wonder if he's trying to convince me of a lie.

What does it matter? "I just need a phone so I can call a cab."

He nods, looking out across the cemetery. The flowers he was holding are gone. I think about the grave that might belong to his mother. The empathy I want to feel for him is missing in a way I can't explain. Maybe because I've never had a grave to visit before.

"As I said, I do not own a phone," he says, pulling my attention back, "but I will escort you where you need to go."

The way he speaks hinders my ability to understand things. I respond with an eager nod after an awkward, lengthy pause.

"That-that would be great. It's just down the street, but I . . ."

I'm being stalked by a demon who may or may not chase both of us down, but hey, it's better than going it alone.

His eyes darken into a stormy, sea-foam color. "You can no longer travel alone."

It's not a question; it's a warning. He starts walking toward the main gate, and I stumble after him like a lost puppy.

"Wait." I catch up to him as he steps outside the cemetery. I hesitate only a second before squeezing through the gate and crossing the invisible barrier of safety. "I'm Róisín, by the way."

He stops so suddenly that I nearly bounce into him. His eyes are still clouded over like the sky above, which is threatening a downpour.

He doesn't look at me when he speaks. "Róisín? This is your birth name?"

I just nod, not knowing what else to say. It's the name that I told the authorities when they found Darren and me. We had been abandoned for two days before anyone bothered to check in on us. I don't remember much more than a blur of blue-and-red lights pulling up to the window and heavy footsteps leading to the door.

"You must be of Irish descent." He keeps walking, his shoulders hunched over as he jams his hands into the pockets of his shorts.

"Cináed."

The word flows off his tongue like melted chocolate. When he says nothing else, I assume that it must be his name.

I researched my name years ago, so the idea that I have Irish heritage is nothing new. Róisín: pronounced Row-sheen. It's Gaelic for rose.

None of that means anything to me, though, other than giving me one more reason to hate my parents. It wasn't enough of a crime to abandon us—they had to go and name me something ridiculous.

The Roberts' house—and their SUV parked in the driveway—has never looked more welcoming. At this point, I don't care if Juliana corners me with list of invasive get-to-know-me questions. I'll sit through a family dinner with zero eye rolls. Whatever the Dread Parents Roberts dish out will be a cakewalk compared to the last twelve hours.

"Here is fine," I say, stopping a couple houses away. I don't want to add to the trouble I might be in by being seen with a guy. Heat creeps up my neck, and I kick my sneaker into the sidewalk to vent my nervousness.

"Pleasure to meet you, Róisín." He offers me a small smile. These drastic mood swings are starting to give me whiplash.

"Same. Thanks for—"

"As I told you before, your gratitude is wasted on me." The words should have come across as rude, but his voice is gentle and sincere, and all I can do is kick the ground.

Before I muster up the courage to do something reckless like ask if we can see each other again, I hear a hiss of sprinklers spitting to life and sidestep into the road. When I look up at Cináed, he's disappeared.

Things just keep getting weirder.

I stare down the empty street before turning toward the Roberts' house.

{ 4 }

As life becomes more orderly, more deliberate, the supernatural world sinks further away.

- William Butler Yeats in the Preface for *Gods and Fighting Men* by Lady Gregory (1904)

A few months ago, I'd faked sick to get out of school, catching a bus ride to visit Darren. He'd just moved in with Howard and Juliana, and I was excited that we were living closer to each other.

When I showed up here, I planned to wait until the school bus dropped him off, and then maybe we'd go see a movie or walk to a park and laugh at the ducks on the pond. The kind of stuff we usually did whenever I came to visit.

But I quickly realized my normal self-appointed visiting hours were not going to work anymore.

I didn't knock on their door and introduce myself or ask if Darren could come hang out with me. Instead, I crept into the backyard so I could find his room and sneak him out, thus avoiding the painfully awkward "foster parent" talk.

When the people who are paid to look out for you ever start to act like they really care, I get extremely uncomfortable. Whether those people genuinely care or not doesn't matter. I want nothing to do with it.

The first time I skirted around the fence and into the back-yard, Juliana was there, planting flowers and wearing a wide-brimmed sun hat. She glanced up at me from under her sun-glasses and smiled a red-lipstick, whitened-teeth kind of smile.

Not only was my cover blown, but I later found out that she had known I was coming all along. Darren had apparently told her all about me, the little snitch. I couldn't be too upset, though. His grin melted away any anger I felt at his betrayal. Even if he *was* grinning because I was sitting inside "his house," drinking lemonade and having a blatantly one-sided conversation with Juliana.

Darren was happy. He *is* happy. And that's something I don't think I've ever been able to say about my brother be-fore.

That being said, as I walk up to their house today, I know I need to see Darren first. I need to make sure he's okay and take a moment to see if *I'm* okay. That can't happen if I walk through the front door and get bombarded by the Robertses. So I creep around the side of their great brick house and peek into the backyard.

The lawn retreats into a perfect line of trees that creates a natural barrier between their yard and the neighbors'. I step around the corner, remembering the eerie feeling I had when I stood on their back porch a few hours ago. Like someone was watching me.

Darren is sitting at his desk, reading one of his many books. Dark hair swoops across his forehead and around his ears. I haven't seen it this long before. His eyes and hair are a few shades darker than mine, and his skin a few shades lighter. It's our signature button nose that proves we're siblings.

I pause, taking a moment to watch him. His baby face is pressed into the palm of his hand, and no worry lines crease his skin.

I'm transported to other times and places when our lives were still crappy but somehow a lot simpler. I wasn't trying to manipulate years of poor grades in order to graduate on time, and Darren still thought I was the only girl for him because all the other girls had cooties.

There were roughly the same number of miles between us, but somehow we didn't feel so far apart. I look at my brother now and see a young man who will soon be living his own life, dreaming his own dreams, with or without me.

I feel a small tug in my chest and blink against the sudden moisture in my eyes as I tap on the glass.

He jumps in his chair and looks up from the book. I smile and wave, and his eyes widen as he slides the window open.

"Hey," I say.

I resist the urge to punch the screen out from between us and hug him. After nearly two months of no visits, it feels so good to see him again.

"Where have you been?" He meant it as a scolding, but his tone is laced with concern. Looking at my wrinkled clothes and messy hair, he adds, "You look awful."

"How about you let me in, and I'll tell you all about it?"

Although the last thing I want to do is tell Darren what happened, I also can't ignore the disturbing chill that's inching up my spine the longer I stand here.

Darren obediently pops the screen out and lets it fall at my feet. I wince at the loud clatter, waiting for Juliana to come bursting on the scene at any moment.

I clamber inside and slide the window shut, locking it just in case. Darren's brow furrows again as he looks at me.

I cross my arms to hide my trembling hands. "Can I use the phone?"

He shrugs and starts down the hallway, and I exhale in relief. The fewer questions from him, the better. Lying has always come pretty easy for me, except when it comes to my brother.

"Where are Juliana and Howard?" I ask, trying to sound casual.

"They always have date night on Saturday, but they said to call them when you got here so they can come see you."

"No need," I say, unable to hide my intensity. Darren shoots me a look as he reaches for the home phone. I add, "I'll only be here for a bit, and besides, I came to see *you*."

He hands me the phone, and I wait until he makes himself a bowl of cereal and saunters back into his room before dialing Sue's number. The phone rings once.

"Hello?"

She sounds tired but hopeful. Meaning she thinks I ran away and has been stressing about it all day.

I take a deep breath through my nose. "Hey Sue, it's Róisín."

When she starts shouting to someone on the other end and I can tell she's trying not to cry, I lean against the wall. A thick wad of guilt lodges in my chest like a sticky ball of chewed gum. Out of all my foster parents, Sue is definitely one of the more attentive and caring people I've lived with. I hate freaking her out for no good reason, especially because I know she thinks I disappeared on purpose.

I tell her the condensed, slightly modified version of what's happened in the last several hours, leaving out the parts about my personal demon stalker, of course. It would sound like the dumbest excuse in the world.

I can tell she's calming down, and she agrees to let me call her back in an hour. I know she'll hate the idea of me spending the money on a cab ride home, but there's no way I'm walking to a bus stop, let alone more than a few feet, without someone beside me.

When did you turn into a kid afraid of her own shadow? protests my voice of reason.

It's not my shadow that terrifies me, I retort with a grimace. *Just the ones that want to kill me.*

I hang up with Sue and walk down the hall, pausing to look at a large, framed photo hanging above the living room mantel. Howard and Juliana are holding hands, flashing their pearly whites at the camera. What catches my attention is the boy standing slightly in front of them, his dark hair combed neatly to the side. Darren's smile is slightly anxious, probably because this is his first family picture debut. His sidelong glance makes it look like he's smiling up at Howard and Juliana.

My teeth tug on my bottom lip as I turn away and continue down the hall to the bathroom.

The house is peaceful and pristinely clean, as always. Letting my pack fall to the ground, I lock the door and hesitate before resting my hands on the countertop. I feel like I contaminate everything I touch in this place.

Even though getting home will be stressful and expensive, the real issue is trying to continue like life is normal from now on. Inside, I'll be in constant fear of what might happen if these . . . hallucinations won't go away.

My exhausted mind jumps from condemning myself to a life of protected isolation to calling an exorcist or a ghost hunter. I finally force my body to move, stripping down and turning on the shower. I try to be as dainty as possible as I wash away the sweat and ocean salt, and I sing random song lyrics under my breath to keep my brain distracted.

When I'm clean and dressed in my damp shorts and a spare shirt I managed to find tucked in my bag, I finish toweling off my hair and return to Darren's room.

He's right where I left him, sitting at his desk with an empty bowl in his lap and a book in his hands. I make out the words *Celtic Myths* on the cover before he closes it.

"So, what happened to you anyway?"

I set my bag down and move to the window, feigning casual interest in the view. When my searching gaze comes up empty on demons, I finally turn around.

"Well, when you said you guys were gone looking at fish—"

"It's called 'the aquarium'," he interjects, and I can hear the excitement bubbling inside him. "There's this extra-credit summer course, and one of the assignments is to do a research project on any aquatic creature, so I chose to write about green sea turtles. The aquarium has one named Myrtle who's eighty years old, and we went to see her."

I smile, not surprised that Juliana enrolled him in summer classes. He's brilliant, and they're rich. I'm sure she realizes how easy it is for him to excel when supplied with the right resources.

This is yet another area where Darren and I couldn't be more opposite. While he likes to curl up with a book or visit the aquarium to study turtles, I'm aching to be done with school. Every semester feels like an eternity, and avoiding the school counselor, who wants me to look into colleges, is getting more difficult.

College sounds like another four years of misery. And for what? With no real talents or interests, why would I invest all of that time and money? In the end, I'll probably spend the rest of my life working as a waitress or a taxi driver—or whatever pays enough to get me through.

I sit across from Darren on the bed, not wanting to miss the opportunity to distract him from my poorly made-up explanation of why I disappeared today.

"What's so special about this turtle?"

His face lights up, and he sets the book down, grabbing another from off his nightstand.

"Well, first off, green sea turtles have a lifespan of a hundred years," he rambles, flipping to a page featuring a huge turtle. "Can you imagine living that long?"

This kid has more passion in him about one little turtle than I do for anything I've ever learned in school. Let him be the one who goes to some fancy college and lands a high-paying career.

Sunlight reaches the bedspread as the sun continues to set. I rest against my hand while Darren turns to the section on sharks, his brown eyes sparkling as he reads out loud from the pages.

All I need in life is sitting right here with me.

{ 5 }

[Faeries] could make themselves seen or not seen at will. And when they took people they took the body and soul together.

- *The Fairy Faith in Celtic Countries* by WY Evans-Went (1911)

"When are you going to tell me what's going on?" Darren asks.

I'm lounging on his bed, eating from his second bowl of cereal while he idly spins around in the swivel chair.

Propping myself up on one elbow, I trace patterns in the bedspread and stall.

"Are you ever going to tell *me* what's going on?"

One dark eyebrow quirks on his forehead, and I watch as his confusion settles into a resolute glare. "I'm not a kid, Raisin," he starts, and I roll my eyes at the ridiculous nickname he gave me years ago, before his toddler self could say my actual name.

Unfortunately, it stuck.

He continues, "You can't change the subject. That kind of stuff won't work on me anymore."

I smirk. "It worked when I asked you to tell me about Myrtle the turtle."

He groans, but I catch a glimmer of amusement in his eyes. "You really are a pain in the butt."

A flash of white light and a boom of thunder answers him. Darren and I both jump as we look out the window. Sure enough, the ominous storm clouds I saw this morning have settled over us like a thick blanket.

Darren moves to stand in front of the window. "Those are some intense cumulonimbus clouds."

A handful of raindrops streak the glass. Once again, I'm glad to be indoors and not wandering the streets. If a demon chased me down on a warm and peaceful afternoon, I don't want to know what this kind of night would bring.

I disguise my shudder with a feigned yawn as I sit up. "Do you know anything about, um, demons and stuff?"

My attempt at casualty doesn't pass. Darren's head snaps around, his eyes cautious and guarded. "Demons? Like ghosts or something?" He turns back to the storm outside the window.

My brow furrows, and I choose my next words carefully. "Not necessarily. Just anything about hellish creatures that, you know, could potentially exist?"

At this point, all of the blood has drained from Darren's face. He hasn't moved from the window.

"Darren?"

Another flash of lightning segues into a deep, rolling thunder. This time Darren's feet leave the ground as he leaps away from the window. I catch onto one of his arms and make him face me.

"Hey, what's up with you?" I hold his chin as our eyes meet. The depth of fear I find in his gaze unnerves me.

When he looks over at the bookshelf, I follow his stare and see the book he was reading earlier, the one about Celtic myths, and reach to pick it up.

"Have you been reading scary stories?" I flip through the book's yellowed pages. My thumb stops on a dark, pen-sketched drawing, and I let the pages fall open.

The illustration is simple, but what it portrays clenches my gut.

"It's a Sluagh," Darren murmurs distantly.

My fingers itch to tear out the page and burn it. Anything to erase those glowing, hollow eyes from my memory. "And do you believe in this Sluagh? I mean, do you think it exists somewhere?"

When Darren doesn't respond, I look up to see him staring out the window, wide-eyed and frozen. My periphery tells me the truth before my head turns to look.

It's here.

The demon sits outside, perched on the windowsill like a freakish gargoyle come to life. The light in the room casts a glare on the glass, but I can still make out more of the demon's features than I have before.

A gaping mouth rests beneath large, wide-set eyes that shimmer like oil, and its black teeth drip with rainwater. Two pointed ears frame its hairless, seemingly skinless head. The rest of its body is equally taut and naked. When it shifts, I catch a glimpse of something protruding from its back—a pair of dark wings with feathers that glint like sharp blades.

"Darren," I whisper, not taking my eyes off the creature. "Darren, get out of here now."

Neither of us move. The demon lifts a clawed hand and starts to trace a nail along the glass. The noise sets my teeth on edge and slaps me into action.

In three steps, I manage to pull Darren out of the room and throw the door closed behind us. Darren, thinking faster now that the monster is out of sight, leaps and knocks down a key from above his doorframe. It clatters to the ground, and I fumble for it, shoving it into the door handle as I order Darren to call Howard and Juliana.

He sprints down the hall, and my sweaty hands pause as I listen for the shrill sound of glass being cut. Silence buzzes in my pounding ears, and then I hear Darren scream.

My heart plummets to my feet as I tear down the hall and slide into the kitchen, shouting my brother's name. As I round the corner, I see that the Sluagh has punched a fist through the screen in an open window. It has Darren by the throat in a death grip. One of its black claws has punctured a small hole near his jaw, and a line of blood trickles onto the collar of his Spider-Man T-shirt.

The demon looks at me, seeming to smile before lifting Darren out of the window in one swift movement.

My screams are lost in the angry thunder as I wrench the sliding glass door open. The demon, the size of a grown man, has managed to lift Darren into the sky with grating swooshes of its dark wings. I cry out for it to stop, but the creature flies up and over the trees lining the backyard.

I sprint across the soggy grass, tearing through the tree line that snags my shirt enough to tear the sleeve. I keep running, and when I reach the front gate of the neighbor's yard I throw myself over it, barely breaching the top before I land with a solid *thud* on the sidewalk below. As I scramble to my feet, I search the sky in a wild panic, making out a distant form several blocks away.

"*No!*"

The desperate plea is useless, but I continue my chase down the empty sidewalk, trying in vain to formulate some sort of plan.

I'm running so hard, my gaze focused on the sky, that I don't see the person in front of me before I've hit him like a head-on car crash. We ricochet off each other, and I land with a splash in the gutter. Rain blurs my vision as I squint at his face.

Cináed.

Curls are plastered to his skin, darkened by water. As he stands and looks at me, I see something in his eyes that stops me in my tracks.

The vibrant sea green from before has shifted to a bright, glowing neon. A small detail, but a feature that's undeniably abnormal.

"You have to help me!" I scream through the sheets of rain pelting us. I point to the sky where I last saw Darren. Sure enough, a hazy outline of the demon battles against the storm, my brother hanging beneath it in its claws.

Before I can explain myself, Cináed sprints down the sidewalk. In my shock, I hesitate for half a second, but I catch up. We run in silence as rain hisses down from the sky, and an occasional crack of thunder vibrates through my chest and out my feet.

Despite our pace, the demon is getting further away. Cináed grabs my hand in a solid hold, and immediately I feel my legs move faster. My blood pumps harder, and a weightlessness seems to carry my feet over the ground as if I'm moving too fast for gravity to keep up. One glance at Cináed's glowing eyes confirms to me that he is no ordinary summer tourist.

We close the distance, and Cináed doesn't take his gaze off of the demon when he says, "Hurry, hand me your shoe."

"My shoe?"

At this speed, I doubt I can stop altogether in order to pull my shoe off, not without face-planting into the cement. When he doesn't respond, I try to add a skip in my step, giving myself an extra millisecond of time to throw my foot high enough to grab the shoe off without tripping.

As I reach my free hand around and kick my foot so high that it hits my backside, my fingers close around my shoe and tear away the slick sneaker.

Naturally, I stumble. In a motion so quick it leaves me stunned, Cináed grabs the shoe from my hand, catches my fall, and sits me on the ground.

Then he shouts something up at the Sluagh, waving the sneaker above him.

I cup my hand over my eyes as I peer into the sky, holding my breath. The demon circles back around. I see Cináed's teeth flash in a grin as he tosses my shoe high in the air.

Several things happen simultaneously. First, the Sluagh releases Darren from its grip, and I scream as my brother free falls to the earth. In the next instant, the demon swings down and snatches my sneaker from the air, shrieks, and flies away. Cináed takes three steps and holds his arms open wide, catching my brother's limp body like a bag of flour.

I lurch to my feet and jog over to them on wobbly legs. A sob escapes my lips as I reach for Darren, expecting the worst.

When I hold my hands to his pale face, I gasp as his eyelids flutter open and he groans.

"Darren!" I cry, knowing my tears blend with the rain on my cheeks. "Darren, are you okay?"

Cináed watches me with his glowing eyes. "Your brother was just stolen by a shadow faery. I suspect that one of you encouraged this by drawing too much attention to yourself." His tone is curt and slightly smug, as if what he's saying is common knowledge, what anyone with half a brain would know.

"Come," he says, still holding Darren in his arms. He starts down the sidewalk at a quick but much more normal pace.

"We need to take him to the hospital," I say, speed walking next to him, trying to reach for Darren.

Cináed guffaws at me under his breath. "What you need is to hide yourselves. You have attracted the attention of some of the darkest fae. The Sluagh will not be appeased with a shoe forever."

The reminder of my missing shoe makes me register the sensation of my drenched sock soaking up the puddles on the sidewalk.

"Then where are we going?"

"To a place where the shadow fae dare not enter." He glances at me, rainwater dripping from his nose and lips. The tip of a pointed ear pokes out from beneath his wet curls. "I will take you to King Rauri's kingdom."

{ 6 }

[T]here is no part of this world which does not impinge upon or act as a gateway into the otherworld. The Celtic otherworld is contiguous to ours, overlapping it, its waters forever seeping through the barely perceptible cracks which mark the unseen borders.

- *Encyclopedia of Celtic Wisdom* by Caitlín and John Matthews (1994)

"King who?"

I stumble along beside Cináed, who walks as if he's carrying a cantaloupe, not my brother's sprawling body. I watch Darren's pale face, praying he'll be alright. At least he's breathing steadily, but he's soaked through and probably bleeding from the demon's claws.

"King Rauri," Cináed says. "He is High King of the Otherworld."

I feel like I'm treading through mud as I try my best to internalize what he's saying.

"And tell me again"—breath—"why we can't just"—breath—"go to the hospital?"

What I really want to do is demand that he take us to the hospital, but I'm terrified that Cináed will ditch us and the demon will come back to claim its dinner. As much as I hate it, I know I'm indebted to Cináed, and I'd lose my mind right now without his help.

He raises his arms, gently shifting Darren's head so that it rests more comfortably on his chest. "Mortal physicians cannot protect you against the Sluagh and other dark faeries. You must seek refuge in the Otherworld."

Otherworld. King. Faeries.

A wave of nausea surges through me, burning in the back of my throat.

This can't be happening. This isn't real. This is a nightmare.

Cináed, noticing my lagging pace, looks back at me. He glances me over, probably wondering why I always look like a drowned rat.

"Hurry, Róisín."

He nods toward the growing fog. The rain calms into a light drizzle as we walk, but it bites more than the downpour did. Or maybe my adrenaline rush reached its peak, and I'm on the downhill dive when your muscles freak out and you start to feel things like temperature again.

I swallow and take deep breaths through my nose, letting the sharp air cleanse my brain. Cináed keeps walking. His voice echoes in my ears. The way he said my name somehow made it sound not so entirely lame.

It's the accent. He knows how to use his foreign charms to his advantage.

But after what he did, how he rescued Darren . . . My previous judgments about him don't sit right anymore.

That and his glowing eyes, pointed ears, and awareness of everything crazy in my life.

Through the hovering mist, I make out the familiar outline of shops near the water. The air is musty and humid, and I shudder against the growing chill seeping through my wet clothes.

Dim lamps line the docks, and ship beacons cast yellow beams on the waves lapping against the metal-and-wood framings below. The dark, alluring water makes me want to retreat somewhere solid and secure.

Cináed stops partway down a dock. I follow his gaze, tipping my head back until my neck aches.

The fog shifts, clearing my view of an ancient cargo ship tied to the end of the dock. Rusty metal smeared in barnacles looms above us, and a limp flag with strange symbols hangs from a mast.

Do cargo ships even have masts?

"What kind of contraption is this?" I say, peering up at it with a furrowed brow. The ship seemed to appear out of nowhere. I didn't see it was here until we stopped in front of it.

Cináed grins. "Meet Branna. She is the noblest, most beautiful vessel of the sea."

Branna. Again with the name from the gravestone.

"My crew is away for the night," he continues. "I will escort you to your sleeping quarters."

"*Your* crew?" I stare at him. "You own this thing?"

Darren moves in Cináed's arms, moaning. I leap forward, pressing my face closer to my brother's.

"Darren, Darren, it's me, Róisín."

Heavy footfalls rattle the dock beneath our feet, and I turn to see a man stomping in our direction. "Hey you!" he bellows into the night. "I see you there! You're not supposed to be down there."

I open my mouth to retaliate when I feel something hit my shin. With a wince, I snarl at Cináed, who gives me the death glare in response.

"Grasp my arm and stay silent," he says between his teeth. I hesitate for only a second and then clamp my hand onto his bicep.

Cináed faces the man, now only a few yards away, with a smooth expression. "No need for concern. I am merely passing through, out on an evening stroll." His voice rushes through the air like the waves, reaching the man who stops walking, glancing over Darren and me as if we aren't here.

The man breathes hard, blinking and wiping at his sweaty, bald head with a coat sleeve. "But I—I swore I saw some kids here and—"

Cináed's easy laughter stops the man short. "My apologies. I am often mistaken for someone much younger."

The man smiles, and his panting breaths turn into a low chuckle. "Must be all this sea air." He grins and pats his belly. "My wife says it keeps any man youthful."

Darren groans, this time scrunching his nose like he's about to wake up. The man blinks again, looking at Darren.

Cináed's forced smile disappears for a moment, but then he laughs and glances down at Darren in his arms.

"I see that my stomach is also enjoying this salt air you speak of. Would you mind if I take a moment here alone before retiring for the night?"

Still staring at Darren as if trying to see something he can't quite make out, the man nods and mumbles about sea ghosts before walking away. We stand there, holding painfully still until he steps off the dock and disappears into a shop.

"What . . . the . . ." *That's it. I have officially lost my freaking mind.*

Cináed lowers Darren to the ground, and I cradle my brother in my arms as I sit on the dock. Then he reaches for one of the thick ropes tied to the ship.

"Wait here, and I will lower the plank for you."

Like an agile monkey, he uses his hands and feet to clamber up the rope and onto the deck.

I run my fingers through Darren's wet hair, whispering soothing words to him. Panic rests just beneath the surface of my shattering composure.

If I had taken the first incidents with the demon more seriously and hidden in my room all day instead of trying to go to the library, none of this would have happened.

Darren moans again, and I brush a hand down his face.

If I had told him about the demon the moment I climbed into his room, would he have known what to do? He knew about the Sluagh from that book, as if he'd been studying it for a specific reason.

I spot movement along the ship's deck, and what I guess is the "plank" lowers at an angle to the dock. Cináed slides down the rope he'd climbed and swoops Darren into his arms, nodding for me to follow.

"Make haste." He glances around the empty pier. The only disturbance comes from the tethered boats floating nearby.

"Night is particularly dangerous, for shadow faeries revel in their own company."

My skin prickles as I hurry behind him, balancing on the slender plank until my feet hit the deck. Cináed stops in front of a door, and I open it so he can step inside.

He lays Darren on the twin-sized bed, and I rush over and sit beside my brother, holding his hand and watching his face for any sign of discomfort. All previous eye-fluttering and nose-twitching has stilled. His breathing gives me hope that he's sleeping peacefully. Moonlight glows through thin linin curtains covering the small window beside the bed.

The demanding edge to my tone surprises me when I say to Cináed, "If you're so anti-hospital, you'd better have another plan to get my brother some medical attention."

Cináed's stare doesn't waver. In fact, I swear his expression shifts into something resembling appraisal as we watch each other in the smoky shadows.

If Darren wasn't lying beside me, potentially seriously hurt, I would have nothing anchoring me to the ground, keeping my heart steady. Cináed has to know the effect he has on girls. I'm sure that beneath his god-like mask, he's mocking me, ridiculing me for even entertaining the dream of what it might feel like to be noticed by him.

"I will return shortly," he says coolly, silencing my inner dialogue like a cold rag tossed onto a flame.

The small room darkens when he disappears. I hold Darren's hand tighter, brushing his hair back as I inspect the cuts on his face and neck. None of them will need stitching. The wounds from the demon's claws on his back will be more severe.

As I gently roll Darren onto his side, I lift up his shirt and gasp when my fingers come back dusted in blood. It's not enough to soak through his shirt, and I take that as a good sign.

I remind myself to keep breathing. The last thing Darren needs is for my nerves to short circuit as I lose all control. After a day like today, I know I'm dangerously close to a full-blown freak-out session.

Movement flutters on the other side of the curtains, and my insides freeze over with jagged icicles when I catch a glimpse of something floating past the window. I'm not sure if it's the demon or some other hellish being, but I do know that Cináed is right about one thing.

Darren and I aren't going home until we find a way to protect ourselves from whatever monsters are out there. And although it goes against my code to trust a stranger, Cináed is the one person who might be able to help us.

{ 7 }

Witness the nature of the creatures, their caprice, their way of being good to the good and evil to the evil, having every charm but conscience—consistency. Beings so quickly offended . . . yet so easily pleased, they will do their best to keep misfortune away from you.

- *Irish Fairy and Folk Tales* by William Butler Yeats (1918)

My consciousness begins to latch onto the noises and sensations around me as my eyelids flutter open. Without moving, I see that I'm still lying on the bed in the tiny room on Cináed's old boat. And with a start that launches my stomach into my throat, I also realize that Darren's side of the mattress is empty.

I fling myself from the bed and take one step toward the door. Instead of walking in a straight line, my legs wobble like a bowl of Jell-O, and I stumble into the wall. The floor shifts beneath me, a strange sensation that reminds me of riding an elevator.

Voices float through the cracks in the doorway, along with a fresh scent of cool saltwater. The rushing sound that had turned into background noise while I slept is just now registering in my ears. I spin around to look out the window.

I know next to nothing about boats, having never stepped foot on one, but it's clear this boat is hauling. Considering how clunky and weather-beaten it seemed last night, it tears through the giant, foaming waves below with unnatural speed.

I tumble out the door in a mad dash, my eyes blinking against the sharp glare of the sun.

Water. As far as I can see in every direction.

I feel several pairs of eyes on me as I turn around. A lot of new and, quite frankly, horrifying faces stare at me. Some of the creatures balance crates on their backs, while others swing from the ropes above. One mops the floor just a few feet away, his skin the color of a cartoon corpse—grayish blue— and his cheekbones and elbows so sharp they could stab me. The monster grins, revealing rows of razor-like teeth.

It sounds like his throat is coated in ice when he speaks. "Are you the captain's trinket, lady?" His teeth glint in the sunlight. "If not, I'd be happy to oblige."

A few others laugh in response, and I run past them, taking the stairs two at a time, nearly colliding with someone at the top.

I shove against the form, fighting to change course before a pair of monster hands can grab me.

"Good of you to join us," Cináed says, stopping me in my tracks.

I look up at him, his cheery expression telling me he's either oblivious or calloused to the terror in my eyes.

"I am demonstrating the art of sailing to your brother."

I glance past him and find Darren standing at the wheel, holding onto it with both hands. A wide smile creases his cheeks while a breeze tosses his dark hair around like long grass.

"Darren," I breathe, my rapid pulse slowing.

Darren doesn't lose his focus on the horizon. "Hey Raisin, Cináed says I have a knack for sailing." Pride oozes from the words. "He says I can be the helmsman all day if I want."

Cináed's tone is chiding, but his eyes sparkle with amusement. "I said you may help as long as the weather fares well. Now keep her so, sailor. Straight and true."

Darren's grin melts into a firm line, and his knuckles wrap around the wheel. "Aye, Captain."

Cináed's feet are bare, his pant legs rolled to his calves, and the top buttons on his loose shirt are undone. Wind catches at his clothes and tendrils of hair like a playful kitten. Cináed seems more at home standing here on this deck in the middle of the ocean than I can ever remember feeling in my life.

Now that I know Darren is safe, and his health miraculously improved overnight, I remember my second concern. Squaring my shoulders, I glare at Cináed.

"The only thing you should be teaching Darren is how to turn this boat around. We never agreed to sail anywhere with you."

He eyes me with a touch of annoyance, and my fists ache to wipe that pretty-boy smirk right off his face.

"You are no more hostages here than I am someone whom you can command. This is my ship, and while you're standing on it, you will obey the orders of the captain."

My eyebrows disappear into my bangs. "You're the one who brought us on here in the first place. How was I supposed to know you were going to sail away in the middle of the night?"

He faces me, lowering his voice. "You foolishly attracted the interest of the shadow fae. I am merely escorting you to safety."

My teeth grind together. A handful of creatures from the deck below glance at us, pausing to watch the scene.

"That wasn't my fault! All I want is for you to tell me how to stop all of this"—my hands motion around us in a loose gesture—"and take us back home."

Cináed catches one of my arms at the wrist, pulling me a step closer. He leans in, and for a terrifying moment I think he might kiss me. But instead he presses his jaw against my ear, his whisper matching the intensity of a shout.

"Do not speak openly of things you do not understand. I cannot save you from the consequences if my crew recognizes your gift of Sight."

I squint at him. "What are you talking about?"

"The beings on this ship are not using glamour to hide or guise themselves. I ordered them to reveal their true selves, knowing you could not feign blindness to them, as you both seem to see through fae glamour."

He pulls away and disappears down the stairs, leaving Darren and I alone on the upper deck. Everyone resumes their tasks when Cináed cuts through them. I watch him go, his hands locked behind his back.

A corpse-man, a chubby, rat-like creature climbing a rope, a beast hoisting a crate on his shoulder, looking like a scary blend of buffalo and human . . .

One demon was bad enough. *How in the world has this gotten worse overnight?*

My toes flex, one foot gripping the inside of my sneaker, the other digging through my sock. I step back from the railing and bend forward, trying to keep fresh air pumping in and out of my lungs as my vision temporarily fades to black.

"You're blocking my heading, Raisin."

Darren's voice somehow grounds me again, and I pull myself upright. I glance at the *heading*—aka open ocean for hundreds of miles—and try not to roll my eyes.

"Can you let the ship steer itself for two seconds while I make sure your bandages are okay?"

His wide eyes flicker to me before settling back on the horizon. "Captain left me in charge of the wheel."

By *Captain*, I know he's referring to my least favorite person in the universe. I go to lift Darren's shirt, wanting to inspect the cloth I wrapped around his back last night to stop the bleeding. Before he can shift away, I see that the bandages are gone, replaced with some sort of cream.

"What's this?" I demand as Darren uses one hand to pull his shirt back down.

"Cináed had one of the crew, an apprentice druid, make me a poultice."

I barely hear what he's saying. My insides flare like an out-of-control wildfire, and without thinking, I stomp across the deck, down the stairs, and in the direction in which I last saw Cináed.

Corpse-man catcalls me as I move past him, and several others make like they'll stop me from crossing the deck. But despite their threatening actions, none of them touch me as I tilt my head high and walk with determination.

I don't stop till I see Cináed at the front of the ship, facing the horizon. As I get closer, I hear a soft whistling tune coming from his direction.

I shove his shoulder, and the wooden flute he's playing falls from his lips.

"How dare you!" I shove him again with both hands.

He doesn't budge, holding his ground like one of the ship's masts. "You had no right to use some weird voodoo crap on my brother. I don't care how much you think you're helping us"—I jam a finger into his chest—"you don't touch him ever again."

"Druid."

His one-word response throws me off. "What?"

"The one who healed your brother. She is called a druid."

A bitter, joyless laugh escapes me as I shake my head.

My life is in shambles and he's concerned about titles?

"Listen here, I don't know what your ulterior motives are, but Darren and I don't want any part in this."

He quirks one eyebrow, and I see the skin near his mouth pinch in a small smirk.

"You do not intimidate me, Róisín. You do, however, annoy me. You claim you have no choices. I am offering you two: Continue to disregard my generosity and be tossed into the ocean, or follow the example of your younger brother and behave yourself."

A gust of wind whips my loose bangs around my face, and he lifts a hand to tuck them behind my ear, his touch softer than the ocean breeze.

His hand drops to his side, and he leaves me standing there, my rebuttal stuck in my throat.

{ 8 }

The name 'faery' has acquired unfortunate connotations, evoking images of butterfly-winged and saccharine creatures slightly bigger than insects. [W]e must . . . understand that they have a far greater stature and power than we can conceive. Immortal, able to pass between the worlds at will, with resources that seem magical to humans.

- *Encyclopedia of Celtic Wisdom* by Caitlín and John Matthews (1994)

The rest of the day drags on without incident. Eventually, Darren joins me in our room, replaced at the helm by the buffalo-man. The squatty rat creature waddles in soon after, bringing a tray of food and showing all of its sharp little teeth in what I guess is a smile.

After splitting the dense bread, we each take an apple, sitting on the bed with our backs against the wall and our feet dangling over the end while Darren tells me about the different creatures he's seen.

"And the minotaur is called Manny. Do you know which one the minotaur is?"

I vaguely recognize the word. "Is that the one that looks like a buffalo?"

"Yes. But don't call him a buffalo. He likes to be called First Mate Manny."

"Mmm-hmm." I bite into the apple, my mind wandering to our parents, of all things.

Darren inspires the thought—rattling off random facts about monsters while my instincts scream to get out of here ASAP before something eats us. I wonder if our parents were opposites too. Maybe one of them was an adorable nerd and the other a . . .

A what? What label defines my messy existence?

Several terms come to mind. *Street fighter. Orphan. School flunky. Thief. Tomboy. Rebel* . . .

"Hey Darren," I say, "why were you reading that Celtic book?"

I feel his body tense. "It showed up in my room. I thought Juliana bought it for me, but she said she didn't."

I continue, aware of the anxiety in his voice. "When I was there, was that the first time you'd picked it up?"

He shakes his head, his dark eyes reflecting the fading sunlight from the window.

"I read parts before. That's how I recognized that thing from the drawings."

"The demon that came to your house?"

He stares ahead at nothing. "It came once before and watched me through the living room window. I was going to tell Juliana and Howard about it. I was just so scared they'd think I was lying . . ."

He looks at me, tears shimmering in his wide eyes. "I didn't know what to do. I thought I was the only one who could see it."

I pull him against my side, wrapping my arms around him. "Hey, it's going to be alright. Whatever it was is gone now." I want to tell him he's safe, that he has nothing to be afraid of anymore. But the words stick to my tongue, tasting as wrong as they would have sounded out loud.

Instead, I coax our conversation back toward the less horrifying creatures, and Darren obliges.

"Well, the goblins were easy enough to pick out," he begins. "But I'm still not sure about the captain."

My stomach contracts. "Cináed?"

"Yeah, I thought he might be from Greek myths. Like a demigod or something."

I'm glad Darren's head rests on my shoulder so he can't see my face turning red. *A demigod?*

Darren continues. "Manny says we're sailing to the Otherworld, where Cináed is from. But I don't know where the Otherworld is."

"Well, we know he's Irish," I say, remembering how he weirded out over the origins of my name.

Darren's eyes are closed now, and the waves rock us gently as lines of vibrant pinks and yellows streak the sky.

"Then he's probably a faery," he murmurs.

"A faery? Wouldn't he need wings or something?" The image of Tinkerbell glitter-bombing everything crosses my mind, and I shake my head. There couldn't be anything further from Cináed.

"Faeries come in all shapes, sizes, and colors."

Images of the demon resurface, chilling me to the core. Cináed *did* call that spawn of hell a faery, so maybe Darren is right.

He yawns, fading fast. "But, the more normal they look, the more powerful they are."

I don't ask any follow-up questions, letting sleep take him. His theory jump-starts my brain into high speed, leaving me with plenty to think about.

The demon never came across as "normal." From the moment I first saw it outside my window, I knew I had to be hallucinating, or that I'd somehow invited a demented soul into my life because of my sins—according to the people running foster home #5, I'm ripe for damnation—or maybe because of that one party where I played around with a Ouija board.

Cináed is the second faery to enter my life. Sure, he's drop-dead gorgeous but otherwise seemingly human. The way his eyes glow in the dark and how he can move scary fast and turn people invisible totally freaks me out. But sure, he's pretty normal. At least, way more normal than the demon.

The more normal they look, the more powerful they are.

Conclusion: Do not underestimate Cináed.

After nodding off into a restless sleep and dreaming that buffalo-man threw me from the ship while Cináed laughed, I wake up with Darren still snuggled against me. The sky tells me it's early morning, and I slowly extricate myself from Darren and tiptoe out the door.

If Cináed says we're trapped on this ship and any complaints from me mean I'll be swimming with the sharks, I need to try another tactic. As much as I want to know how to protect Darren and me back at home, I also have no intention of sailing to some fairytale world in order to find the answers.

A group of creatures work on the deck, but since I chewed out the captain, none of them have even made eye contact with me. This gives me a small twinge of satisfaction as I take the tie from my wrist and pull my hair into a ponytail.

I look around for a moment, and when I come up empty, I decide to investigate the top deck.

Cináed doesn't acknowledge me as I move to stand beside him at the helm. His white shirt matches the sails above. One hand rests casually on the wheel, and for a moment he looks like the hot boy in school, driving his car with perfect cool-guy finesse.

I tug on my now-stiff, filthy T-shirt, once again feeling like a loser for thinking that I have the right to talk to someone like him. Appearance isn't everything, but from experience, I know what it's like to constantly land on the bottom rung. Hand-me-downs and self-given haircuts haven't done me any favors.

I bite my lip and force myself to focus. As long as I can get Darren and myself home safely—with a guarantee that there won't be any more demons snatching us up—nothing else matters.

"Hey." The word interrupts the awkward tension between us with as much delicacy as a belly flop.

"Good morrow."

I cross my arms to stop my hopeless attempts at fixing my clothes.

"I want you to teach me how to sail or whatever."

He looks at me, and I cringe when he smirks, his eyes dancing with dark humor. "The Demanding wishes to be Commanded, does she?"

I swallow hard, not sure what I've just gotten myself into. "I just figured I'd rather learn to sail a ship than be used as fish food." I shrug, playing the careless teenager card like my life depends on it.

Because it just might.

He hesitates, and I hope I didn't just remind him about his threat from yesterday. He turns and bellows something I don't catch, and the scary-huge buffalo comes stomping up the stairs. I look into the creature's beady, black eyes and divert my gaze as he snorts through large nostrils.

"Yes, Captain," he grunts.

"Manny, our passenger here would like to become a part of the crew." Cináed winks at me. "Today is as good a day as any to inspect the high mast, is it not?"

"Aye, Captain."

The beast reaches for me, and I jump back with a squeal. They both stare at me like I'm the one who's strange, and I clear my throat before saying, "I can walk by myself."

Manny grunts again and turns to stomp down the stairs. I glance at Cináed, and he motions for me to go. "First, learn how to follow orders. Then we shall see if you are able to—how did you so eloquently put it? 'Sail a ship, or whatever.'"

His accent shifts into a mockery of my own. I clench my fists, itching to give him the bird, then turn and hurry to follow Manny onto the bottom deck.

Reaching the last step, I see Darren shuffling out of our room, yawning and rubbing his eyes. When he smiles at me, I'm reminded once again of my failure to keep him safe—to be the big sister he deserves.

"What's going on?" His arms stretch above his head of tussled hair. His Spider-Man shirt stained with blood and shorts splotched with dried mud remind me of a younger Darren, tossed around the foster care system just like me.

It's little wonder that he loves his life with the Dread Parents Roberts. They give him everything I've failed to provide, and I hate myself for getting him into this mess. I wish I could say it's the first time my choices have landed us both in some serious trouble.

The buffalo *moos* at me to keep up.

"Why don't you help Cináed steer the ship?" I say to my brother, trying not to sound too eager.

Darren looks over at my hairy cohort who won't shut up. "Why is Manny calling you?"

I sigh with an audible groan. Once my brother notices something interesting, he cannot and will not be talked out of tagging along. Sometimes I wish he acted more like the dweebish little tween he's supposed to be at this age, and less like a hyperaware smarty-pants.

Manny waits with his bushy arms folded over his broad chest. I stop in front of him, maintaining my own glare to demonstrate he's not the only one pissed off at this situation. Darren, of course, hops along right behind me.

"Hi Manny," he starts, then adds quickly, "I mean, First Mate Manny."

The beast's eyes seem to light up as he focuses on Darren. "Good morrow, Darren." Then all niceties disappear as those eyes rove back toward me.

"Captain wishes for you to learn the task of managing the riggings."

Judging by his ominous tone and Darren's small gasp, I know this can't be good. Both of them stare up into the mess of ropes and sails at the top of the mast. I try not to swallow my tongue as I follow their lead.

"So, you expect me to climb up there or what?" I smother the question in sarcasm, tacking on a little laugh that comes out sounding slightly hysterical.

"Precisely," he grunts.

The mast reaches taller than a two-story house, its width thicker than a tree trunk. As if adding insult to injury, the rat creature leaps from the top of a sail and latches onto a dangling rope, swinging like Tarzan through the air.

"Right," I say, feeling my body turn to mashed potatoes.

I'm going to die long before I ever win Cináed over and convince him to bring us back home.

{ 9 }

The faeries, beside being revengeful, are also very arrogant, and allow no interference with their old-established rights.

- Ancient Legends, Mystic Charms, and Superstitions of Ireland by Lady Francesca Speranza Wilde (1887)

"Hurry along," the buffalo says. "Captain ordered all sails to drop, so you best start climbing."

My eyes are still staring up at the never-ending mast that stretches into the sky like a redwood tree. *Climb this? What does he think I am, some sort of monkey?*

As if reading my thoughts, Manny adds, "You use the riggings, human. Once you reach the first landing, you untie the sail."

Darren nudges me and points to our left. "Those ropes are the riggings. You climb it like a ladder."

"Aye." Manny almost smiles down at Darren. "You learn fast, young one." Then he nods to me. "Jarlath will meet you at the first landing and show you how this is to be done. Begin climbing."

Darren pipes in. "Can I do it too?"

"No way, Darren." I take him by his small shoulders and look him in the eye. "You stay down here."

His brow and button nose scrunch up. "But that's not fair—"

"I need you down here to tell me what to do," I continue, desperate to keep him on the deck. "Can you do that for me?"

His disappointed face softens as he nods. "Yeah, I guess I can."

Before I realize what I'm doing, I pull him to my chest and plant a kiss on his head. His hair is warm from the rising sun. I don't want to forget the little things like that. Just in case.

Just in case I fall to my death in a few minutes.

Releasing Darren, I step over to what they call the riggings. Manny stands right behind me, and he starts to instruct me in his low, gravelly voice.

"As your brother said, place your hands along the ropes, and your feet will be supported by the wooden beams. Climb at a steady pace, and once you reach the first landing, you will assist Jarlath in lowering the sails."

I nod instinctually, not sure if I actually caught any of that. Brushing my bangs behind my ears, I grab one of the ropes and step up onto the side of the ship. The ocean blurs below, churning and foaming like a giant hot tub. If I fall onto the deck, I know the impact will break me. Falling into the water means there's a slim chance of survival—as long as Cináed turns the boat around to rescue me.

My feet move like deadweight along the ship's edge, inching me around so that my back faces the open ocean. I start to climb. One hand, one foot. Next hand, next foot.

It doesn't take long before I wish Cináed had used something other than my shoe as demon bait. Without any support, my socked foot already aches from standing on the slender beams.

I make the mistake of glancing higher than the next hand-hold. The first landing is even further away than I thought. I'll be climbing all day if they expect me to reach the top sails that blend in with the white clouds.

I duck my head and focus on the ropes in front of me as my stomach rolls like the ocean. *Just get to the first landing, and worry about the rest later.*

The sun glares down on me, making it harder to see the next handhold. It doesn't help that my fingers are clammy. Or that every step rocks the riggings, like I'm on a grown-up version of the rope obstacle course I used to play on at the park.

"You're almost there!" I hear Darren call to me, and I look down between the gaps in the ropes. I can almost see the entire ship below me now, and Darren's small form blurs as my vision fades in and out. I clench my eyes shut.

I take it back. This is nothing like a playground obstacle course.

When I open my eyes, I see Cináed among my small audience. I can't make out his expression from here, but something tells me an annoying smirk is plastered on his adorable face.

How I hate that adorable face.

With an internal push that escapes my lips in a grunt, I continue to climb. Just when I think that the mysterious landing doesn't exist, my hands close around solid wood. My arms tremble as I claw my way onto the platform and hug the mast like a lifeline, glad that no one can see me unless I peek back over the edge of the small landing.

"Well, looksy here," a voice squeaks from the other side of the mast. "And I thought Captain told me a falsehood when he said a young lassie would be dropping the sails alongside ol' Jar."

My sweaty cheek unsticks from the mast as I turn my head to see where the voice is coming from. Sure enough, the creature named Jarlath stands beside me in all of his squatty, rat-faced glory.

He blinks two maroon eyes at me, his fat tail curling behind his furry backside. He's dressed in a pair of tattered overalls that would fit a large toddler, and several sharp teeth poke out of his long face.

Jarlath leans closer until I can smell his wet fur, and when he opens his mouth to speak, the scent of sardines triggers my gag reflex.

"Do you have a voice in there, lassie?" Jarlath yells at me while I cough and turn my face. "I have the rights to know if I'll be teaching a mute. Did the king slice out yer tongue?"

I hold my breath. "Can we get this over with so I can climb down?"

Rat-face leaps back a step, and I wince as he teeters on the edge of the landing. His paws grip the wood as he starts to fall. Then his tail, as if with a mind of its own, latches onto a rope and steadies him.

"Mercy be, lassie! Ye almost scared the Goddess Aine out of me little heart." Jarlath places a paw on his chest. "Well, let us be dropping the sail then, shall we? I'd hate to miss my noon-time pandy."

With stiff limbs that don't feel like my own, I inch one knee up after the other and pull myself into a standing position, still gripping the mast like a vice. Rat-face stands on the pole that spans the width of the ship. I can see the white, tent-like material of the sails lashed to the pole with ropes.

The chubby rat points to one of these knots. "It is our task, lassie, to untie each knot and let the sail loose. Then we retie the rope around the nubs here. We start at the furthest ends and move in toward the mast."

His little paws point in both directions, and I crane my neck to see where the first knot has to be untied. It might as well be in another galaxy.

Cináed can sail us wherever he wants—this isn't worth my life.

I shake my head as I kneel and crawl to the edge of the landing. "Nope, nope, nope," I repeat over and over, reaching for the riggings.

Enough of this madness. Time to climb back down and face the humiliation.

The wind catches away Jarlath's voice as I peek over the edge and see Darren waiting in the same spot. When he sees me, he gives a little shout and waves his arms as if calling out to a lost ship in a storm.

I was only out of sight for a few minutes, and everyone else, including Cináed, apparently moved on to more interesting things.

My jaw clenches, and I scan the deck to find Cináed. I glare at the back of his golden head as he talks with Manny, pointing toward the horizon.

He sent me up here and doesn't even care if I can make it back down.

As if sensing my glare, Cináed turns and lifts his face into the sunlight, staring right at me. He folds his arms over his chest and just stands there, not saying a word. At least not that I can hear.

It's as if he's using his body language to speak to me. And from what I can tell, his message is loud and clear.

He prefers to have me out of the way. To him, I'm just an annoying girl who won't shut up about wanting to go home.

Huffing a loud breath through my nostrils, I push away from the edge and rest my back against the mast.

"Let's do this thing," I mutter.

Jarlath's face contorts to show all of his sharp little teeth. "Aye, lassie."

After Jarlath gives me a few more instructions, I take one side of the sail while he takes the other. Kneeling on the platform, I reach for the pole, which is about half the width of the mast, and clutch onto it as I lower one leg after the other onto a rope suspended beneath the pole like a tightrope.

As I rest my feet on the rope, I feel the open air beneath me. Nothing but this rope stands between me and my death.

Both of my arms wrap over the top of the pole, and I move one arm and then one foot to the left as I make my way to the end where I can start to untie the knots. Beads of sweat drip down my back, and pressure builds behind my eyes. The breeze is a lot stronger up here, but it keeps fresh air flooding into my lungs and eases my queasy stomach.

When I reach the end, I lift one shaking hand and tear into the knot. The roughness of the rope scratches my skin, and by the time I've reached the third knot, my fingers are raw.

Jarlath is making fast progress. He scampers along like a trapeze walker, using his tail to right any missteps.

The fourth knot is especially stubborn, and as desperation surges up from my core, I try to use both hands to untie the rope. In a heartbeat, I feel one foot slip off the rope beneath me, and I start to fall backward.

With a gasp, I hug the pole as my other foot loses its grip on the rope. Dangling, I swing my legs, searching for the rope out of sight beneath me.

"Róisín!" someone shouts from below.

My neck and arm strength have to hold. I'm in a race to get my feet back onto the tightrope before my screaming muscles give out.

A thumping vibration shakes the pole, and my chin bites hard into the wood. Fur brushes past my face as the rat appears by my head, and then he disappears from view. I try to hold still so he can situate the rope back underneath my feet.

Hot breath burns my top lip, and my fingernails claw at the sail material in my fists.

I feel something tugging on my right foot, the one with the sneaker. My shoe settles on something more solid than air. The socked foot comes next, the rope pressing into my sole as I carefully ease some weight down.

As if guiding me out of a nightmare, Jarlath walks backward on the pole, calling to me whenever I stop moving, until I reach the landing.

Strong, tanned arms grasp under my armpits from behind and hoist me onto the platform.

"Róisín." His voice is gentle, and maybe it's my own terror projecting itself into his tone, but I swear I hear a touch of fear.

I lay in Cináed's arms, almost feeling secure on the landing now that I've experienced walking the tightrope of death. My muscles spasm and tremble in random bursts, and Cináed holds me closer, his legs forming walls around me.

"Why?"

I know he understands when he answers, "Because I did not think you would try."

His jaw rests against mine, and I'm glad I can't see his face. I don't want to try and read his thoughts through his eyes. I rest my head on his chest with another shuddering breath.

For this brief, foreign moment, I don't want to think about anything at all.

{ 10 }

The host is riding from Knocknarea
And over the grave of Clooth-na-bare;
Caolte tossing his burning hair
And Niamh calling, 'Away, come away:
Empty your heart of its mortal dream.
The winds awaken, the leaves whirl round,
Our cheeks are pale, our hair is unbound,
Our breasts are heaving, our eyes are a-gleam,
Our arms are waving, our lips are apart;
And if any gaze on our rushing band,
We come between him and the deed of his hand,
We come between him and the hope of his heart.
The host is rushing 'twixt night and day,
And where is there hope or deed as fair?
Caolte tossing his burning hair,
And Niamh calling, 'Away, come away.'
- "The Hosting of the Sidhe" by William Butler Yeats (1899)

I lean against the side of the ship, a firm barrier that reaches above my hips, and stare into the stars scattered across the deep indigo sky.

This is the first time I've wandered onto the deck after what happened in the riggings.

Whenever I thought about leaving the room, my wounded pride kept me trapped, pacing beside the bed. I imagined running into Cináed. Or worse, not seeing him at all and being reminded of my failure by the monsters he calls crewmen.

As I gaze into the great expanse where the sky and ocean collide, stretching forever in every direction, I'm overwhelmed by my own blindness. If all of this ended right now, and Darren and I magically reappeared in our homes, would I wish any of this back?

I've been so focused on my mission that I didn't stop to think about what this chance could mean. Wherever Cináed takes us, this orphan girl, who's never experienced a life beyond foster care and skipping class and not fitting in, has been offered a chance to know something different.

The facts are these: Cináed brought us on this boat, promising safety, and then sailed off without my consent.

But I think I believe him when he says we're not prisoners here. After all, he lets Darren and I roam freely around the decks—freedom that Darren took advantage of for the last three days while I seethed in our room—and Jarlath brings us plenty of food.

Cináed did demand that we never go below deck without either himself or Manny—as if we needed a rule to keep us from exploring a ship full of monsters—but otherwise, we're probably safer here than we would be back home with a demon stalker on the loose.

Maybe it's not too late to let my pride go and, as Cináed put it, see this from a more Darren-esque perspective.

Speaking of my brother, he's been keeping track of our days here in a small notebook the buffalo gave him. If not for that, I wouldn't be able to tell if we've been on the ocean for an entire month or just a week.

Darren says it's because faeries follow a different time than we do. He knows a lot of random facts about the creatures we've been living with. Most of them don't make any sense. But I remember the one he murmured before falling asleep that first night.

Cináed is a faery. A powerful one.

The ocean sprays droplets of salt water over the ship, and I shudder against the refreshing nip in the air. I step away from the edge, slightly reluctant to return to our room where Darren is fast asleep.

I turn around and see Cináed standing a few feet away, like he's been watching me. My heart jumps to my throat and stays there. His hands are tucked into his pockets, his hair catching the light of the nearest hanging lantern, turning the curls a more fiery gold.

I stare at the deck, looking at the stars reflected in the dampened wood. It's almost like we're standing in the sky. At that thought, the same weightless sensation I experienced on the tightrope rushes over me, turning my gut. My knees shake, but I force a deep breath, remembering why I ventured out here tonight.

To see Cináed again, without anyone else around.

I can do this.

"Nice night," I say, my voice raspy from underuse.

Cináed's expression is unreadable, and he pauses before responding, "It is that."

A strong gust of wind punches my back, and my wavering legs take a step in his direction. I'm still brushing my hair from my eyes before I see that he's closed the remaining space between us. I stare at his chest as he tucks my overgrown bangs behind my ear, his hand resting on my upper arm to steady me.

"You have not yet recovered," he says.

I know he's talking about my near-death experience. Embarrassment creeps up my neck.

"I'm fine."

Before I can react, he drapes one of my arms across his shoulders and holds my waist against his so that my weight rests on him. His movements blur together, like they're happening too fast for me to register them.

He walks us toward the stairs that lead to the upper deck—the opposite direction from my room. We pass Manny at the helm, and the beast nods at his captain, glancing at me with a softness he's only shown to Darren until now.

He probably pities me. The weak human who can't even untie a single sail.

Cináed winds us through a narrow hallway and into a room similar to the one I share with Darren. Maps and books are scattered across a sturdy desk lined with lumpy candles melted into the wood. A bed leans against the window, and he sits me down on the mattress. The moon beyond the glass offers the only light in the room, and then the sharp snap of a match illuminates Cináed's face, and he spreads the small flame over the hungry candlewicks.

Putting out the match, he rummages through a drawer in the desk. He finds whatever he was searching for and sits across from me in a wooden chair. The moonlight lands on him, and the nearby flames dance in his eyes, currently a deep shade of blue.

Any remaining doubts that Cináed is something other than human vanish away. Sure, he doesn't seem to have wings or a tail, but tonight there is something downright otherworldly about him.

"So tell me, Róisín." He pulls the chair closer until our knees touch, and he holds a cloth bundle to my forehead. "Would you consider yourself an especially stubborn human?"

"Excuse me?"

His eyes lift to my face, and the corner of his mouth tugs upward.

Nope. He's definitely *not normal.* Normal people don't have such frustratingly adorable smirks.

"It takes an especially determined, albeit prideful, person to reach the first landing with no previous tutelage aboard a ship."

The smell of flowers fills my nose, and a soothing sensation spreads over my body. It must be from the cloth pouch, some sort of voodoo medicine like the stuff he gave Darren. I fight it, deciding I'd rather feel seasick than let Cináed's jab pass without a counterattack.

"Do you like giving orders to people you know can't handle the job?" I snap. "You said you didn't think I'd try, so why even ask?"

All humor drains from his face, replaced by an unexpected seriousness.

"Róisín, I—" He stares at our knees and then refocuses on me. "I meant it only in jest. I know now that you take things quite literally."

Then he adds, with a dimpled smile that melts my iron pride, "You are unlike any human I have ever known."

My pulse races, and I swallow hard. "If you aren't human, then what are you?"

His grin contrasts with the inky darkness of the room. "I am a faery, of course."

I don't know if it's the magic floral medicine, or if being alone in Cináed's bedroom is getting to me, but I start giggling like a total loon.

"Seriously?" I shake my head and it rubs against the cloth. "Y-you don't even have wings!"

Cináed stares at me with humor etched into his face. Like he's watching a strange animal in a zoo exhibit.

"You are correct, I do not have wings. But other faeries do." He sits back, instructing me to hold the cloth in place, then tugs his fingers through his hair with a sigh. "I have withheld information until now for your own safety, but you must understand some things before entering the Otherworld."

I sit up straighter. Getting Cináed to spill about what's going on is all I've wanted since the night he rescued Darren from the demon.

His eyes wander to the window, and he watches the waves rolling behind the ship as he continues in an even tone.

"The beings you see on my ship are similar to others that exist in every country around the world. Our kind remain invisible to humans for our own protection.

"But for reasons unknown to me, the veil that hides us from human eyes no longer works on you or your brother. It is very curious, and apparently the shadow faery who took your brother thought the same. I assume you revealed your Sight to the Sluagh, thus encouraging it to pursue you because you appeared to be a threat."

His voice trails off, and I feel like he's speaking his thoughts out loud, forgetting I'm even here. I mull over his words as I play with a strand of red-tipped hair that sprang loose from my ponytail.

"The demon that stalked me." I pause, remembering the night all of this began. "It was watching me sleep, and it woke me up. What was I supposed to do? Just ignore it?"

He disregards my question. "And that moment was the first time you saw a faery?"

My mouth opens and then closes again. "I mean, I've always noticed weird things." When I realized that no one else hears the voices in the wind or can see how lightning bugs have tiny human faces, I ignored it all to stay sane."

"You and your brother are, as you would say, orphans, correct?"

I can't count how many times those words have blindsided me. But coming from Cináed—who sits like an untouchable god in a beam of moonlight—I somehow can't ignore their sting.

"Yeah," I mumble at last.

"Do you know anything about your parents?"

My tone is laced with ice. "Why should that matter?"

"Róisín." He leans closer, lifting my chin. "I do not mean to offend."

After what seems like an eternity of painful silence, staring into each other's eyes as I hold my emotions together, he releases me and moves to the desk. I sink against the wall, madly tamping out the fire blazing inside me.

Stop it. You're not his type, remember?

I bite my lip and shrug. "I'm fine. It's really not that big a deal."

"Never make excuses for them," he begins, glancing up at me as he uses a mug to hold down the corner of a map on the desk. "I will not presume to understand your pain. But for what it's worth, I feel for your loss."

The way he says it closes the conversation. I leave the cloth pouch on the bed, feeling surprisingly energized, and move to stand near the desk.

"I know you hate gratitude," I say, "but I want to thank you for saving my brother."

His eyes reflect the candlelight around us as he looks up at me. When he doesn't cut me off, I continue, my voice wavering a little.

"Darren means the world to me. I don't know what I would have done if that demon had . . ." I clear my throat. "Thank you. Truly."

He nods. "You are most welcome. To clarify, it is not your gratitude, but your mode of expressing it that makes me uncomfortable. The fae prefer to express such feelings with actions, not words. We are a," he pauses, lips twitching, "physical species. At times to a fault."

Then he adds, in a voice that reminds me of the ocean at night, both dangerous and enticing, "But I recognize that we have our differences, and therefore promise to accept your thanks however you wish to bestow them."

My face burns in the dark.

Is he baiting me to make a move?

Just when I think he's serious, he winks and chuckles, his focus returning to the map.

I clear my throat, feeling both disappointed and relieved. *If he were serious, what would I have done?*

So I start a new conversation, saving my confusing feelings for later. "Tell me about this Otherworld."

His smile widens into a grin, and he places his finger on the map in a spot encased by open ocean. "We are here."

He traces a line to a smudge of land off the west coast of England. "And here is Ireland, as the humans refer to her now."

I smirk too, noticing his accent sounds more prominent when he's talking about Ireland.

"King Rauri will hold a feast upon our arrival. He will be most pleased to welcome you and Darren." Cináed smiles, his gaze distant. "It is tradition to feast on the provisions we bring from our voyages. And the dancing, the music . . ." He looks at me. "Oh, Róisín, how your ears will delight in fae music."

I set my hand on top of his, bringing his attention away from some far-off scene. "Will the king tell me how to get rid of the demon and any other dangerous faeries back home?"

Cináed nods, and I start to remove my hand, but he holds onto it—another casual gesture he doesn't seem to think anything of.

"Aye, he shall grant you safety in the Otherworld until we can discover more about your Sight. He will be just as curious as I to learn the cause of such an occurrence. That is why he bids me to travel as often as I do, in order to learn what I can from the human realm, to understand how we may better protect ourselves and our kind."

"Is that why you saved Darren? Why you're bringing us with you?" *As research projects?*

"For these purposes, as well as for your own safety."

He watches me, gauging my reaction as I read between the lines.

I might mean more than a research project. But I'm still a helpless human.

When I don't respond, he continues.

"Most of us would kill you for your Sight rather than trust you and what you've seen. Humans have not been kind to the fae and other magical beings in the past. We are slow to forgive those wrongs, and we do not want humans to be aware of us. While I believe in your innocence, know that you are a threat to us. We can only survive in secret."

He lifts our hands and walks around the desk until he stands in front of me. Once again I feel my insides ignite, and my heart takes off like a bullet train. Standing so close to him,

I catch what must be his scent—a perfect blend of clean ocean air and warm sunshine.

"Enough questions for tonight." He traces a line along my jaw, and a thrill runs down my spine. "Come." He steps back but doesn't let go of my hand. "I will escort you to your room."

He holds me close as we walk onto the deck. Part of me still resists his touch, knowing there's no way he could ever have feelings for me. But another part of me, a voice that grows stronger the longer Cináed is near me, says that this is unlike anything I've experienced before. Keeping my feelings in check so I don't end up with a broken heart has worked in the past. But Cináed makes those other guys I used to swoon over look like piles of garbage.

As I watch him from the corner of my eye and feel his arm around my waist, I sense a portion of my reserve crumble away. At this point, resisting is futile. Whether he's out of my league or not, I'm already too far gone.

{ 11 }

The Tuatha De Danaan, the People of the Goddess Danu, were a divine race who possessed great magical powers and were learned and gifted, according to Irish legend. [T]he Tuatha De Danaan ruled Ireland for many years, until they were defeated by another wave of invaders, the Milesians. Although they were banished by these newcomers, they did not leave Ireland. Instead, they went underground to live in the *sidhes*, mounds and earthworks that are scattered all over the country. Above them, the human inhabitants of Ireland, descendants of the Milesians, lived and died, and were helped but sometimes hindered by the Tuatha De Danaan, who became known as the People of the Sidhe, the Faery, or the Little Folk. From time to time, these mysterious beings would enter the mortal world . . . But they always returned to their kingdom under the earth, that happy otherworld, the Land of Youth.

- *The Names Upon the Harp* by Marie Heaney (2000)

"Róisín, wake up!"

Someone shakes my shoulder, tearing me from my dreams.

Bolting upright, I see Darren next to me on the bed. Now that I'm awake, his attention returns to the window, where soft sunlight caresses the water with a warm yellow glow. I hear seagulls crying and lots of noise coming from the deck.

As I try to regain my composure, letting my pulse quiet as I realize there's no immediate threat, one memory solidifies in my mind, expanding till it swallows me whole.

Cináed brought me to his room. He didn't almost kiss me, did he?

"You can see it!" Darren's nose presses against the grimy glass.

"See what?"

"The rocks! That means we've reached land." He looks at me with wide eyes, full of excitement and fear. "The captain's taking us to the Otherworld today, isn't he?"

All of my irrational feelings for Cináed dissolve. How do I tell my kid brother that it might be a while before we can go home?

If we ever go home, my cynicism interjects.

"Once I figure out why we can see faeries and how to protect ourselves from them, we're going straight home, okay?"

Darren glances out the window again, his expression more solemn. "I just don't want Juliana and Howard to worry. I know they'll worry about me."

As much as I hate to admit it, I know that the Robertses are Darren's best shot at experiencing some semblance of a family. It's no secret that the adoption process is well under way. He belongs to them now, more than he does to me.

I pull him closer, making a silent vow to get him back safely, no matter the cost.

Everyone is hurrying around the deck, busy with their tasks and shouting to each other. I see Jarlath swing past on a rope, landing on a stack of crates carried by several green, hairless creatures that Darren calls goblins. They're loading three smaller boats the size of a wide canoe.

To the left of the ship, I can see large, sharp rocks jutting from the ocean. A heavy mist crawls over the cliffs, and white seagulls dive in and out of the fog as deep green waves overtake the dark stone. Above the rock face, I can barely make out a thin layer of greenery dipping over the edge in a splash of color.

"Good of you to join us." Manny shakes the deck as he stomps over to us. "Captain just ordered me to retrieve you as we are preparing to sail ashore."

"Are we coming?" Darren asks.

The buffalo's head is so far above us that I have to peer up into the growing sunlight to look at his hairy face. His black nose twitches as he snorts. "The captain deems it best for you to join the group going ashore." In a softer tone, he adds. "Besides, the crew members remaining behind include those least fond of humans, and the captain would not be here to stop them from . . . acting on their opinions."

His beady eyes dart around the deck. I take Darren's hand.

"We're coming with you."

Manny brings us to the small boats, two of which are full of crates. The third is empty, and I see Cináed standing near it, giving out orders.

Seeing him immediately sets off an embarrassing number of fireworks in my stomach, and I turn away, scared that someone will see me blushing.

"As this is one of our larger hauls," Cináed is saying, "our journey will be slow and my return delayed. But keep a steady watch for me, as I plan to sail north while the weather is warmer. After this next voyage, we shall take a much-needed reprieve."

"Aye, Captain." Jarlath gives a gravelly squeak.

Cináed's gaze latches onto me. For a moment, everyone else fades away, and I imagine I'm in his arms again, smelling the summer breeze on his skin. He turns to Manny.

"First Mate, you will journey with the mortals in the empty vessel. The goblins and I will take the crates."

Buffalo repeats Cináed's instructions in a bellowing voice. Creatures hustle to obey.

I look down at Darren, squeezing his hand. I can tell he's trying to be brave, but his eyes are an open book, displaying all of his emotions to the world. I've always been better at masking my feelings, but right now I'm so far out of my element that all I can do is keep breathing and try not to panic.

This is it. Once we reach land, you can either follow the faeries or make a break for the nearest human authorities.

I think Cináed would let Darren and me go. Even if we represent a flaw in the faerie-protection program, he said himself we aren't prisoners.

All I have to do is ask to be directed toward the nearest humans. The Robertses will take care of the plane tickets back home. It's simple, really.

As my mind whirs like a hot machine, Manny herds us to the side of the ship. He and some other creatures lift the first two boats onto the railing, where a pulley system of ropes guides the first boat down and into the water. The goblins disappear over the edge, and Cináed climbs into the next boat.

His eyes find me, and even though we're surrounded by monsters and crashing waves and I can barely hear myself think, for a moment I know he sees only me.

A playful smirk spreads across his face, his eyes glowing green.

"Keep your wits about you," he says, his voice just loud enough for me to hear. "You will soon enter a land beyond anything you have dared to dream of."

Then, still standing in the small boat, he raises a fist and shouts across the deck, "May the blessings of Dea be with us!"

Darren and I step up to clamber into the last boat. My socked feet make me wish I still had a second sneaker, but walking around with one shoe is somehow worse than no shoes at all.

Manny waits until we've both climbed inside. Then he hands the ropes off to the next monster in line and I wince as his huge body lurches aboard.

"A land beyond anything you have dared to dream of."

Cináed's melodic voice whispers through my mind, speaking to some part of me I didn't know existed.

We can't go back yet.

Not only do we need answers from Cináed's king, but a strange pressure between my lungs is filling me with longing, curiosity, and a thrilling terror.

If we turn back now, who knows what we'd miss?

The ropes lower our boat, and we jerk to a stop several times along the way until we finally hit the water with a *splash* that shakes my bones and almost throws me into the ocean.

Manny watches as I right myself, his hands busy untying the ropes and releasing us from the mother ship. Darren curls into me, already wet with ocean spray.

The ocean is even louder down here. It beats against the rocks with a deafening roar. A wave retreats from the cliffs, rushing at us and tossing the boat around. Another wave moves toward the rocks, and we drift closer to the cliffs again.

I hold Darren with one arm and the side of the boat with the other, biting back a cry every time the waves threaten to tip us.

Maybe I spoke too soon. Maybe all I want is to go home and take a nice hot shower. Not be torn to shreds in a deadly game of ocean tug-of-war.

Manny holds an oar in each hand, his huge arms flexing with each stroke. His buffalo face doesn't convey much expression, but I swear his black eyes look brighter. Water drips down the horns above his cow ears, trickling into the creases around his mouth.

Is he smiling?

The cliffs stand taller than the highest sail on Cináed's ship. Waves roll around us, collapsing against the unmoving rocks. I want to close my eyes until the roaring, hissing, thundering madness stops.

Through the fragments of morning sunlight, I see a divot cut into the cliffs. Sure enough, we paddle on between the waves and the fog until a passageway appears. It's big enough for us to enter but rests at an angle that blocks the waves from crashing in.

The second our boat crests the passageway, a dark blue shadow falls around us, and a deep chill ices the crisp air. I untie the jacket from my waist and wrap Darren up in it.

"Captain, are the mortals to be used as servants?" one of the goblin asks, its grating voice calling from further ahead.

Another one adds, "Aye, they are rather young and scrawny, Captain."

"They will be welcomed by King Rauri and receive his hospitality and protection," Cináed says. "They owe me less than you do, Bins, and deserve your utmost respect."

Manny snorts white puffs from his nostrils, his chest rumbling in a laugh.

I can't see Cináed behind the pile of crates in his boat, but I don't need to. His protective tone quells my fear. Well, some of it.

"Move steadily now," Cináed calls.

A piece of stone falls from the cliffs above and plunks into the water, echoing around us and heightening the strange stillness.

The scene changes so subtly that I don't notice we're drifting through a tunnel until darkness consumes us. The smell of mildew and damp earth stings in my nostrils.

A distinct *thunk* vibrates the boat, and I jump in my seat.

"Do not fear, Róisín." I can hear Cináed's smirk in the dark. *How did he know I jumped?* "It is only the sound of our vessel reaching land."

Manny snorts again. It's true that the boat stopped moving, but my vision can't decipher between the tunnel walls and the murky water to see where the land begins.

"Lead the way, then, and let's get back above ground," I say, already feeling claustrophobic.

Now all of them are laughing. Well, the goblins' laughter sounds more like shrieking. I sit there, exasperated and annoyed.

"What did I say now, huh?"

A furry hand rests on my arm, and with Manny's help we all manage to shuffle off the boat. When my feet hit the sand, I feel more secure, even though I still can hardly see anything besides the faint outlines of our group. Apparently all of them can see in the dark.

Great. Just one more human weakness that proves I'm worthless.

I'm surprised when it's one of the goblins who responds to my question. It blinks up at me with neon yellow eyes and a voice like bits of glass grinding together.

"To dwell with the fae is to never see the day."

I hear murmurs of agreement, and Manny nods. I know because I can feel his chin hair brush my head with the movement.

My throat constricts. "What, so we're trapped in this tunnel now?"

No one answers me. They're all facing a glowing orb of red light bobbing toward us from deeper inside the tunnel. It casts strange shadows along the rock walls, and it seems to be humming as it hovers beside Cináed's head.

"We come with gifts for the king," he says to the orb, and it zooms out ahead of the group.

Everyone follows at a steady pace, our feet crunching into the sandy floor. Darren's hand is wrapped in mine, and with every step I contemplate spinning us around and sprinting for the boats.

The mysterious Otherworld that Cináed bragged about for days can't be a bunch of tunnels, right?

It absolutely could be. Who knows, maybe this king is nothing more than a washed-up faery drug lord hiding down here. The goblin mentioned human servants. Maybe I'm leading Darren into an underground human trafficking system.

Maybe—

Cináed silences my inner dialogue, glancing at me as he starts talking.

"Long ago, our race was known as the Tuatha De Danann. We roamed this land, tilled the earth, and grew prosperous. Then another race, the Sons of Mil, arrived, rousing us to war in order to protect what was ours.

"After many lives were lost on both sides, the Sons of Mil defeated our kind. When they took control of the earth above, those of us left alive were forced to retreat underground. Our knowledge of magic makes the conditions bearable, but we are still prisoners here. Trapped in the land we can no longer possess but cannot bear to leave behind."

The crunch of feet and the humming light create a kind of eerie rhythm. The way Cináed talks about this history almost makes it sound like he lived it himself. But that's impossible.

I've never heard about any of these people groups, which means this story has to be hella ancient.

"What happened to the Sons of Mil?" I ask.

"They still possess the land that we lost," Cináed says. "They are what you would call the human race."

Okay, so maybe not as ancient as I thought. Is that why faeries seem to hate humans? Because we took their land and forced them underground?

It doesn't explain why the demon tried to kill us, though. That thing lives in another country across the ocean. Did the Sons of Mil take over everything on that continent like they did here? There has to be more to this story. A more logical explanation for this universal hatred.

I'm saved from having to respond when the orb of light swirls around Cináed's head, humming louder. We all stop, and Cináed approaches the wall blocking our path. Right when I think we'll have to turn around and find another way, Cináed places his hand on the stone, and the ground rumbles.

I pull Darren behind me, my eyes glued to the shifting stone beneath Cináed's touch.

When the rock and sand particles settle again, the once-immovable blockade forms an open archway. The red light zooms through it and joins a million other lights flickering between tree branches that reach as far as I can see in a lush, misty forest.

Wait.

A forest? Underground?

Cináed turns, watching me with a fierce glow in his eyes.

"What just happened?" My voice sounds small and foreign in my ears.

"Darren. Róisín." Cináed nods to each of us with a smile. "Welcome to the Otherworld."

{ 12 }

Mortal who has danced with the fae,
has seen the danger and delight with glee,
and entered a realm and lost their way,
will soon find what used to be.

- Verde

Cináed steps through the archway. Darren manages to wriggle away from me, and he hurries after Cináed, his dark eyes bright and his mouth forming a small *o*.

Manny holds the goblins back, gesturing for me to go next.

I hesitate. If I cross that line, if I step inside this underground world, I'll be signaling to everything sensical in the universe that I believe in something . . . well, something *non*sensical.

Cináed tells my brother to stay close, and then he watches me, his smirk masking something deeper in his eyes. Curiosity?

He still doesn't know if I'll go through with this. Which proves yet again that this is my choice. Even now, standing on his faerie doorstep, he won't force me.

An inhale rattles my chest, and I feel something pulling me from my core, like a far-off voice calling my name. One step at a time, my socked feet cross over from the tunnel and onto the cold soil floor.

Rows of bark and moss surround us, their colors more vivid than anything I've ever seen. Branches block out most of the ceiling, but the subtle yellow glow and patches of blue I glimpse through the tree limbs couldn't be more similar to a sunny afternoon sky.

Under the ground.

Manny and the goblins step through the archway. On this side, there's no stone wall supporting the passageway. The arch stands on its own, surrounded by trees. A portal in the middle of a forest.

I force myself to take another deep breath. I know I'm in shock, and for now I prefer it that way. Dissolving into panic because my life has turned into one of those fantasy movies I ruthlessly make fun of won't get me the answers I need.

I'm walking toward Darren when a swarm of colorful lights stops me in my tracks.

They hum a series of notes, vibrating the air around them. A deep purple light moves close enough that I can see the source of the glow. A minuscule body, more slender than my pointer finger, flutters on a pair of sheer wings. The creature's skin is also indigo, the same color as the light pulsing from it like a heartbeat.

And its tiny face, overwhelmed by large, black eyes, is staring right at me.

"Pretty, this one," her voice chimes like a tiny bell.

"Pretty for a human."

"Human child, come to dance with the fae."

"Who might her faerie lover be?"

"She will make the perfect summer bride."

"Pretty girl needs a pretty gown to be a bride."

Heat flames in my cheeks. I look past the lights at Darren and Cináed. Everyone is watching me with unreadable expressions. Only Darren shows his true feelings, looking like he'd offer up a kidney for the chance to be interrogated by these talking light bulbs.

"Surely she is more than a summer bride," the indigo light says, hovering in front of my face. *"Do you not see her glow?"*

I step through them, waving my hands like I'm warding off a swarm of bugs. The lights zoom away, chittering through the trees.

Darren takes my outstretched hand, and we start walking. All I want is to put some distance between us and the archway before I change my mind and run back through it.

Summer bride? I laugh under my breath as I stomp through the underbrush. I won't be caught dead in a dress, let alone marrying some faery.

After walking for what seems like hours through soft undergrowth shrouded in swirling mist, Cináed calls back at us to stop for a break.

I lean against the dampened trunk of the nearest tree and catch my breath. Orange and yellow mushrooms grow along the mossy bark. A pair of small eyes blinks in the nearby brush before darting off.

Darren sits beside me on a boulder. His skin glistens, the hair bridging his forehead darkened with humidity. Everything in this forest is either sticky or squishy. I can't set my foot anywhere without the ground swallowing it.

As the other members of the group talk amongst themselves, I nudge Darren's arm.

"Hey, you alright?"

It's a stupid question considering we're traveling through an underground forest to find answers from a faerie king.

Darren glances at me. The vibrant greens of the forest are reflected in his brown eyes.

"I think something's wrong with you," he says finally. "You look really different."

My brow furrows. "Different how?"

"What that will-ó-the-wisp said, about you glowing?" His eyes flicker across my face. "Well, you kinda are."

"Will-ó-the-wisp?" I sit next to him on the boulder, rolling my tight neck and shoulders. "You mean the blue flames on *Brave*?"

The foster kids I live with, Angie and Garrett, love that movie. Whenever Sue leaves the house, the TV turns on, and for the last several weeks I got to watch a cartoon redhead ride a pony and chase after cute blue flames. The lights at the archway didn't look a thing like those will-ó-the-wisps.

"Come, we are nearly there," Cináed interrupts before Darren has the chance to rant about how modern society has warped our views of mystical creatures.

"But we must hasten." Cináed watches the trees like he sees or hears something we can't. "Many of the creatures in these woods are not kind to travelers."

The vulnerable feeling of being watched sends a cold shiver down my spine.

We keep walking, and I notice my brother is taking in our surroundings with the keen eye of a researcher. It makes me wonder just how much of this is anything like the fairytales he's read about in those books back home.

I duck under twisted branches and navigate through deadfall. A light mist curls beneath my soaked feet, and with every step I feel a growing heaviness in the air, like I'm trying to inhale the shadows around us.

I glance ahead at Cináed and his posse of monsters, all of them looking outright nightmarish as they travel through the layers of trees and brush.

No, this kinda scene wouldn't work in your typical fairytale book.

And it would be naïve of me to treat it as such—to let the magic, and strangeness, of this place distract me from a potential trap.

"You know," I say as I work through a particularly dense patch of wet moss, "I don't think this place is everything you made it out to be, Cináed."

His screeching halt should shut me up. Who knows what an angry faery might do?

But I ignore the tension in my gut, choosing instead to test the line. He needs to know that even though I'm human, I'm not stupid. If he plans to sell Darren and me off as servants, he's messing with the wrong girl.

Cináed's eyes burn through me. I jam my nails into my palms to keep from flinching. "I mean, where's the public transportation? Where I'm from we don't have to hike through the woods unless we want to. Don't you at least have a bus system?"

Darren hides his snicker while the goblins shriek with laughter. Cináed just stares.

"Hold your tongue, human," Manny bellows, his cow ears twitching.

I raise my eyebrows, gesturing to the mud caking my feet. "I'm just saying, how come us *humans* have something you don't, huh?"

Cináed finally looks away, his jaw flexing. Manny takes a step closer, snorting and pawing the ground.

"I said hold your—"

"First mate." Cináed stretches out a hand, and the buffalo goes silent. Those sea-green eyes find me, only this time, I can't find any semblance of anger burning inside them. His defeated expression hurts me more than if he'd used his powers to turn me into a toad, or whatever faeries use as punishment.

"You are correct," he begins. "The fae are unable to match the human race in terms of science and discovery. This does not mean, however, that there must be a battle of words today in order to determine the superior race."

I exclaim, "We won't be anyone's servants." *Or brides.* I wish I sounded demanding instead of desperate. "All we want are answers, and then we're going home."

He sighs, brushing the curls from his forehead. "So that is what this is about." His anger resurfaces faster than I can blink. "You may think what you will of the fae, Róisín. But never question my loyalty to a promise again. Now, do as

Manny ordered and hold your tongue until we reach the castle. Goddess Morrigan knows we've already drawn enough attention to ourselves here, and I do not wish for any of us to die before we reach the castle."

Cináed turns on his heel, and the other creatures follow their captain. Although I got the confirmation of safety that I wanted, I'm left feeling unsatisfied.

Probably because you overreacted, again.

No one talks again until Cináed halts, and Manny pulls back a layer of hanging vines and twisting ivy.

Darren steps closer, and I slowly follow him, peering out into a huge sea of rolling green hills. Far off, I see two horse-drawn carts racing each other. The horses' coloring alone tells me they're unnatural, one's platinum gold and the other sunset pink. The riders inside the carts have to be some kind of warriors. Both wear armor, and their long hair splays out behind them like the horses' tails.

After they dip below another hill, I focus on the distant structure that must be the castle. It glints in the light, the smooth walls reminding me of cream-colored marble, crowned with sharp spires that pierce the clouds like knives.

But it's the pale golden orb in the sky that clenches my stomach. *How in the world can all of this be under the ground?*

Temporarily forgetting about my orders to be silent, I ask no one in particular, "I thought the fae never see the light of day?"

It's the goblin's quote, and one of them answers, "That's no sun, girly. The fae use magic to create everything your little eyes can see."

Cináed adds without looking at me. "As I said before, you cannot begin to understand our mysteries. At least not during your first days here."

We leave Manny and the goblins at the edge of the forest and follow Cináed into the open expanse of grass. When Darren asks why the others are staying behind, Cináed explains that they will return and bring the crates of food and other provisions through the doorway. Once that happens, King Rauri's druids can transport the crates from the forest and into the castle.

I look at Darren to gauge his reaction, but he just stares ahead at the castle. I think shock's getting the best of him too.

We reach the castle faster than I anticipated. The grass shifts like water underneath my feet, helping me walk. Only once does the ground get ahead of me, almost pushing me over.

Our feet touch the shimmering cobblestone path trailing around the outer wall of the castle, and the ground behind us settles back into itself with an audible sigh that tickles the backs of my legs. Standing on solid stone steadies my trembling knees.

Before we go any further, I reach out to Cináed and hold his arm. He looks at me, and even though I can tell his focus is elsewhere, I can't ignore the painful knot between my lungs.

"Cináed, I'm-I'm sorry." He blinks at me, as if truly seeing me now. "For what I said about your people. It was wrong."

His smile doesn't reach his eyes. He rests a hand against my face, the touch both warm and gentle, gone in the same breath it arrived.

He turns and tells us to keep walking. The ache in my gut relaxes just enough to make room for a new onslaught of anxiety.

Something's not right here.

My feet, regaining their feeling after walking for hours through cold mud, grip the stone path as I try not to make a sound. I thought by now we'd run into someone. Another faery who lives in the castle. Maybe I haven't seen enough medieval movies, but I can't be the only one who feels how the air is heavy with a creepy, unnatural silence.

Cináed stops in front of a break in the cream marble. A small frown pulls at his mouth as his eyes scan the area. His fingers rest against the wall, his body blocking my view of the archway that seems to lead into the castle.

"What darkness has entered here in my absence?" he says, as if talking to the stone, not us.

I pause on the balls of my feet, readying myself to run at the smallest sign of danger.

When nothing happens, Cináed steps away from the wall, motioning for us to follow.

We round the corner and walk through the archway choked with greenery. It forms a tunnel of glass, and thick ivy winds around each marble pillar supporting the passage.

It reminds me of the greenhouse I used to hide in at foster home #2. The greenhouse belonged to the old couple next door. One time the old man found me hiding in there, and instead of ratting me out, he picked me some cherry tomatoes from a vine and let me be. I can still remember the slight tang of dirt in the air and the moisture streaking the glass.

With each beam of sunlight and line of shadow, the tunnel seems to be getting smaller. Long thorns encroach on the path. One of them cuts me, and I hug my arms closer to my sides, overwhelmed by the strong smell of decaying plants.

Darren slows, looking at an orange rose so wilted it might fall to the ground at his touch. When his fingers cradle the soft petals, a distinct spark passes from his skin and into the flower. Immediately the rose lifts its head, and the thorns nearest to it retract into the ivy. Darren flinches away, his eyes wide.

"Come, mortals."

Cináed waits ahead. His once-slight frown is now a deep scowl, and his shifting eyes never settle on any one thing. We hurry to catch up.

The tunnel ends, and the air grows cool as we step inside the castle. Cináed is nearly running now, his head turning left and right like he's searching for something. I pull Darren to a faster pace, refusing to lose Cináed and end up wandering alone in this gorgeous but eerie castle.

Tapestries, jeweled weapons, and other archaic decorations you'd expect to see in a history museum line the smooth walls. Regret sits like a boulder on my chest as we reach the end of a wide hallway full of windows and drooping chandeliers.

We never should have come here. We never should have stepped through that portal. We never should have—

Cináed shoves a set of ceiling-high double doors wide open. He pauses in the doorway, and I peer into the room, shielding Darren with an arm as a joint gasp rushes over us.

{ 13 }

There is a double-edged relationship between mortal and faery in Celtic tradition: reciprocal respect and mutual aid can easily slip into jealous overlooking, theft and greed. The faeries expect respect and exact retribution if the rules of common inter-species politeness are transgressed.

- *Encyclopedia of Celtic Wisdom* by Caitlín and John Matthews (1994)

A crowd stares at us, their beautiful, athletically curvaceous bodies draped in silk gowns and long shirts. Light hair falls loosely around proud shoulders, and jeweled hands holding golden cups hover in front of curled upper lips.

Despite the throng of godlike creatures—clearly powerful faeries like Cináed—my gaze falls on the front of the room. A line of faeries sits in high-backed chairs, and from their scowls I think we've interrupted something serious. One in particular captures me with an icy stare before he turns to Cináed.

"The final advisor has decided to return at last," he says, his voice both alluring and cruel. His pale, angular face and raven-black hair stand out against the throng of sun-kissed, golden-haired faeries.

Cináed takes two more steps, slow and deliberate. "Where is he?"

I can barely hear his words. Tension threatens to burst through the windows as everyone looks from Cináed to the dark-haired faery.

"I see that you are uninformed of King Rauri's death." The cold tone and wicked gleam in his eyes freezes my blood.

Cináed's shoulders slump as his face lowers into his hands. I notice an empty golden throne behind the dark-haired faery, where I imagine the king must have sat. Blood pounds in my ears, and my skin itches to grab Darren and bolt for the nearest exit.

"Compose yourself, Wanderer," the dark-haired faery continues, his mouth pressed into a faint, douchebag kind of smile that tells me I'm going to hate this guy for the rest of my life. "You shall have ample opportunity to mourn at the festival of Lughnasa."

I hear a breathy snicker from somewhere in the room. The female sitting beside the dark-haired faery folds long fingers on top of the table. Her taut-lipped face reminds me of a strict teacher.

"Cináed the Wanderer." The way she says his name tells me they must know each other well. "We sent word to you as soon as Rauri grew ill. We are currently examining the cause of his and Queen Finnabair's sudden deaths."

She gestures to the long table where she and seven others sit. "The advisors have been gathered for this purpose—and to discuss the future of our kingdom."

"So I see, Orla," Cináed says, some of the hostility returning to his voice. "The advisors also chose to invite an additional member to the table in my absence."

The dark-haired stranger lifts a heavy eyebrow, daring Cináed to make him move from his seat.

Orla gestures to him. "This is Naoise of the Western Moors. He has accepted the role of prospective king. The advisors have all agreed to include him in our quest for answers concerning these recent deaths."

"How convenient for Naoise to have appeared in such an hour of need." Cináed doesn't hide the sarcastic drawl in his words.

Naoise opens his mouth to respond, but Orla continues, ignoring the power struggle in front of her.

"As one of King Rauri's closest advisors, and as someone who has experienced personal loss as a result of this strange sickness, I believe we can expect your full support as we deliberate together to decide what—or quite possibly *who*—is causing these deaths."

Her voice cuts through the room, and when she stops, the silence settles on my chest like a cage. Has our chance to find answers died along with Rauri?

I stare at the back of Cináed's head, my breath stuck in my throat. Even his golden curls seem limp and lifeless. As the room waits for his response, I can't help but feel like I don't know anything about him. The king's most trusted advisor? And what's this about losing someone to the same sickness that killed the king and queen? The image of Cináed kneeling in front of that strange gravestone flashes in my mind.

After five heartbeats, Cináed lifts his head. His voice is resolute, laced with suppressed emotion.

"If you believe that whatever stole Branna's life is connected to the deaths of the royal family, then I make it my personal quest to find the source of this sickness and destroy it. We will purge it from our lands forever."

His words build in power, and his fists clench at his sides. Orla nods to Cináed. Naoise stands, and his eyes stare past Cináed into the shadows of the corridor where Darren and I wait.

"It seems the Wanderer has brought gifts from his travels," he says.

Cináed glances at me and then turns back around. "Their presence is of no concern to the council. They are in my care."

Even from a distance, Naoise's clear eyes send shivers down my spine, and I'm overcome with the sensation of stepping into a body of ice water. Just like me, the other faeries seem to be entranced by every calculated word he speaks.

"They are human?" Naoise asks.

Cináed hesitates. "Aye."

More gasps punch through the stagnant air as one by one the entire room directs their attention to us.

Naoise continues, "Not only has Cináed been absent from us during this *hour of great need*, as he calls it, but he has betrayed us by leading two human children into our kingdom."

"Betrayed?" Cináed looks at the terrified faces around him, his voice rising above the chaos. "They were brought here at my invitation. No harm has been done."

"No harm?" Naoise shakes his head like a disappointed parent. "How much you have missed, Cináed the Wanderer."

Orla chimes in, filling my panicked heart with hope before I realize the meaning of her words. "We shall treat our guests with the same generosity they have bestowed on our kind."

Not good. Not good. Not good.

Faeries hate humans. We took their home. *Why did Cináed bring us here!*

Everyone nods and voices their consent. Everyone but Cináed, but no one is listening to him anymore.

Naoise smiles at me—the kind of smile that belongs to a snake. "Yes, Orla. Let us show these humans how pleased we are by their presence."

Stares bite at us from every direction, stinging like hot knives. Naoise's eyes linger on mine for another moment before he turns away dismissively.

Golden-cloaked figures appear out of nowhere, flocking toward Darren and me and forcing us out of the room. Cináed watches, shouting words I can't hear over the ringing in my ears.

The tall doors swing shut with a shuddering *thud* that kicks cold air into my face, and the cloaked beings wrap strong, gloved hands around us, leading us back down the castle hallway.

Dripping liquid from somewhere above plinks incessantly, fraying my agitated nerves. I look up from the bottom of a dank hole underneath the castle—a godless place Darren calls the dungeons—and glare into the black void of nothingness.

The only light leaks in from the trapdoor in the ceiling of the prison—or the floor of the castle. When the guards opened the trapdoor to throw us down here, I noticed a pair of eyes peering up from the darkness. Now I'm not sure if I really saw anything at all. Over the dripping and my own beating heart I haven't heard a single sound.

Darren's arm rests against mine in the dark. We're sitting together, our backs pressed into a wall of earth and mildew. I hope he's managed to dose off. He has to be in serious shock. I know I am. I guess I have been ever since I laid eyes on the demon sitting outside my window.

From that moment till now, my life has been a downward spiral. The kind you see when you flush your crap down the toilet. That disgusting metaphor is basically my life.

And now everything depends on how I manage the aftermath of the toilet flush.

I hear something shuffle in the shadows. I tense, shifting my body to shield Darren.

"Hey newbies, did you manage to swipe any food before you got caught?"

The feminine voice is dry and croaky, but it projects itself with shocking forcefulness. I blink hard, trying to detect a face through the curtains of blackness.

A hand appears in one of the beams of yellow light, followed by the rest of her. "Are you deaf or something? I asked if you had anything to eat."

Hair hangs in greasy strands around her sallow face. Her dominant features and sharp eyes—along with her broad shoulders and muscular arms—tell me she used to demand a certain level of respect.

I know Darren is wide awake because he shivers against me.

"We don't have anything," I say to the girl.

I thought I'd already hit rock bottom, but somehow she's managed to knock me down another rung. I didn't even think about swiping food, or water, or anything to keep us warm. The one thing I considered myself decent at—being ready for anything—and I'd flopped hard.

"Great." The girl drags her legs around to sit cross-legged. She winces before straightening her spine. "The last thing we need are more useless mouths to feed."

The darkness moves, and another voice carries through the musky air. "Enough, Margarette. The last thing *they* need is for you to make them feel worse than they already do."

It's another girl, only her voice is softer, lilted with a Spanish accent. My eyes seem to finally be adjusting because I can see the outline of her body, propped up on one elbow.

Margarette rolls her eyes, but the Spanish girl talks over her rebuttal. "Where were you hiding when they found you?"

"Um . . . I don't know what you mean."

Margarette rolls her eyes harder this time. "The faeries must have messed with these ones, Es. They look as forlorn as newborn calves—"

"You arrived here how long ago?" Es interjects, and I hear her scooting closer.

I glance down when Darren says, "Not even a day."

Both girls stiffen, their eyes bulging. Es's black hair falls around her like a blanket as she leans closer, her voice lowering.

"You have only just arrived in the Otherworld?"

Margarette tips her head back and shouts, "What in the name of all that is holy is going on in this place?"

More movement presses on my ears, and I'm forced to speculate how big this pit actually is and how many people might be down here.

"Markie, hush!" Es pulls on Margarette's arm, but the ranting continues.

"Who knows how long we've been living here, serving the fae, fighting in the king's name. Then they dare to hunt us down like animals, mocking every sacrifice we made for them."

She turns, her sharp eyes cutting straight through me. "And now they're bringing more humans here. Tell me, Es, how that makes one lick of sense. After what they have planned for us, why increase the bloodshed—"

"Hush!" Es slaps Markie's arm, hard. Markie stops talking, but I think it's because she's fuming too hard to formulate words, not because of the slap.

"Esperanza, who's here?"

The Spanish girl turns toward the new voice in the shadows. "Two humans. They just arrived."

A man in his late twenties crawls closer, rubbing the sleep from his eyes. A light English accent laces his words. "What do you mean, just arrived? Surely no humans have survived this long."

"Sterling," Es scolds again, but this time with a gentleness she didn't waste on Markie.

Sterling looks at us, placing his arm protectively around Esperanza's waist. His bright blue eyes inspect Darren and me with curiosity. He brushes a strand of his blond hair from his face back toward the loose bun at the nape of his neck.

"Forgive me," he starts, "I am Johnathon Sterling. And this is my fiancé, Esperanza Fierro."

Es's cheeks flare red, and she ducks her head into Sterling's shoulder, hiding a dimpled smile. Margarette clears her throat with a growl.

"Ignore the lovebirds. I am Markie of the Strong-arm. When you've lived in the Otherworld as long as I have, you learn to move on from your human name."

I want to ask just how long *is* a long time here, since Markie looks to be about twenty-seven or so, but Sterling asks, "And what about you? You must have quite the story to tell of how you arrived. Were you stolen, bribed, intoxicated? Or perhaps you fell down the wrong abandoned well?"

Darren moves to sit beside me. "We sailed across the ocean on a faerie ship. The captain brought us here to try and keep us safe."

Markie's laugh is dark and slightly maniacal. Sterling talks over her. "Safe? Dear boy, what in the world could be worse than the dangers here?"

I want to punch Sterling. Can't he see my brother is terrified enough?

"We were being stalked by a shadow faery," I snap, silencing Markie's laughter. "It tried to kill us."

"So you sailed across the ocean to escape it and decided to step inside the place where those demons are born?" Markie chuckles under her breath. "Smart."

"No more questions," Es says. "They have experienced enough darkness for one day. Let them rest while we inform the others."

"Others?" I ask.

"Thirty-seven total, including both of you," Sterling says.

Esperanza gives us another sad smile. "We will introduce you after you have rested from your journey."

Sterling helps Esperanza stand. Markie crouches and slowly rises to her feet, noticeably favoring her left leg. She's almost taller than Sterling, and both of them look like giants next to Es, who is closer to Darren's height.

When they disappear into the shadows, I turn to Darren and see that his eyes are swimming with tears.

"Hey, hey, it's alright." My soothing tone fights to hide my lie.

He sniffs and shakes his head. "They're right. We never should have come here." A single tear spills from each eye as he looks up at me. "What if I never see Juliana and Howard again?"

I wrap my arms around him, tucking his head underneath my chin. I can feel my own tears drying up inside me as my emotions solidify to iron in my gut. A deep anger presses on my chest, making it hard to breathe.

This is not how it ends. This is not how Darren spends his life.

"Don't worry," I whisper into his hair. "We're going to get out of here. No matter what it takes, I'm getting you home."

{ 14 }

[B]eware of eating the fairy food or drinking the fairy wine.

- *Ancient Legends, Mystic Charms, and Superstitions of Ireland* by Lady Francesca Speranza Wilde (1887)

Eventually Darren drifts into a restless sleep, his tears dried on my shirt.

I doze off once or twice, dreaming of faceless monsters with sharp teeth. Every time I open my eyes to escape some nightmare, the dank hole provides no relief. My mind plays tricks on me, telling me that the monsters are always here, no matter if I'm asleep or awake.

When I'm pretty sure I'm about to go insane, a noise cuts through the rhythm of dripping liquid and Darren's heavy breathing, startling me but also saving me from the maddening solitude.

Judging by the fading speckles of skylight filtering through the floorboards, the day must be ending.

I peer into the shadows as Markie and Esperanza come shuffling over. The limp in Markie's left leg slows her down, and she mumbles curses with every step.

"We pray you rested well." Esperanza smiles, and Darren stirs beside me.

Markie grunts. "Keep your prayers to yourself, Es." Then she looks at me. "Let's get moving. We want to ask a few questions."

My brother's muffled yawn creates a burst of warmth on my shoulder. We stand and follow, often using the scrape of feet against the dirt as our only guide through the darkness.

Then I notice a pale face, the whites of someone's eyes, a bright blue shirt. One by one, a group of outcast humans appears before us.

Sterling nods. "Welcome. A few of our friends wish to make your acquaintance."

A set of metal bars connects the floor to the ceiling, and on the other side of the bars, a single torch flickers, casting a yellow glow over the sea of hollow faces. People line the dirt walls or stand near the prison bars. I scan their faces and see a terrifying emptiness in their eyes.

Esperanza turns to us, standing next to Sterling at the center of the group.

"We told them of your arrival, and everyone wants to hear your story—the entire story." She glances at Sterling, and he holds her hand. "Any knowledge you have about"—she looks at the ceiling and her voice lowers—"*them*, could be of help to us."

I clear my dry throat. The anger burning like hot embers in my core reflects back at me in the eyes of the other prisoners. They hate the faeries who did this as much as I do.

A girl sitting in the far corner catches my attention; her doe-eyes smolder with rage. That same fury twitches in

Markie's jawline and in the way Sterling holds Esperanza close.

"I'm Róisín, and this is my brother, Darren." My voice is raw, but I make sure that my expression is resilient. I want to show these people that I'm not about to give up.

I do most of the talking as we tell our story. Darren pipes up now and again, adding specifics about the creatures on the ship or things he heard from Manny. After explaining our final moments before they threw us into the pit, my gaze settles on Sterling, Esperanza, and Markie in turn.

"That's all we know," I say. "Now, who can tell me what we're all doing down here?"

"It's . . . complicated," Sterling begins, glancing at Es.

"I've got time." The double meaning in the phrase stings. From the looks of it, the only thing I have left is time. Time to sit and waste away like the rest of these empty carcasses.

"Who's the faery who brought you here?"

The question comes from the girl sitting in the back. Her large black eyes remind me of the floating lights, the will-ó-the-wisps, in the way they take up too much room on her soft face.

"His name's Cináed."

I can tell this sets something off in her. A tormented blend of emotions dances across her delicate features. It's easy to see how beautiful she is, even though the torch behind her shadows her face.

I want to ask how she knows him, but I also don't want to make myself vulnerable. My gut pinches at the thought that she could be his significant other. Which is something I can't say about my strange relationship with the golden-haired faery.

Loud footfalls above make everyone wince, and dust and chunks of dirt fall from the ceiling. Several people crawl away, back into the darkness like rats. Markie shields her eyes, her hand fingering a small knife tucked into her belt. I wonder where she got it.

A door on the other side of the bars swings open, casting painful rays of light into the pit. Two males walk down the stairs, each carrying a wooden spear.

"Lord Naoise requests the presence of the girl who appeared in the courtroom with Cináed the Wanderer."

I don't dare take my eyes away from the glaring light because I know that everyone else is now watching me.

No, no, no, no.

I swear under my breath.

Naoise. The dark-haired faery.

I can still feel the way his eyes held me captive while his wicked smile chilled me to the bone.

I hear scratches across the floorboards, followed by several longing yelps.

"If she does not make herself known by stepping forward, we will send the hounds in to fetch her."

A pause.

I look at Darren, bright spots dancing in my vision from where I stared into the light.

"Go now, you idiot," Markie says to me. "Those hounds negotiate with their teeth. Don't waste your bravery."

I squeeze Darren's hand and stride toward the door.

Sterling takes my arm. "Have you had fae food?"

"What's that?"

"If you must ask, then you have not had it," he says. "No matter what, do not partake of the fae food unless you wish to spoil your chances of ever returning to the human realm."

A guard unlocks the gate while the other forces everyone back by jabbing a spear through the bars. Sterling retreats with the others and leaves me with one more thing I have to worry about.

How will I know what's fae food and what isn't?

Doe-eyes snarls at the guard, her teeth surprisingly sharp. Her long white hair and gray-brown skin make me think that she might not be human. That, and her unnatural beauty that's even more stunning up close.

Instead of crawling past me like the others, she discreetly tucks a piece of paper in my hand and whispers in my ear.

"Get this to Cináed, and I will be in your debt."

Before I can respond, she fades into the crowd behind me. The gate opens just wide enough for the guards to pull me through.

We reach the top of the stairs, and that's when I see the hounds. They look more like small horses than dogs. Each paw is bigger than my hand. The one closest to me fights the rope around its neck. Its tongue lolls, and its eyes roll back as it howls, clawing the floor to get to me.

I retreat a step, my eyes darting around for the nearest exit, when strong hands grab me from behind and press something sharp into my back. I can smell alcohol on the faery's breath, along with a sweet scent I don't recognize. A different kind of wine, maybe.

"One wrong move, and this knife finds its home in your gut."

These faeries don't wear golden cloaks like the ones who brought us here. Instead, they're clad in black-and-brown leather lined with blades and other knickknacks. They all reek of alchohol and wet dog.

I'm dragged down a new corridor bathed in a purple sunset. Despite the ethereal glow, this hall somehow feels even darker than the pit.

We stop. A rich purple mist curls out from around the cracks in the doorway in front of us, and a foreboding chill pierces my body like a thousand invisible needles.

The door swings open, revealing an unlit room and a floor blanketed in knee-deep mist. I half expect to hear a smoke machine whirring in the background as I'm pushed through the doorway, the knife in my back biting through my skin. I yelp, spinning my head around to glare at the guard.

"You little jacka—"

He slaps my face so fast that I only realize it happened after I hear the *smack*. Bright splotches invade my vision, and heat burns in my cheek and down my neck.

One of the dogs whines, and the faerie heckling falls silent. Every pair of glowing eyes trains on something behind me. I can't hear what's coming over the ringing in my ears, and I hesitate to look over my shoulder. Even my assailant tucks his knife away, dropping his grip on my arm where I know I'll have welts to match the mark on my face.

"What is this?" Naoise's voice is smooth and dark, like ink spilling onto paper or blood seeping through fresh snow.

One of his hands cups my chin, gently lifting my face. I lock my gaze onto his clear, gray-blue eyes and feel entranced. A helpless bug flying too close to a dangerous, beautiful trap.

If he knows about his influence, he doesn't show it. He lets me go, turning his full attention to my escorts. The dogs cower in the doorway while the faeries quiver and turn sickly shades of blue and green. I think one actually pissed himself.

"You dare lay a finger on her, knowing I summoned her here for my own purposes."

The one who slapped me stammers, "B-but your greatness, she was disrespectful, and—"

"And you are not authorized to punish anyone within my lair." Naoise frowns, glancing over the faery. "Be gone before I disembowel you like the worthless maggot you are."

They ditch the room faster than a bunch of kids running from a haunted house. The door closes behind them. Nausea roils in my gut as my heart jumps to my throat. Something tells me my street-fighting skills won't last a second against this guy.

The faery's pale body is draped in a black cloak, revealing only his hands and his head in the fading light from one uncurtained window. He watches me, his dark head of hair tilting to the side. What can only be genuine intrigue sparkles in his eyes.

"Tell me, human, what do you call yourself?"

{ 15 }

Do not sign any contracts or agree to any bargains with faeries. Faeries love to haggle but will usually do so only if they are sure they will win.

- *The Shadowhunters Codex* by Cassandra Clare and Joshua Lewis (2013)

"Róisín," I choke.

My gaze lingers on the door, wondering if it locked when it closed.

"Róisín," Naoise murmurs, almost to himself, "but of course."

The shrouding smoke obscures the size of the room. My gut tells me that running blindly into the dark will only play into the faery's hands. The window, however, is open to the evening air. I might have a chance if I slip through it when he's not looking.

But right now Naoise stands between me and my escape. Which means I need him to move in my direction so I can switch places with him.

I gather what's left of my rapidly disintegrating composure, forcing the conversation to keep going. "Why was I brought here?"

When he smiles, I bite my cheek to keep from either crying out in fear or swooning over his devilish beauty.

How can someone so terrifying be so drop-dead gorgeous?

His black, shoulder-length hair swoops back from his fore-head, tucked behind his pointed ears, and the dust of a beard frames his square jaw. The cloak draped over his broad shoulders shifts around his boots as he takes a step closer to me.

"You are not wondering who I am?"

"I've been wondering a lot of things since I got thrown in the dungeons."

I sidestep toward the window, hoping he won't detect my intentions. But he takes another step in my direction, seemingly unaware of my plan as he laughs under his breath.

"You may call me Naoise," he says, humor etched into the lines around his mouth and eyes. "Soon, I will take the throne as the High King of the Otherworld, but for now I am simply a creature who has been struck by your innocent beauty."

My stomach plummets to the ground. I blink, trying not to burst into wild hysterics like a deranged hyena.

Me? Beautiful?

He lives in a world of faerie supermodels, and he wants to flirt with the grungy human teenager. I'm not buying it for a second. At least, that's what I tell myself over and over again, trying to drown him out. By now I know he's using some faerie voodoo magic on me, luring me out of my protective walls.

Just three steps away from the window. *Focus, Róisín.*

"I thought humans were off-limits." I pause, letting him circle closer to me. "I heard about the king and queen."

He clasps his hands behind his back as he stops walking, as still as a statue. "The fae are an irrational, irreverent, and incapable race." His smile mirrors the pity in his voice. "They chase after what they want, knowing not what they truly need."

By now my base instincts should have kicked in, pumping adrenaline through my veins, barreling my body through the window. But the longer I stand here, the more sluggish and complacent I feel.

I order my legs to move. But my body ignores me, acting with a mind of its own.

"If faeries are blind and illogical, where does that leave you?"

A different kind of humor dances in his eyes—the kind that, if prodded too much, will bite back and make you regret your words. "You mean to ask what qualifies me as the ruler of the incompetent?"

I swallow, unwilling to retract my slant but also not wanting to set him off. Thankfully, he continues without a response.

"My beginnings were less than ideal." He cuts across the room and looks out the window, just an arm's length away from me. "A being of shadow for a father and a mother ashamed of her child's lineage. She left me in the Shadowlands, abandoned as some wandering beast's next meal. But the gods intervened, and a childless faery of the moors found me and raised me as her own."

The last touch of sunlight glows against the green hills, but it's the sliver of moon that captivates me. It hasn't always been this bright or this large before, has it? Then I remember that technically, all of this is underground. That concept makes just as much sense as a parent leaving a baby to die.

I realize Naoise is watching me watch the moon, and I clear my dry throat. "Parents suck," I say.

As a foster kid, I grew up hating the sympathetic phrases.

I'm sorry.

That must be so hard.

Call if you need anything.

I know what they really want to say sounds something like, *Wow, your life is crappy. I don't have anything to say to fix this, so I'll say whatever gets me out of this conversation the fastest without revealing how uncomfortable I am right now.*

Better to say nothing at all than something that means nothing.

Naoise lifts his dark brows, the momentary surprise on his face somehow making him even more attractive.

"Aye, Róisín. It is often from a past shrouded with sorrow and pain that a warrior, a leader, emerges. The past hovers as a constant reminder of where I began, fueling me toward a different future. Only I can create my own legacy, here and throughout eternity."

In spite of myself, the passion in his words leaves me breathless and enthralled. He might be a devilishly handsome faery living in an underground world, but his speech touches a deeply rooted nerve in my core, making it impossible to deny the strange sense of familiarity between us. Magic or not, something about him pulls me closer. I grip the windowsill, willing my restless body to behave.

He watches me with that same sparkle of curiosity and humor in his eyes, like he can see the internal struggle written across my face in neon lights.

"I sense that something important has led you to the Otherworld."

I nod, unclamping my jaw. "I want to know how to protect myself from faeries."

And I want to know why Darren and I can see faeries who are supposed to be invisible.

The second question clings to my tongue as I remember Cináed's warning to never reveal that secret to anyone. I don't know what someone like Naoise would do with that information. Possibly nothing. But until I know his true motives for bringing me to his *lair*, as he calls it, the less he knows about me, the better.

He looks away with a hint of a smile. "You have experienced a degree of fear and pain at the hands of the fae, and now you wish to retaliate. Very well."

"Can you help me?"

The question hangs in the cool air, and I immediately regret asking it.

He already sees me as weak and helpless no doubt, simply because I'm human. And now I just gave him extra leverage.

In a split second, he closes the space between us. He doesn't touch me, but his presence surrounds me, holding me in a blanket of darkness that feels like cool silk on my skin.

A breeze shifts the sheer black curtains over the window, prickling my arms and legs with goosebumps. I can tell he knows he has me trapped. Not with physical walls but with an irresistible and dangerous fascination.

His gaze shifts, and his voice is quick, just above a whisper.

"I will aid you in your cause, Róisín. To learn the ways of the fae, one must be joined with them. You will train to compete in the Festival of Lughnasa." His hands reach for mine, and I realize how much I'm shaking as he grasps my hands between his. "As a result of your training, you will no longer be a prisoner here. You will know how to fight against the fae, and you will feel more at home in the Otherworld."

I shake my head. "I need to bring my brother back to our real home. All I want is to know how to protect us both from faeries and to go back where we belong."

I sound so young, so fragile. I bet his hands could crush me in a heartbeat if I gave him any reason to. My gut tells me with a sickening nosedive that I'd be smart not to disappoint him. That I should be grateful he wants to help me at all, and that I'm better off complying with his plans and not asking any questions.

But there's one thing I won't abandon, not even now as he stands in the moonlight like a marble statue of the world's most desirable man.

I will bring Darren back home. I will protect him and make sure no demon faery ever touches him again.

"Then I will make you a deal, my human rose."

I blink, taking a moment to register what he said.

"What kind of a deal?" I ask slowly.

"A simple agreement between two reasonable beings. A deal that offers both of us what we most desire."

When I don't respond, he continues.

"Train for the games and compete in the festival of Lughnasa nine sunsets from now. Learn how to fight, dance, and behave like the fae. If you win two out of three events of your choosing, you may return to the human realm with your brother."

I swallow. "And if I lose?"

His bright eyes glance between mine, a new intensity shimmering within them. "You will become my summer bride, my eternal rose, to rule with me as my beloved queen."

I gasp in a pocket of air, and it fills my mouth with the taste of moonlight and desire—as if that's even possible.

For a brief moment, I forget myself and almost fall into his arms like some lovesick juvenile. But I rock back on my heels, separating us as I chomp down on the inside of my cheek. Clarity pushes against the fuzziness in my head, and Naoise's intoxicating aroma is replaced by the metallic taste of blood in my mouth.

His eyes don't leave me as I regain my composure. I feel my face flame, knowing what he must be thinking about me.

His mouth twitches in amusement. I retract my hands, turning toward the window and folding my arms across my chest. My mind races, replaying his words, searching for a loophole, some ulterior motive I've missed. He can't honestly want me of all people as his bride, his queen.

Another shiver drizzles down my spine.

He wants me to marry him.

I tamp down on my bubbling mess of emotions. Does it matter why he chose me? If this means I have a chance to save us and get Darren back home, why question his motives?

On the other hand, I'd be a fool not to at least learn the terms.

"And what if I won't make this deal with you?"

Cold wind blasts into the room, howling as it kicks up the mist around our feet. I watch as Naoise's godlike beauty transforms into a terrifying perfection. A monster capable of the impossible.

His tone is cold, calloused even. "Then you shall remain imprisoned, and after years of human time have passed on and everyone who cares for you lies dead in their graves, you and your brother will be offered as sacrifices to appease our ancestors, the Tuatha De Danann. Thus your meaningless lives will end, and no one will be there to mourn your passing."

Hair flies around my face, and the curtains swirl against me. Naoise lowers his hands, and the wind starts to calm. Mist resettles on the floor, a few wisps left floating between us.

My reckless infatuation for him flew out the window in his display of rage and power. The tantrum was meant to scare me, but it did more than that. It reminded me of my own festering anger—for everything the faeries have done to ruin my life and put Darren in danger.

I glare at him, forcing as much disdain into my voice as possible. "Then I agree to your deal. And once I win, I'm taking my brother home, and I want nothing to do with you or any other faery ever again."

His mouth twitches as he clenches his fists. But he quickly assumes a cool mask of indifference.

"We shall see, Róisín." The door to the room opens wide, and he gestures for me to leave.

I can't make my feet walk fast enough as I run into the corridor. Sprinting down the hallway lit with flickering torches, I hear his voice pulsing through the shadows, pressing in on me from every direction.

"We shall see."

{ 16 }

Games and competitions were the chief occupations at [Lughnasadh], with contests held for horse riding, chariot racing, competitions between nobles . . . and more.

- *Lughnasadh: Rituals, Recipes, & Lore for Lammas* by Melanie Marquia Llewellyn (2015)

The next morning, I wake up in a bed with sheets the color of butter and pillows the tint of expensive wine.

After running away from Naoise like a crazy person, I found myself back in the arms of the leather-clad guards. Only this time, they took me down a hallway full of doors and left me in one of the guest rooms before locking me inside.

I pounded on the door for a while, but when I got no response, I turned around to examine the softly lit space and found a bedroom, complete with a large armoire, a golden bathtub on legs, and a queen-sized mattress cocooned by curtains hanging from the high ceiling.

I was more than a little shocked that they locked me in this fancy room instead of throwing me back in the pit. And as I examine the room in the early daylight, that shock still hasn't worn off.

This is Naoise's doing, no doubt about it. But why?

Our deal didn't include five-star accommodations. If I'd known, I would have demanded Darren be brought up here with me. I refuse to leave him down there while I live like a queen.

A queen.

Moaning, I drop my head between my knees, nauseated. Naoise wants to be king, and he wants me to marry him. And if I don't win some sort of game, his request becomes my new reality.

Why didn't I keep my mouth shut until I found Cináed?

The entire time I was with Naoise, Cináed never crossed my mind. It wasn't until I landed in this room that I finally rid my head of Naoise's face, voice, and even his smell, and had room to think clearly again.

I reach for the crinkled paper in my pocket. The one doe-eyes gave me. I huff and roll my eyes, imagining what her secret love note might say. Did she really expect me to just hand it over as if I respect her privacy? *Please.*

I feel every speck of dirt on my skin and under my nails as I crawl out of bed. A soft pink will-ó-the-wisp floats closer to me, but when I look at it, it shoots back toward the ceiling near the tall, glass-paned window that reminds me that as long as I'm here, I'm a prisoner.

I can only hope that making a deal with Naoise will help me escape.

The small paper is grooved and grainy, and as I open the fold, I scowl. A single sentence scrawled in charcoal smudges the paper, but not a word of it is written in a language I can read.

Thoughts of what it might say compete with memories of my maddening conversation with Naoise last night. Dread swallows me despite my cheery surroundings. This room belongs to a princess—or at least someone obsessed with frills and gold and all things floral.

I pace back and forth, bare feet stomping against the cold, honey-colored marble.

"I should have stood my ground." I pound a fist on the armoire, intricately painted with trees and wildflowers. "I should have bargained for a better deal. I should ha—"

A light knock cuts me off. I stare at the door blankly, not knowing who—or what—could be coming to see me. All I know is that I'm supposed to be training for a competition. A competition that I stupidly signed up for without knowing a single thing about it.

I lean on the armoire, wanting to throw up but knowing my stomach is completely empty.

Another knock. "My lady?" The door clicks open, revealing a pretty porcelain face with heart-shaped lips.

When I make no motion to speak, the girl smiles and prods the door open wider. Two more girls file into the room. They all have pointed ears and skin with a subtle but constant glow. I sit on the bed as they glide over to me, pastel skirts floating around their ankles. All of them stand about my same height and look to be in their mid-to-late twenties.

"The poor dear." One of the girls *tsks* at me, her lashes splaying around her blue eyes like butterfly wings. She tugs on my T-shirt. "What terrible circumstances you must have been through to end up in such a state."

I want to laugh at her. My looks are on the bottom of my priority list right now. But I doubt these perfect beings would understand.

I begrudgingly let them strip me naked. While I have no sentimental attachment to my clothes, I'd rather not start this horrible day by standing in my birthday suit in front of three Barbie dolls.

Butterfly-eyes pinches two fingers into my clothes, carries them out the door, and drops them in the hallway like a bag of garbage. The other girls bring buckets of water from the hall and pour them into the golden bathtub. I try my best to hide behind one of the bed poles, noticing the flowers molded into the metal tub.

The girl with braids wrapped on top of her head—she looks like an adorable milk maid straight out of a movie—takes pity on me and tells me I can get in the bathtub now. I step over and slide into the water up to my shoulders.

Butterfly-eyes starts to work through the knots in my hair with a comb. I sink lower, letting the warm water ease my tense muscles. How long has it been since I've bathed, anyway? I cringe when I realize I can't remember.

"Oh!" The comb clatters to the ground. They all look at my head like my hair just turned into a bunch of snakes or something.

"Is there a spider on me?" I swat at my head, splashing water around the tub.

Milkmaid points at me, and heart-lips slaps her hand down.

"We were ordered to prepare the girl," heart-lips says. "It is not our concern where she came from."

Butterfly-eyes trembles as she picks up the comb. "But Hafwin, she is a human."

Their ringleader stands her ground, placing her hands on her hips. "Whether she is human or the tips of her ears were chopped off is none of our concern, Lana."

I hear soft sniffles as the comb continues tugging on my hair.

"I think I know just what you need," Hafwin says to me, her heart-shaped lips pursed. She turns to milkmaid, who's staring at the floor. "Bring the Ura petals."

The girl nods and disappears out the door. I try to hold still as Lana tugs harder on my hair. I'd offer to dislodge the comb myself but my mouth feels glued shut. I can sense Lana's fear toward me and it makes me squirm, unsure what to do about it.

Milkmaid comes back holding a cloth bag, and she dumps its contents into the water. Pieces of dried purple flowers that smell like heaven float around me. The water starts to bubble and froth, and the scent wafts over me.

I sink down into the bath until my head goes under. When I pop back up, Hafwin's lips pull into a wide smile.

"Ambaiste," she says, "you were hiding a rare beauty underneath all that filth."

After they scrub me down and a floral smell exudes from my skin, the girls dress me in leather pants and a long cotton shirt. They pair the outfit with a leather vest and a belt that cinches below my ribs. Milkmaid, whose name I learn is Fodla, helps me tug on a pair of soft leather boots while Hafwin braids my hair down my neck.

When I'm done, they stand back, beaming as they admire their work. Fodla hands me a small mirror.

My hair trails down my head in a braid woven with a leather band and tied in a knot at my shoulder. The flaming red dye must have been leached away in the strange, bubbly water. I finger the ends, now a muted pink, trying and failing not to look at my face. My skin still possesses the same olive tone, but a soft glow pulses beneath my cheeks, reminding me of what Darren said in the forest.

"You look really different."

Is it possible that Naoise wasn't lying? That he actually thinks I'm beautiful?

"You will be the prettiest competitor of all," Lana says, seeming a little braver now that I no longer resemble a zombie.

"Thanks." I set the mirror down, ready to be done with dress-up and figure out how to win these games. "Now, can someone tell me what I'm competing in?"

"Select the events in which you will compete."

A male faery with a red beard and a thick fur vest points at a line of wooden signs. Another faery sits below the signs at a table, writing notes.

Red-beard turns on his way out, his eyes narrowing to slits as he meets my gaze. A thick fist clenches around the weapon at his belt. I look away, hoping I never have to compete against him.

"Next."

I step up, replaying my conversation with Hafwin about the events I should choose.

"What are your skills?" she asked me.

"My what?"

"Your strengths, child. What skills are you known for in your homeland?"

Punching Melissa Bryant and breaking her nose. Stealing random stuff from the local gas station without ever getting caught. Winning a hotdog-eating contest against the high school champion of three years.

"Um, I can fight okay, I guess."

Hafwin looked me over. "Perhaps this is true in your homeland. But here, we faeries fight differently. Do not enter events dependent on physical strength unless you wish to fail the first day."

The faery at the table commands my attention. "State your name."

"Róisín Montes."

"Your full name, complete with your title."

"That is my full name."

He looks up from his notes, and the eye roll he was about to give me freezes. "Y-you must be the human—I mean, the competitor—that I was made aware of just recently."

He scrambles over the words as his eyes shift to the waiting competitors behind me. Heat crawls up my neck, but I take a deep breath and refuse to turn around to see who's staring.

Probably just, you know, everyone.

He writes my name with a feather pen.

"Select the events in which you will compete."

Each sign is painted with a symbol. I find the storytelling symbol, the one Hafwin said only requires that I recite a story. I point to the sign, and he notes it.

"And will my lady be competing in any other events?"

I sigh internally. If only I could score our freedom with one event. My gaze scans across the symbols, resting on the one that shows two painted figures fighting with sticks.

"That one."

I hear a small yelp and see Lana, blue eyes wide with fear. Hafwin shakes her head in earnest protest. But I ignore them. If I can't rely on what I know, I don't stand a chance. Faeries might fight differently, but at least I have somewhere to start.

"For your second event"—he writes my choice—"staff sparring."

Just one more event.

The only painting that doesn't show figures either dancing or throwing large objects is the one nearest me.

"That one."

"For your third event, horse racing."

Horse racing. Can't be too hard, right? Have I ever been close enough to a horse to touch it? Nope. But it's either that or dancing.

And I'd rather fall off a horse a thousand times before dancing—aka awkwardly flailing around—in front of a crowd.

I join Hafwin and the others, who quietly escort me through the crowd with their eyes lowered. It's obvious I'm the freak show here. No one wants to stand too close or look at me for too long. But I catch an earful of conversations, whispered just loudly enough for me to hear.

"All humans are vermin. Their kind plague our land."

"Why would Cináed the Wanderer bring her here?"

"She should not be allowed to compete. She could infect us all with the sickness."

And the last words, muttered by a warrioress standing next to the male with the fur vest, inject me with the kind of fear that urges my feet to run as fast and as far away as humanly possible.

"Come Lughnasa, we will make sure she regrets the day she entered the Otherworld."

{ 17 }

Queen Maive was handsome, and overcame all her enemies with a bawl stick, for the hazel is blessed, and the best weapon that can be got. You might walk the world with it.

- *The Celtic Twilight* by William Butler Yeats (1893, 1902)

After leaving the crowd of angry competitors, I tell Hafwin I'm going to see my brother. She tries to blow me off, but when I make it clear it's not up for debate, she offers to send Fodla to the dungeons with a note.

"You are expected at the first sparring lesson," she explains. "You do not want to fall behind from the start."

Translation: You need as much help as you can get since you were born behind.

I tell Fodla my message, and she nods before turning down another hall as Hafwin guides me toward a section of green grass inside the castle walls. I hear Lana call it a courtyard.

Two males circle each other on the lawn, holding slender sticks taller than their bodies. They rotate around each other, completely focused on the opponent. A small crowd watches from behind a protected overhang on the opposite side of the courtyard. Tall, glassless windows loom over all four ends of the grass, and an occasional archway connects the stone floor and the lawn.

One of the two fighters performs a quick spin maneuver. His opponent tries to lunge forward but tumbles to the ground. A few spectators clap as the fighter left standing brushes his forehead with his sleeve. Even from a distance, I notice how the sunlight glints off his curls.

A burst of anxiety explodes in my stomach. I try to get a better view, but the crowd is dispersing, and I lose sight of him in the throng.

Could it be Cináed?

"Halt, ladies."

I'm forced to peel my gaze from the courtyard, pressing into the soft parts of my feet to keep from barreling into Hafwin and Lana.

Orla, who reminds me of every disappointed teacher that's ever lectured me, walks toward us. Her feet glide across the stone floor with quick, precise steps as her gray gown bends around her womanly curves. The graying hairs in her updo don't match the youthful strength in her movements.

"What is this? Who instructed you to remove her from the dungeons?"

The girls quiver like flowers in a storm.

Hafwin says, "My lady, Naoise of the Western Moors called on us to prepare the girl."

Orla lifts a slender eyebrow and folds her arms. "He did, did he? And what exactly did you prepare her for?"

"To compete at the festival of Lughnasa, my lady."

More of Orla's age shows in the lines that branch off her scowl and between her glaring eyes. Although fuming, she manages to keep her voice emotionless. "I see. You may proceed."

The girls give a low curtsy. I stand tall, look Orla straight in the eye, and don't so much as nod my head in respect. I feel the anger billowing from her like a snowstorm, but I walk past her without flinching.

That encounter told me everything I need to know about my standing here. While I'm probably the only human competing, no one will dare throw me out because they'd be going against Naoise.

Images of his perfect, pale face, his gray-blue eyes watching me, send a shiver down my spine. I blush, mortified at his control over my emotions even when he's not around.

He's just a means to an end, I tell myself. *Take advantage of his interest in you in order to get out of here alive.*

Whoever he is, I know now that he represents a significant level of authority. For the first time, I'm glad I made that deal. The head honcho of the faeries left a mark on me that says, *Don't touch.* And with that protection, I plan to learn the faerie ways so I can take care of my own.

Hafwin waves her hands to shoo me onto the grass.

"Your sparring lesson begins now," she says, as if that's all the explanation I need. "Your instructor will meet you in the courtyard."

The previous fighters, including the one who looked like Cináed, are nowhere in sight. Only a few spectators linger, conversing underneath the overhang.

I ease myself across the lawn, squinting against the sun that warms my leather pants and vest. Someone moves from the shaded covering, and two bare feet step into the sunlight, followed by a lithe body and a head of golden curls.

Cináed wears an outfit similar to mine, minus the boots. Now that I think about it, I've never seen him wear shoes.

His expression is impossible to read as he nears me. I know my face, on the other hand, reveals just how much I've missed him. The feeling comes on strong at first, surprising me. Then I remember the scrap of paper tucked beneath my belt, burning a hole through my ribs. The note from his girl-friend.

He stops a few feet in front of me. If we were alone, I wonder if he would close the distance.

It's better this way. My nails bite into my palms. *His heart belongs to someone else. No need to make a fool of yourself.*

"Good morrow, Róisín." His voice is tight, distant.

"What the heck is going on? I'm supposed to be training for a competition."

He kicks a stick up from the grass with his toe, catching it in his hand. "I heard. I have been assigned to be your sparring trainer." The stick flies at me, and I jerk my arms forward to stop it from hitting my face, grabbing it before it tumbles back to the ground.

His smirk doesn't reach his eyes. "The moment has come for you to learn to fight as the fae."

I grip the staff and plant my feet. Cináed never should have brought us here. Maybe he didn't know about the king's death or that humans would be blamed for it. But Markie said shadow faeries are born here. Add that to Naoise's messed-up childhood, and it's clear we never should have stepped foot in this terrifying, human-hating place.

So yes, I choose to blame the individual who could have prevented this waking nightmare. And you can bet if he's my sparring teacher, I'm not going to be the kind of student who plays nice.

"Are you ready to get your faerie ass handed to you?"

He raises an eyebrow but gives no other reaction to my taunt.

"Good foot placement," he says without breaking eye contact. "But your posture is too eager. Stand tall or risk falling on your face like my last opponent."

I flex my jaw but comply, straightening my spine. He moves to my left, and we circle each other.

This dance has a different flavor than my face-off against Naoise. Instead of predator and prey, we are like two lions about to lunge.

I slide my hands down the wooden staff to wipe the sweat building on my palms.

"You are not attacking a dragon." He cuts through the circle toward me with the staff at his side. "If you aim the weapon too high, you expose your core to the opponent."

He reaches out to readjust my position, and I pounce forward, throwing the side of my staff into his chest the way he attacked his last opponent. He stumbles back, eyes wide. I advance, shoving him harder until he's forced to circle back around or fall down.

When I spin around and face him, his bright eyes no longer reflect anything but frustration. Hot adrenaline pulses through me as we continue our dance.

I inhale and swallow hard, waiting for him to make the next move. In an instant, I'm shoved to the ground. I didn't even see what he did. After scanning over my torso for injuries, I stand up and resume my stance.

I'll be ready for him this time.

My feet fly out from under me, and my back collides with solid earth, knocking the air from my lungs. That time I at least managed to see how he shifted the spear into an angle instead of coming at me head-on.

I'm slower to get up this time, wanting to give myself a moment to strategize and to make sure that no one is watching us. Sure enough, the small crowd stuck around, enjoying this joke of a fight.

I doubt I'm strong enough to withstand another blow and keep myself from falling down. Instead, I'll dodge him and let him chase my shadow, and then aim a solid blow at his back.

He moves as soon as I lift my staff into position. When I shift my hands around and place the stick between us, he angles his blow lower instead, aiming for my exposed stomach and sending the staff into my gut.

I fold forward, collapsing across his weapon. He lets it go and kneels in front of me as I cough and strain to take in air. His words are low and fast, blending with the ringing in my head.

"I beg of you, Róisín, do not compete in games you cannot win."

My face presses into the grass as I manage to inhale a breath that smells like dirt.

"Watch for my signal. I will come for you and get you both out of here."

He stands and pauses before picking something up from the grass. Doe-eyes' note must have fallen out of my belt. A miserable blend of humiliation washes over me, both from losing this fight and letting Cináed invade my heart.

He leaves, and I wait until sweet breath reenters my aching chest before I lift my head. The courtyard stands empty except for a few stragglers going about their own business.

Then I see Orla. She stands in front of one of the windows, watching me. The shade blankets her features, making it impossible to read her face. But I don't need to.

I already know I've proved that I pose zero threat to anyone in these games.

After a moment, she turns and walks away, leaving me alone.

{ 18 }

And so they lived for a hundred years and more, for by their enchantments they could resist the power of death.

- Ancient Legends, Mystic Charms, and Superstitions of Ireland by Lady Francesca Speranza Wilde (1887)

When Hafwin and Lana find me, I wordlessly follow them to my room.

They strip me down again, towel off my skin sticky with sweat, and cover my nakedness in a thin slip. Hafwin walks over, bearing a bundle of green cloth and a sympathetic expression. I'm sure they saw how I made a complete idiot of myself in the sparring lesson. I don't have the courage to ask if the practices count against me in the competition.

It takes both girls to lift the dress over my head because I swat at their hands in protest. After our mini-battle—where I finally give up, distracted by a tray of mouth-watering food brought in by Fodla—the dress settles around me in a rush of fabric.

While they fuss over my dress, I reach for the food. Sterling's voice replays in my ears and I drop the warm pastry in my hand like it's poison.

"Um, is this fae food?" I ask carefully.

"Fae food?" Hafwin glances at the tray. "As opposed to human food, you mean?"

I have no clue. "Yeah."

She eyes the tray, this time biting her lip. "I believe that other than the hazelnuts and cherries, everything else is from the human realm." Then her amber eyes find mine. "Why?"

I hesitate, feeling once again like I'm walking on egg-shells. What if I reveal too much and they use it against me? Or what if I offend them and they make my life miserable?

"I heard that fae food might keep me from being able to go home."

Holding my breath, I wait for the repercussions.

Instead Hafwin nods and removes the small bowls of hazelnuts and cherries from the tray, handing them to Lana who takes them out the door.

"Then we shall bring you human food and nothing else."

Hafwin gestures toward a floor-length mirror and asks my opinion of the gown. My eyes scan across the green material that matches the colors of a forest floor, and the skirt is airy around my legs. An elegant bodice of creamy lace trails from waist to collarbone.

I shake my head, the strawberry pastry caught halfway down my throat. "This is way too fancy."

But Hafwin and Lana ignore me, twirling around my head like sparrows, twisting my dishwater-brown hair into a braid decorated with white blossoms and green ribbon.

When Fodla returns, she kneels in front of me, knotting my boots with nimble fingers. I listen to her gentle voice explain how they will be bringing me to my first horse-riding lesson soon, after the sun "begins its descent in the sky."

At this point, I know they're helping me because it's their job, but I doubt that treating me as kindly as they have is required. Faeries hate verbal thanks, so I make a mental note to find another way to show my appreciation.

"Did you find him? My brother?" I ask Fodla.

She nods, finishing up the laces. "Aye, your brother is being taken care of. He told me to tell you not to worry, that he will wait for your return."

Tears prick my eyes as I imagine Darren giving Fodla such a brave response. I need to find Naoise and renegotiate our deal. I refuse to leave him down there.

My hand reaches for a goblet and—after double checking it's safe for me to drink—I drain the sweet water while eyeing a steaming bowl of mush that smells like a better version of oatmeal. Getting pushed to the ground over and over must have worked up my appetite.

I munch on food as the girls tidy up the room. It feels wrong to let them gather up my dirty clothes, but once again they ignore my protests. I'm reminded of when foster parents acted like my maid no matter how many times I resisted the help. Sue was especially attentive to my needs like that, and I always felt guilty.

I take the bowl—which is, in fact, something similar to but better than oatmeal—and move to the window ledge, redirecting my thoughts to Cináed. Specifically to what he told me after knocking me around like a punching bag.

"Watch for my signal. I will come for you."

Sunlight sparkles on the glass, and I blink against the glare. Humiliation weighs me down, making me feel sick that

Cináed could be right. Maybe I have no clue what I've gotten myself into, and I should toss in the towel before it's too late. Darren's safety and my freedom are the kind of playing cards I don't want to gamble with.

Then again, Cináed never believed I could do anything before. It shouldn't surprise me that he wants me to give up before I even try, just like when he told me to let the sails down.

And because you were stubborn enough to try that, you almost died.

I stop chewing as my stomach churns. The green hills blur together, and I wipe my face with the back of my hand. The tears dry as quickly as they formed.

I will not feel sorry for myself.

"Lady?"

I turn and see them watching me, their eyes full of pity and concern. While I don't need their sympathy, I could use their insider knowledge.

Moving to sit on the bed, I pick around the remaining bits of fruit and pastries on the tray, keeping my tone neutral.

"How many competitors are there in these games, anyway?"

Hafwin answers as she hands Lana a pile of folded linens. "It depends. This year might be different considering the royal family's deaths. Judging from the crowd at the event selection, I would say each event could have a dozen or more competitors."

"Do most of them compete in several events?"

Fodla answers from her seat near the armoire, where she's mending a tear in my cotton shirt.

"Aye, most everyone enters at least two. My brother traveled from the north to enter three events at this year's festival."

"Is he still trying for the chariot race?" Lana asks with a giggle.

Hafwin sighs. "Three decades might have taught a less thickheaded fae to invest in a more reasonable dream."

"Unreasonable or no," Fodla glances up from her needlework, "I dare not squelch a younger brother's dream."

Three decades?

"Just how old are you guys?" I look at each of their youthful faces. "If you don't mind me asking."

Lana giggles again. "But of course! Humans are such fragile creatures, are they not? Living for a fraction of our time." Her butterfly eyes bulge as she looks me over. "You must be *so* young!"

Hafwin shushes her, then turns to me with an apologetic look. "We are each in our first century, but some faeries live hundreds of years."

"Our longevity fades a little more with every passing season," Fodla says, the shirt forgotten in her lap. "After King Rauri's death, I—I doubt any of us will live half as long as our ancestors."

I lean on my hands, overwhelmed with images of Cináed kneeling in front of that mysterious grave. Whoever Branna was, she died over twenty years ago. Up until now I thought that meant she had to be a relative who died around the time he was born.

But until now I also assumed Cináed was close to my age. I look at Lana, seemingly the youngest of the three. Could Cináed be her age too? Anywhere from twenty to ninety but frozen in a college freshman's body?

"I would not be so certain," Hafwin says to Fodla, cutting through my thoughts. "This Naoise of the Western Moors stands as one who knows what it is to pass through countless seasons of time."

Lana squeals, and I'm not sure if it's from delight or fear. "Oh, do not speak of him. We should not discuss any fae with such power."

Hafwin winks at me when Lana turns to the window with a shudder.

"Forgive her." Hafwin's heart-shaped lips pull into a smile. "Arguably the most superstitious faery to ever walk the earth."

"Am not."

Fodla talks over Lana, her face turning bright pink. "Surely he must take a summer bride? He cannot wait until the council crowns him. He must choose a companion like all the rest."

Before any of them notice me blushing, I get up and pretend to retie my boot, speaking from the other side of the bed. "What's the difference between having a summer bride and any other marriage?"

I hear Hafwin answer behind me. "Tradition deems it necessary for every companionless fae to choose a lover during the festival. If not, they will be partnered at random at the close of Lughnasa."

I stand up slowly, my gut tight and my head spinning. "So the couple stays together until the summer ends or what?"

"As long as both faeries desire to be together."

She makes it all sound so simple. But the dread I feel says otherwise. Getting Darren and I out of here was already bad enough without adding a complicated tradition to the mix. Knowing that Naoise said he wanted me not only as his summer bride but his queen skyrockets my emotional stress to a new level I didn't think existed.

A knock on the door makes all of us but Hafwin jump. She answers it and steps back to let Orla, of all faeries, into the room. Up close, the texture of Orla's gray dress reminds me of a pair of nice suede shoes that foster dad #1 wore to service on Sundays.

"Well done, ladies. You are dismissed," Orla says.

The girls hesitate for a moment, then they move toward the door, curtsying on their way out. Hafwin looks back at me with a reassuring smile.

"Follow me," Orla says, not bothering to wait as she takes off down the hallway in the opposite direction. I gather my skirt in my hands and hurry after her.

"Where are we going?"

She doesn't look at me when she answers. "Your horse-riding lesson. The festival is nearly upon us, and you have much to learn before you can compete in the games. I assume you have never ridden a horse before?"

I'd like nothing better than to stick it to her condescending tone and tell her that I *have* ridden a horse before.

It's not like orphan cast-offs can choose expensive hobbies like riding lessons. I was lucky Sue let me borrow some money for a boxing class every Friday.

We step outside the castle gate, and I breathe the sweet air into my lungs, glad the heat from earlier has dissipated in the cloudy afternoon.

Fog hangs from the branches in the distant forest. I never should have crossed the grass between those trees and the castle. Part of me screams to sprint toward them while I have the chance.

Not yet. Not without Darren.

A two-wheeled cart waits for us near the outer castle walls, and I follow Orla until she steps up into it and rests her hands on the railing. There's someone sitting in front of the cart compartment on a little bench. If he fell, nothing would stop him from being plowed over by the wheels.

"Take us to the high pasture," Orla says. Then she looks at me, still standing a few feet away. "Climb into the chariot, girl."

I glance at the cart, then back at her cold, expectant stare. In another life she could have definitely been one of my teachers. She has the same calculating eyes that miss nothing.

"Why are you doing this?" I say. "The other girls could've brought me to the riding lesson."

What I really want to say is that I don't trust her for an instant, not after she tried and failed to throw me back in the dungeons. How do I know she's not taking me out behind the castle to kill me?

We stare at each other for several heartbeats. She breaks the silence with an audible exhale from her nose before she says, "If you must know, I wished to observe you. Naoise speaks highly of you, and I want to know why."

I duck my head, letting my bangs fall in front of my face as I swear under my breath. As if this day couldn't get any worse, now Orla wants to be my shadow, watching my every move like a hawk.

Without another word, I climb into the chariot. The boy clicks the reins, urging the two chestnut horses into a trot.

The sound of hooves colliding with earth and the wheels whirring through the knee-high grass does little to ease the awkward silence. I'm too angry—too confused—to talk. Orla seems fine to stare straight ahead into the endless sea of green.

The castle disappears as we crest a hill into a shallow valley. A tent made of golden fabric billows like a sheet in the breeze. The driver stops the chariot, and I follow Orla to the tent.

Naoise's face appears when the sheet shifts in the wind. He didn't see me, and while part of me wants to bribe the faery boy to drive me away from here, I need to get Naoise alone and renegotiate our deal. Darren belongs with me, not alone in that pit full of strangers.

Orla waits at the tent entrance, like she's about to start tapping her shoe and checking a watch she doesn't wear. I step inside with my heart in my throat.

{ 19 }

And the breed of horses they reared could not be surpassed in the world—fleet as the wind, with the arched neck . . . and the large eye that showed they were made of fire and flame, and not of dull, heavy earth. And the Tuatha made stables for them in the great caves of the hills, and they were shod with silver and had golden bridles.

- Ancient Legends, Mystic Charms, and Superstitions of Ireland by Lady Francesca Speranza Wilde (1887)

As soon as our eyes meet, Naoise rises from his chair and reaches for my hand. "The lost child has blossomed into the rarest rose." He kisses my fingers, leaving a tingling sensation behind.

One female and two male faeries sit at Naoise's table. I recognize them from the group of advisors in the courtroom.

Naoise places a hand on the small of my back and motions toward them with his other hand.

"May I present Róisín, the human girl who desires to learn our ways and compete in the festival of Lughnasa."

Everyone has leaned away from me in their chairs. I'm tempted to start coughing just to see them panic. At least, that's what I'm guessing they mean by my humanness infecting them.

"Naoise, if I may," a male starts, his brown beard clinging to his concerned face like dark cotton swabs, "should not this girl be kept with the others?"

"Aye, if only until we know for certain what caused these recent deaths," the female adds, her gaze flickering from me to Naoise.

I eye the exit, but Naoise's hand presses on my back, grounding and immobilizing me. Orla's tight mouth twitches, observing the situation with the same enjoyment as someone watching their favorite movie. I wish I could spit in her symbolic popcorn bucket.

Naoise's hand flexes against my skin. I can feel his anger vibrating through the air. I hold my breath, preparing to make a quick getaway if things take a turn for the worse.

Like if Naoise unleashes his faerie powers I've heard rumors about and seen hints of but have yet to experience in full force.

"Speculation proves nothing," he says at last, his voice barely at a normal pitch. He meets Orla's gaze and seems to check himself, swallowing hard and tugging on his collar. "Whether the sickness is confirmed or not, one human cannot harm us."

The three faeries look at each other, and I can tell Naoise won the argument—for now at least.

"A horse-riding lesson awaits," Naoise continues. "Consider this in my absence: My promise to protect the fae from whatever plagues our lands remains intact. No further deaths have occurred since I arrived."

With one last glare at each of the faeries at the table, he leads me outside where a row of powerful-looking horses stand tethered together. As we get closer, they paw the ground, tossing long tails as their muscles quiver. One horse stands out from the rest, its eyes locking on mine. Before I can get any closer, Naoise points toward the tallest horse, painted an inky black from mane to hoof.

"Meet Meall. I found her as a filly, no more than a few weeks old, in the Shadowlands. She was foaled by a Pooka, a phantom horse that is part animal, part demon."

I stare at the horse's deep red eyes as it snorts through flared nostrils. Meall is the only horse that isn't desperately trying to get away from Naoise. The other horses tug on the ropes, and the golden horse nearest to Naoise whinnies as its ears fold back on its head.

"What's wrong with them?" I ask.

Naoise scratches Meall's thick neck, ignoring the other animals. "Some creatures sense things more deeply than others. Horses are remarkably sensitive to their surroundings."

He turns to look at me, his hand lingering on the side of Meall's long face. "They can also sense great power, the need for revenge, or feelings of overwhelming fear. Meall feeds on such emotions, while any lesser horse will try to flee. That is why I have kept her as a companion all this time."

He steps away from Meall and points to the other horses.

"Now you may choose which beast you prefer."

The golden horse and a white horse with a purple mane and tail are bookends to the maroon-colored horse that first caught my attention. It flinches away from Naoise's closeness, but as I step in front of the faery, the horse lowers its head to gaze at me with one dark brown eye.

"It's pretty," I say, seeing my reflection underneath its long eyelashes.

"Say the word, and he is yours." Naoise waves a saddle boy over.

My hand stops moving along the horse's neck. "But I thought this was just about training for the competition."

"You will train with this horse, yes. And from thence forward, he is yours forever." His voice is soft in my ear. He stands just behind me, ignoring the shifty animals whose wide eyes look at him like he's a hungry wolf about to bite.

Part of me gets their panic. Naoise gives off the strongest predator vibes I've ever felt.

Another part of me, that I'm sickened and embarrassed to admit exists, can't help but be attracted to him. And not just him, but what he offers me.

What if I never had to go back to being the weird orphan kid? Staying would flip the table—it would change everything. No more foster care, no more flunking high school, no more trying to prove myself to anyone.

The years I spent running, fighting, stealing, and failing at life. All of it could be wiped clean.

The servant boy lifts a saddle onto the maroon horse's back. My hand fits in the hollow space where the horse's neck and shoulder join together. I wonder if what Naoise said about horses sensing emotions is true.

Naoise rests a hand on my arm, diverting my attention. "So, my rose, will you join me for a jaunt around the high pasture?"

He doesn't wait for an answer as he mounts his black horse. I eye the space between the ground and the saddle, not sure how to close the gap.

"Róisín," Naoise calls to me, watching another rider come in from the direction of the castle, "excuse me while I converse with this rider."

He takes off, Meall's thick hooves churning up earth like a truck in the mud.

"Interesting choice." I turn around to find Orla standing near the tent. She's eyeing me and the horse with a curious pinch in her thin lips.

"The horse?"

Orla takes one step but doesn't seem interested in being any closer to the animals. "He used to belong to the late king's daughter, Princess Aisling."

She says the princess's name with obvious contempt, her mouth pulling into a small frown.

The horse nudges my shoulder as if he wants me to probe for more information. I try to make my voice sound as passive as possible.

"Did Aisling die with her parents?"

Orla's quick laugh takes me off guard. "No, no. King Rauri arranged her marriage to the prince of the merfolk. It is a fate most fae believe to be worse than death."

My brow furrows, intrigued and disturbed by Orla's satisfaction. Something tells me this is the faerie version of *Mean*

Girls in action. She turns toward the tent, still chuckling darkly under her breath.

"Do you know what she named her horse?" I ask.

The laugh dies as her mouth softens. "She named him So-na. It means, *may fortune smile.*"

She disappears behind the tent flap, and I look at Princess Aisling's horse. His brown eye blinks at me, and he tosses his head of black hair a little as if he knows something I don't.

"Sona," I whisper, tasting it on my tongue. He nods again, and I wish I could read his emotions like he's probably reading mine.

"Okay then." I pat his neck. "Promise not to let me fall?"

He snorts, whipping his dark mane across my face like a playful slap.

"Alright, alright, I'm going." I grab the saddle horn and am about to heave myself onto his back when the advisors exit the tent, deep in conversation. I pull Sona in front of me, blocking everything but my legs from view.

"As I told him, we will not make a decision until Lughnasa," the bearded one says.

"Never mind that," the female says. "What I cannot bear is knowing a human wanders freely. No doubt staying in the castle quarters."

"We all know who allowed that. He's keen on the girl."

This time Orla answers, "Soon enough she will lose her events and be tossed into the dungeon with the others. Do not underestimate Naoise's reasoning. She might have a pretty face, but what she represents is of far more value to him."

"What do you mean?" the bearded one asks.

"Naoise is using the girl as an example. The kingdom must be reassured after our loss, to be reminded that we are the superior race. What better way than to allow a human to compete?"

The group disperses as Naoise rides over. I stay hidden, my fist clenching a handful of horsehair as my teeth grind together.

"My lady, you still have not mounted your beast?"

Naoise stops beside me, and I feel my hands and arms ache as I hold in the revengeful fury.

He's using me. And I was stupid enough to think I meant something.

You do mean something, my inner critic sneers. *You're an example, remember?*

Orla's words tumble around my gut like shoes in a dryer. I swear if Naoise says one more word to me, I'll punch his gorgeous face right here—

"Róisín?" His tone is softer, which ticks me off even more.

Stop being perfect so I can hate you.

"I'm coming." I hold my skirt and thrust a boot into the air, relieved when it slips into the stirrup on the way down. Then I hoist myself up and over the horse's back.

Naoise's horse is taller than Sona, but I still feel too far from the ground up here. The boy unties Sona, and I wait for the horse to move.

Naoise speaks from behind me. "At this rate, you will never learn to ride before Lughnasa."

"Go, horse," I snap. Sona just flicks his tail.

"Simply use your thoughts to tell the beast what you desire. Of course, perhaps that kind of connection cannot be formed with an amateur rider."

I bite my tongue, feeling my neck and shoulder muscles constrict as hot anger runs through me.

Please. I know if I don't get Naoise off my back soon, I'll burst. I'll start screaming at him, throwing punches, telling him that he and his deal can go suck it because this girl is out.

I'm still not ready to find out what the consequences will be if that happens.

Just when I'm about give up, Sona slowly backs out from between the other horses and turns around. Naoise watches us with a small smile, nodding in approval.

"What a joke," I groan.

By now, I know it's in my best interests to keep quiet about what Orla said. What I need to do is wait, bide my time. Use this information to my advantage. Now that I know this deal isn't as black-and-white as I thought, I can organize my own back-alley dealings. A promise means nothing once the initial trust is broken.

Sona must be tired of listening to my inner raging and want to shut me up, because all of a sudden he jumps into a trot. He and Meall keep their distance from each other as we ride away from the tent.

Naoise's black cloak flutters behind him like a crow's wings. Even in the afternoon sunlight, he seems to pull the darkness closer until every shadow connects itself to him. His horse, who he said was part demon, drains the color from the grass beneath her hooves so that she walks on muted greens. I blink, and the colors return to normal.

Everything about this place plays tricks on you.

The floating globe of yellow sun, the blue-gray sky brushed with distant clouds. None of this should be able to exist if we're really underground.

I push those thoughts aside, returning to my present goal.

"Naoise, I want to renegotiate our deal."

He doesn't look at me, but I see his lips twitch. "And what are your terms for this renegotiation?"

I start slowly, handpicking each word. "My brother is still in the dungeons. If I'd known you would give me a room in the castle, I would have asked if he could be brought up with me."

"You wish for me to release him."

"And let him stay with me. I'll watch him."

"He remains in your quarters, never stepping foot outside the door." Our eyes meet, and although his tone is stern, I can't find anything but gentleness in his face. "Keep to that rule, and he shall be taken from the dungeons upon our return this evening."

I smile, unable to hide my relief.

"On one condition."

Smile gone, I wait for the deal breaker. I should have known there would be a catch.

His bright eyes glance over as his voice carries to me. "Race with me to the high pastures. There is a place beyond the horizon I wish for you to see."

Without waiting to hear my response, his horse takes off. I growl, flicking my reins and urging Sona to move faster than a snail's pace.

"Come on!" I cry, watching as Naoise disappears over a hill. "We have to at least try to keep up."

Sona, still lumbering along, turns his neck to look at me with one large eye. We glare at each other for a moment before I throw my hands in the air.

"What? What do you want from me? Huh?"

He snorts again and faces forward.

His slow walk sways us back and forth in a rhythm that makes me sleepy. Maybe I'm not in the mood to gallop anyway. My torso is still sore from this morning, and it's pretty uncomfortable to ride in a dress, even at this pace.

Despite how much I want to show Naoise that I can keep up and have a chance at winning the games, I feel relieved that he's gone. Maybe this was Sona's plan all along. After all, my horse dislikes Naoise even more than I do.

I pat his neck. "You were right. Slow and steady wins the race."

He snorts and breaks into a trot. I squeal, clenching my knees against the saddle and holding onto the reins as I try to stay upright.

Instead of heading deeper into the pastures, Sona veers to the right toward the forest.

"What—are—we—doing?" I grunt each word between bounds, already feeling my backside protesting.

My trusted steed ignores me, increasing his speed into a full gallop. The closer we get, the clearer my thoughts become. I lean forward in the saddle and tense my thighs to soften the blow of each stride.

In my mind, I try to ask Sona, *We're escaping?*

I feel the affirmation tingle in my fingers, and my insides nearly burst with a rush of adrenaline. If we can just make it to the trees, I can find the portal. From there, I can get help. Call for reinforcements. Plan a way to break into the castle and rescue Darren.

We're going to get out of here.

A flash of lightning streaks through the blue sky as black clouds curl around each other, fighting to block out the sun. I feel drops of rain land on my arms, and a few more drip down my neck. Thunder cracks the air in two, vibrating up from the ground and into my bones. Sona jolts beneath me but doesn't stop running.

A sheet of rain meets us head-on, drenching me. I think I imagine it at first, but then I'm sure I can see a rider on a horse, blocking our path. Dread squelches my flickering hope faster than dropping a lighter in a bathtub.

I don't need to see clearly to know who the rider is or to have absolute assurance that Naoise will enact his revenge for what I've tried to do.

Sona senses the threat and rears. I slip from his back, unable to grip the saddle in the downpour. I land with a thud, air rushing from my lungs as a sharp pain spikes through my tailbone.

My vision blurs with rainwater. I can barely make out Sona as he circles me. Naoise is walking toward us, his dark horse standing to the side.

He seems to glide across the soggy grass and through the mud puddles, his cloak curling behind him in a swirl of mist. When lightning threads the sky, it illuminates every angle of his face. I can almost taste his fury snaking its way closer until I'm paralyzed by it.

When Naoise gets too close, my horse bolts. An aching thunder shoves me deeper into the mud. The electric hues of blue and black in the faery's eyes mirror the storm above us.

He stands above me, and with a flick of his hand he summons the mist at his feet to swarm over me. Tendrils of smoke curl around my limbs and my torso, pulling and lifting me until I hover above the ground. My lips feel like they've been stapled shut—otherwise I know I'd be screaming my guts out. The mist doesn't stop lifting me until I'm floating in front of Naoise, my feet dangling just above the ground.

The rain parts between us like a curtain, making it easier to see just how terrifying he really is. The power exuding from him numbs my senses, and I feel my consciousness begin to slip away. I doubt I could survive even the touch of his pinky finger on my skin.

"You would dare defy me?" Each word feels like an icy knife piercing my chest. "You would betray our agreement? Betray my trust?"

His mouth softens as his eyes fill with pain. "I offered you a seat beside my throne. You were to be my queen." My vision is zeroing in and out of focus as his voice lowers to a breaking point. "How could you betray me?"

Raindrops press against my face like eager fingers, rolling my head back. The last thing I hear is Naoise's yell shattering the air in a burst of wind, and everything goes black.

{ 20 }

[T]heir gifts usually have conditions attached, which detract from their value and sometimes become a source of loss and misery.

- *The Science of Fairy Tales: An Enquiry into Fairy Mythology* by Edwin Sidney Hartland (1891)

My eyes refuse to open at first, like two garage doors rusted from underuse. I can feel where my left hip and shoulder ache from lying in the same position for so long. Over my own odor of wet dog—or should I say, wet horse—the faint scent of flowers tells me I'm in my room.

What was I thinking?

Naoise said that the horse would read my thoughts and emotions and act on them. Did Sona pick up on my longing to run through the portal and never look back?

He was obeying my innermost feelings that I've been trying to suppress ever since I left the dungeon. The best way to save Darren is to stick to the deal I made with Naoise, not sprint for the trees the first moment I'm not being watched.

Who knows if I could get back into the Otherworld once I left, let alone convince humans to follow me and attack an army of faeries to save my kid brother?

My side protests as I force my stiff limbs to shift me into a sitting position. As soon as I put pressure on my tailbone, I know my fall off the horse bruised it up bad.

The room is empty. Not seeing Darren adds to my growing dread. If he's not here, that means he's still in the pit. Which means Naoise could have decided to retract that part of the deal.

I've ruined everything.

A groan escapes me as I stand. Between the failed sparring fight and the disaster of a horse-riding lesson, I don't want to know how many injuries decorate my body.

You deserve every single one. You were going to abandon Darren to save your own skin.

I shake my head, tears trembling in my eyes, threatening to spill over. Reaching the door, I realize I'm locked in. I yank on the knob, kicking at the wood.

"Hey!" I shout at no one in particular. "Open this damned door!"

I have to get out. I have to make this right.

Eventually someone hears me trying to beat the door down. A voice tells me to step back, and Lana squeezes inside before shutting the door behind her. Her skin is so pale I think she might pass out.

"My lady," she speaks in a rushed whisper, "you must not draw attention to yourself. Naoise ordered for you to be contained here and for no one to open this door under penalty of banishment."

"But I have to compete." I wipe an arm across my eyes. I'm just now noticing the forest-green dress is gone, and I'm wearing nothing but the light slip. "How long am I in here for?"

"My lady, I-I cannot be speaking with you. I know not how long you will be contained, only that your actions have enraged Naoise."

She shakes her head, staring at the ground, talking more to herself than to me. "They call him Naoise of the Western Moors, but I never believed him to be a marshland faery. He is far too powerful for that . . ."

Her voice trails off, and she shudders. I'm surprised she said as much as she did considering Hafwin called her superstitious.

Images of my visit to Naoise's lair fill my mind. I had no idea he kept his past a secret. Why share it with me—a perfect stranger?

I grab Lana by the shoulders. "Lana please," I plead, staring into her huge blue eyes. "All you have to do is let me out. If I'm caught, I'll lie and say I found a key in a drawer."

She shakes her head, her bottom lip trembling. "The high fae sense treachery. They will know the truth."

I pause, debating for half a second before sinking my fingers into her arms and throwing her behind me. She screeches as she stumbles to the ground. I open the door and close it behind me, searching the empty hall.

Clear.

I jog around the corner, freezing when I see someone coming my way. No doubt he will take one look at my half-naked, mud-caked self and know that something's wrong. I duck behind a tapestry, breathing in a lungful of dust until he passes.

The castle is more deserted than usual, and I manage to reach the dungeons without getting caught. The guard standing at the top of the stairs doesn't flinch when I come barreling through, and I don't stop to think about how strange that is until I reach the bottom and see the group gathered on both sides of the prison bars.

The first person I recognize is Cináed, standing next to doe-eyes. Seeing them together makes my stomach clench.

Neither of them notices me in the shadow of the stairwell, and I listen to the heated argument between Cináed and the humans on the other side.

Sterling's scruffy face presses against the bars. "You release Vera but leave the rest of us to die."

Cináed hands the gate guard a few shiny coins. "I release one who is neither human nor fae, who was captured by mistake. The rest of you"—he turns to look at Sterling—"will only be imprisoned until this ridiculous rumor can be dismissed for good."

"And what if that never happens, eh?" Markie steps up. "What if your kind decide to blame us for the deaths and kill us?"

Several humans gasp, and one of them cries out. I see Esperanza punish Markie's indelicate nature with a pointed glare. Too many faces are clouded in darkness for me to find Darren in the crowd.

If Cináed pities any of them, his stony expression doesn't show it. "I cannot know what will become of you if somehow the rumors stand. No matter the decision of the council, I will come for the boy, Darren."

Hearing Cináed say that name tightens my throat. *He promised to come for us, remember?* Why didn't I trust in that before I took off running?

He continues, "The rest of you mean nothing to me unless you are willing to invest in your freedom. A kingdom's power balances on a thread of hope. My worries are far greater than saving a few helpless humans."

"Without a plan of attack, we are doomed from the start," Sterling retorts, sounding desperate.

Markie kicks at one of the metal poles with her booted foot as she says, "Let's face it. None of these kids would stand a chance against a fae warrior. Hell, even the castle servants have more tenacity and skill than some of these pathetic—"

"Margarette, hush!" Es says.

That's when I see Darren standing right behind her. I ache to run to him, to hold him like I did when we were younger. Like I still do now during the rare moments when he lets me.

Markie kicks the gate again. "I only speak the truth."

"Humans are as melodramatic as the high fae," doe-eyes— Vera—drawls in her sexy voice as she brushes white hair away from her soft, round face. Her grayish skin radiates an almost eerie beauty.

How could anyone mistake her for a human?

She goes on, "Cináed spoke with the guards loyal to King Rauri and bribed a few who were passive. This gate will open whenever you decide you're ready to escape."

Taking Cináed's hand, she starts leading him toward the stairwell where I'm hiding. In that small gesture, her fingers laced with his, it feels like she's clenching a hand around my heart, squeezing until it bursts into a million useless pieces.

Before they run into me, I step out into the torchlight along the wall. They both stop, and Cináed drops Vera's hand, pulling me against him before I know what's happening.

"Róisín." He stands back but doesn't let me go. "How did you come to be here? Naoise had you locked away, and I've been questioning guards all morning to find where he was keeping you."

"I found a key," I say, aware that Vera's reflective eyes are shooting lasers at me.

"Come, Cináed." Her attempt at sounding disinterested can't mask the jealous undertone in her voice.

I turn to her. "He's not your pet. And don't you still owe me?"

At this point some of the humans have seen me, and I hear Markie call out, "The prodigal daughter returns after all. We were beginning to think you were dead."

While Es smacks her arm, I catch Darren's eye. Seeing him solidifies my resolve, reminding me how unimportant any of these people are compared to my brother.

"Tell me the plan for getting us home," I say to Cináed.

He and Vera share another look. Then when his head is turned, she snarls at me before walking up the stairs.

Cináed pulls me onto the first step. Darkness covers us as he talks low and fast. "The plan I had in place no longer stands. Complications arose—one being your recent encounters with Naoise." His eyes match the color of deep ocean waters as he stares at me, almost as if he's trying to read my soul.

Does he think I've fallen for Naoise?

"I tried to run." I stare at the shadows around us, unable to meet his gaze. I haven't fallen for Naoise, but that doesn't mean I can hide the fact that I almost did. "I didn't know what to do about these competitions, and when I panic, my first instinct is to run."

His hand brushes my bangs behind an ear, and just like that I'm transported away from this mess. I can almost smell the salt in the air and hear the waves crashing outside his window as we talk in the candlelight of his room.

"I will do everything in my power to keep you safe, Róisín. Both you and Darren."

"Can we get out of here tonight?"

Now it's his turn to look away. He sighs, tugging on his unruly curls. "As I said, the plan changed. The entire castle knows you are not to be touched. Let alone be aided in an escape."

"But we can't stay here." My voice trembles. "I'll do whatever it takes. Please."

Pain pinches the corners of his eyes. "Do not mistake my words for a dismissal. I have thought of every possibility imaginable. Smuggling you out with the members of my crew. Instructing loyal guards to escort you to the forest. My first choice is to take you myself."

He sighs again, leaning against the wall. "Until I know the depths of Naoise's powers, I do not dare leave you vulnerable to an attack. The moment you step foot outside this castle without his permission, a fate worse than death could await you. And there is no way to prove my theory false without risking your life."

I step away, my panic resurfacing and making it hard to breathe.

"So you just expect me to sit and do nothing? As far as we know, we're just as likely to die here as we are in an attempted escape."

The guard at the top of the stairs leans into the doorway. "Rotations approaching soon."

"We must leave the dungeons before the next watch arrives." Cináed looks at me, then at my slip. "How in the name of Dea did you journey through the castle unseen?"

"I have some experience with sneaking."

Sneaking. Hiding. Stealing. I'm not too proud of any of it, but those skills have been not only helpful but necessary at times.

Like now, for example.

"While I trust in your abilities, let us not tempt misfortune," he says. "I will have the guard admit you into the dungeons, where you will hide until I formulate a new plan."

"But the competition. I can still—"

"There's no time." Cináed takes my arm and leads me down the stairs.

Only Markie still stands by the bars, sharpening her knife against the metal. "Back so soon?"

Cináed ignores her, placing another handful of coins in the guard's hand. "She remains here until I return. If anyone comes searching for her, you saw nothing."

"Aye."

"I won't go in." I plant my bare feet on the dirt floor. "You don't understand—I can still help from out here."

The gate parts, and Cináed pushes me through, his forcefulness taking me off guard. When the gate slams shut, I try to wrench it back open.

Faster than my eyes can follow, Cináed reaches through the bars to hold the side of my face in his hand. Then, in an instant, he's walking up the stairs. I shout after him in vain.

"Oh shut it," Markie says.

I look past her to Darren, who's dozing against Esperanza on the ground. She nods at me, silently letting me know he's alright.

I turn my attention back to Markie. "This has nothing to do with you, so stay out of it."

Her eyes follow the blade as she grinds it against the metal. I see now it's nothing more than a dull butter knife.

"Adorable, really. You're in love with a faery, and you think he's going to rescue you." She peers at me beneath her dark brows. "Hate to break it to you, but he cares as little for you as he does any of us."

I fold my arms. "The reason I've come closer to escaping than any of you is because I refuse to give up. You're the one relying on the faeries to save you."

"Sure thing." She rolls her eyes, fingering the knife we both know couldn't stab a hardened loaf of bread. "Is that what you tell yourself now that you've aligned with the enemy?"

I pause, baffled at how fast news travels around here. "I'm not on Naoise's side."

"Who said I meant Naoise?" Markie motions to the empty stairs. "All of them are the enemy. Don't you get that?"

"Enough." Sterling stands up from his place beside Esperanza. "We must resolve our differences if we are to escape."

Markie snorts. "I cannot stomach another rallying speech. I hate the fae as much as any of us, but Vera is right. We have built our own prison, and fear is the only thing keeping us inside it."

She pauses. "What we need is a plan of action."

"I have a plan."

All eyes turn to me. Even a few people I thought were sleeping are staring at me.

"This should be good," Markie says.

I ignore her sarcasm. "Help me win the games, and in return I can promise you your freedom."

Silence. Everyone looks at each other, and Markie finally asks, "And how do you plan on entering the games, let alone freeing all of us?"

"Because I made a deal with Naoise. If I win two events, the humans go free."

"You mean all of us?" Es asks.

I nod. The lie feels wrong, but since Cináed decided to exclude me from his plan, I don't have another option.

The sooner I can find Naoise, the better chance I have to smooth things over. And maybe, by some miracle, I can still win these games. My gut tells me Naoise has no investment in these humans, which means I might be able to sway him into letting everyone go.

"Look," I continue when no one speaks, "the faeries who were supposed to be sympathetic to our cause have drawn a line in the sand. It's time to stand up for ourselves. Help me win, and we can all go home."

Es and Sterling give each other a silent look. Markie starts chuckling, tucking the knife back into her belt.

"Your plan is just reckless enough to interest me."

Esperanza nods to Sterling, who turns to me. "We are with you, Róisín."

Footsteps sound from the stairs, and two guards step into the firelight. The guard Cináed bribed leaves as they rotate watch.

"Great," I say, lowering my voice. "So, how do I get out of the dungeon?"

"Wait until the next rotation," Markie says. Then she grins, teeth flashing from the torch glow. "Until then, you can begin your training right here with Markie of the Strong-arm."

She walked past him without glancing in his direction, but Naoise saw her, and was so struck by her beauty.

   - *The Names Upon the Harp* by Marie Heaney (2000)

"I told you he was cheating!"

"Keep your eyes to yourself, Alex, or we'll have to start the game over again."

Sterling is the one who gives the warning. Everyone has a handful of cards that appear just as tattered and worn down as the people holding them.

Although most of these humans look about my age, they exude the same sense of oldness that makes me wonder how long they've been trapped in the Otherworld. I know time moves differently here. If it affects humans as much as it does the fae, these people could be decades old.

Darren places his card down, and I smile. "Nice move."

He nudges me, his own smile lighting up his eyes. "Your turn."

I place my card down, and everyone moans.

"What?" I look at my deck, confused.

Darren answers for the group. "You just won the game, Raisin."

"Oh."

I honestly hadn't been listening when Sterling explained the rules. My mind was busy thinking of everything but this card game. Like how on earth I'm going to convince a very angry faery to not only let me compete in the games but, if I win, to release thirty-five more humans than we originally agreed upon.

The cards are gathered, and Esperanza reshuffles the stack in her small fingers. Darren and I bow out, moving to sit against the wall.

"I've actually won four times now," he says, letting me wipe some of the grime from a spot beside his ear.

"Even with Alex cheating?"

My hand brushes the dark locks from his forehead, and I wish I could bring him with me when I go back into the castle. He's in desperate need of a bath, a hot meal, and a real bed.

He laughs once. "Most everyone here cheats, or at least that's what Markie says. That's why she won't play."

Then he continues, and this time I hear the raw emotion in his voice. "I'm scared that if you go, something will happen to you."

"Hey." I wrap my arm around him, but he resists.

"I'm serious, Róisín." More than his stern tone, his use of my real name takes me aback. "I know you won't admit it, but I've learned about the competition. Those games aren't like cards. What if something goes wrong, and you never come back?" His voice cracks, and he turns away.

As much as I ache to comfort him, I can't bear to lie again. Not to him.

Instead, I coax him into my arms, and I try to forget about what I have to do once I get upstairs. The games, Naoise, even Cináed. I let it all go, holding onto what exists in this moment alone.

We wait until Vera comes.

The humans tell me that doe-eyes now works with Cináed to collect information—as they prepare to stage an uprising if Naoise is crowned—and she will bring us any important news from the castle. Cináed had said he would appoint her the job of bringing us our meals so she can keep us updated without raising suspicion.

Vera arrives with a new guard rotation, one that Markie says pledged their loyalty to Cináed as protector of the throne until a proper ruler is appointed.

I stand by the gate, holding Darren's hand. While we wait, he tells me everything he knows about faeries. Most of it comes from his books and some from dungeon gossip . . .

They love making deals to the point of obsession, which explains how Cináed could convince the demon to take my shoe in trade for Darren. And why Naoise wanted to make a deal with me in the first place.

They are separated into two main groups, called courts. Everyone in this kingdom—minus the forest dwellers who consider themselves rogue faeries without a ruler—belongs to the Seelie Court. A huge swath of territory to the west of the moors belongs to the Unseelie Court.

Darren says Sterling believes the rumor that Naoise is Unseelie. While all fae are wild and dangerous, the Unseelie carry darkness with them. Sterling calls them *children of the devil.*

I picked up a few tips from a short fistfight with Markie that ended as soon as it started because Markie dodged my blow while simultaneously swinging wide and hit a kid standing too close. Es flew in like a mother hen, and Markie skulked off, saying something about how she never gets to have a decent fight anymore.

We all watch in silence as the guards change and Vera rummages through the basket on her arm, handing things through the bars. They look like rolls of bread and chunks of cheese. Dirty, eager hands grasp for them. I half-expect to see Vera's face contort in disgust. After all, she made her dislike for humans clear when Cináed released her.

But instead, her large eyes shimmer with emotion as she places a roll in the hands of a girl even younger than Darren.

After the old guard walks up the stairs, Markie taps on the bars with her knife.

"Hark, you there."

The new guard stares back silently from his post.

Markie continues, "One of us will be flying the coop tonight. And Vera"—she points the knife in her direction—"will be doing the escorting. Understood?"

The guard looks at Vera, hesitating. "And Lord Cináed knows of this?"

I can tell Vera is curious now, too, listening to the conversation as she continues her work. Darren moves closer to get food, and that's when Vera sees me in the shadows. The spot between her eyes pinches together.

Good.

She doesn't know why I'm down here. Which means she also doesn't know Cináed ordered me to stay put.

Markie convinces the guard to open the gate, and after a quick goodbye to Darren, I cross through. So far, things are going according to plan. But my stomach still feels like Markie is using it as a punching bag as the gate clangs shut behind me.

Even with enough faerie facts to fill an encyclopedia, I know I'll never feel ready to face all that awaits me outside this pit.

Vera doesn't say a word, but I know her black eyes miss nothing as she empties the basket and meets me at the stairs.

At first I had argued I should go alone, betting I could make it back to my room. But Esperanza reminded me that the room could be locked, and if it is, I'll need someone like Vera to go searching after the key while I stay hidden.

What none of them know is that I plan on turning myself in to the guard at the top of the stairs—who I know is as amiable as the one at the gate—and ask to be brought to see Naoise right away. His room hugs the opposite corner of the castle from where I am now, and while I might be able to make it there, especially in the dark, I can't risk getting locked in my room again.

I hope I can ditch Vera before she decides to ruin anything.

As expected, a single guard stands at the top of the stairs. It's not till I step through the doorway that I see several more guards, including the ones in leather clothes who first took me to Naoise. Most lounge against chairs or the wall, drinking from mugs and laughing at some inside joke.

If any of them see me, this plan could fail. Vera keeps her gaze straight as she walks through them, ignoring the catcalls from a faery slouched in a chair. I glance at the guard by the doorway. Is he the one Markie said could be trusted? Or maybe it's the one standing to the side by the flaming torch, lighting a pipe?

My hesitation attracts several pairs of eyes to me, including those belonging to the guard with the pipe. Now I recognize him as the one who held the knife to my back. I almost swallow my tongue, ducking my head as I turn to follow Vera.

No hands reach out to stop me, but I won't let myself breathe until I round the corner. Vera stands by a window overlooking a small garden, her casual stance telling me she couldn't care less if I didn't make it out of that hall.

Moonlight alone lights this space, and I hope Vera chose it because it's not a trafficked corridor. I rest against the wall to gather my senses and come up with a new plan. Maybe I could convince one of Hafwin's posse to take me to Naoise. Although after what happened with Lana, I can't expect any of them to jump at the chance to help me.

"No one doubts the flower."

Vera's random comment barely registers in my mind. I don't look at her when I say, "Sure."

The half-moon lights up the garden in a soft gray glow. I can smell the flowers, and although they droop like the wilted roses I saw the day we arrived, their strange colors are more vibrant than anything I've ever seen. Blue, orange, pink . . . those names don't apply to the rainbow planted outside.

Vera's gaze moves from the window to rest on me.

"If you wish to be respected, to gain favor with the fae, you must look the part."

I hug my arms around my slip, conscious of my matted hair and exposed, dirty skin.

"You want me to wear a fancy gown?" I say, wanting to laugh at her. She wasn't there to see how the tent of faeries mocked me, even after I was dressed to the nines. "I tried that, and believe me, it didn't help."

Her brows recede into the white hair framing her face. "Because you were dressed as the wrong flower—a mistake just as dangerous as approaching Naoise of the Western Moors as you are now."

I make a sound of protest, but she talks over me.

"You are not a daffodil or a tulip. You are called Róisín, am I right?"

I just nod, feeling too vulnerable to respond. *How can she see right through me, like I'm more transparent than these clothes?*

"Come." She steps away from the window. "Let us find you some rose petals." Then she smiles, revealing sharp canines. "And perhaps a few thorns to match."

When I go to turn the doorknob, it clicks, and the door swings open. Lana must have left it unlocked. Remembering her face when I threw her behind me sends a pang through my chest. After everything they've done, I hated abusing their kindness.

Vera follows me inside. The same will-ó-the-wisp casts a pink glow over the empty room.

Despite the warm glow, the cold air in here bites at my skin. I rub my hands together to create a little friction and move toward the armoire. It swings open, and dresses burst out at me. I shove them aside, feeling exhausted by all the glamour of this place.

Vera kneels by the fireplace and starts arranging pieces of kindling.

I pull out a gown and carry it to the bed. It's just as heavy as the green one from before, and equally old fashioned. I don't know whether I should try to put it on or have it sent to the nearest museum.

After removing several similar dresses, I catch sight of a long white shirt and a short but flexible leather skirt. I dig around for that pair of tall boots and find the same leather vest I wore when I sparred with Cináed. I lay it all out on the ground, away from the mountain of gowns on the bed.

The outfit reminds me of a medieval barista who owns some off-the-chain pub. Or a badass pirate chick who's come to steal your boat. Either way, I dig it.

Vera walks over from the now-crackling fire, placing her hands on her hips as she inspects my choices.

"I know the perfect flourish. Wash and dress yourself. I will return." She exits the room without further explanation.

Once I've removed as much dirt as I can using a pitcher of water and a wadded-up bed robe, I put on the hot pirate costume and tie the boots up to my calves.

"By the grace of Uisce," Vera says when she closes the door behind her, "you are a new sight to behold."

She sits me down and, using the roses she picked, adorns my hair with the blood-red flowers. One look in the mirror shows me she included a few thorns in the twisted updo.

"Holy crap."

I stare at my reflection a bit longer, feeling strange in a good way. The other girls made me look unrecognizable. Now I look, and feel, like the most powerful version of myself.

Like I've finally stepped into my own.

"Okay," I say to Vera. "Let's do this."

{ 22 }

One winter's day, Deirdre's foster father was slaughtering a calf for veal and the blood flowed out across the snow. As Deirdre watched from her window a raven swooped down to sip the blood. Deirdre . . . said, "I could love a man like that, a man with hair as black as a raven and skin like snow and cheeks as red as blood!" "Good luck is yours," [her foster father] answered, "for not far from here lives such a man. He is called Naoise."

 - *The Names Upon the Harp* by Marie Heaney (2000)

I stand alone in front of Naoise's door.

Apparently Vera was only willing to help because she still owed me one. When we reached the *forbidden corridor* where Naoise stays, that favor reached its limit.

"Our debts have been paid," she'd said to me when I realized she'd stopped walking down the moonlit hall.

I nodded, not blaming her for wanting to keep her distance from Naoise. But then she had to go tearing through the rivalry garbage between us, reminding me why I hate her.

"I met Cináed soon after Branna's death. The title of Wanderer belonged to him before those years, but he truly grew to be the seafaring voyager he is today after she died." Each word flowed into the next in her smooth, casual voice. She picked at one of her nails. "He found refuge with me from his endless journey, and we were lovers for a time."

A lump stuck in my throat.

Branna.

The name on the headstone, the name of his ship—she was his partner, after all. As was Vera.

A dark pool of jealousy coalesced in front of me. Part of me longed to dive straight in and let it consume me in equal parts anger and misery. But another part of me sensed that Vera was building up to something, and she would sink the knife even deeper unless I was careful.

Our eyes met. Her top lip revealed several gleaming teeth as she smiled.

"I see by your shock that he never told you this before. Curious. From the way you behaved, I thought perhaps the two of you were closer. Then again, your weak human disposition makes it easy to believe an illusion of the heart."

Then she turned and walked away, leaving me at the threshold of Naoise's lair with nothing but the sound of my own trembling breaths to break the deafening silence.

After calling Vera every terrible word I can think of in my head, I shove my fragile emotions aside and knock on the door.

Naoise's presence carries a distinct aura, a vibe that has me believing in every ghost story I've ever heard. I feel him nearby, and in the next instant I'm standing inside his room.

I cry out, falling back a step.

What just happened?

The door behind me is closed. I feel insane thinking it, but he just used dark magic to transport me through the wall.

Peering through the layers of moonlight, shadow, and mist, I wait for the volatile nightmare of a faery to make himself known.

"Róisín." His voice carries through the air, brushing over my skin. "To what do I owe this pleasure?"

I see him now, standing in the corner furthest from the windows—the area of the room I didn't dare flee into the first night because it melts into a darkness so pure my vision would be useless.

My constricted throat won't release, and I think my voice got left behind in the transportation. Then I catch a glimpse of myself in the glass window. Seeing my girl-power ensemble reminds me why I'm here and what I stand to lose.

I lock eyes with Naoise, refusing to coddle my tangible fear.

"I want to reenter the games. The deal is still on."

He watches me without any sign of emotion, and then his lips twitch into a forced smile.

"You talk as if speaking the words makes them so." He watches the sheer black curtains swelling with the night breeze. "Your fierce passion is what drew me to you, but it is also what blinds you to reason."

"Our agreement never included any deal breakers. You can't call it off without my consent."

His eyes glow through the mist, cutting into me with their cold intensity. "Watch your tongue, Róisín. You forget to whom you speak."

I ignore the reprimand, standing my ground. "You forget that *you're* the one who approached *me*. If you expect me to be queen, we're on an equal playing field. And I say the deal stands."

He doesn't look at me when he says, "And how do I know you will not attempt another escape?"

I bite my lip and decide to use the truth to buoy my argument.

"You don't. But you can't control that part of the deal."

"I disagree." He moves closer, like a panther prowling the jungle floor. "If you flee and do not participate in the games, you forfeit them. Meaning you become my bride, and I am at liberty to hunt after you and return you to the Otherworld."

Shoot. How was I stupid enough to not realize that?

Because he still has you under his spell. You're a bug, and he's the alluring lantern, remember?

Which means no amount of girl power can make me think straight unless he drops the voodoo act. Which he won't.

When I hesitate, he goes on. "Let us propose new terms. Your brother remains in the dungeons throughout Lughnasa. If you so much as try to escape, he will be killed."

He walks until he's so close I could touch him. Even his devilish beauty can't distract me from my loathing. He's using Darren's life as a pawn in this game.

"Then I'm adding something too," I say, swallowing the bile churning in my gut. "If I win, all the humans in the dungeons go free alongside Darren and me."

He glances between my eyes. I can *smell* the shadows clinging to him.

"Agreed."

Before I can mentally celebrate the small victory, he adds, "Night has just begun. Do join me for a ride."

We ride in silence, giving my imagination free reign to speculate how he might kill me tonight.

He'll choke me with that purple mist. Darth Vader style with no hands.

Or worse, what if his horse eats me for dinner? I caught a glimpse of her needle-sharp teeth. No way is she an herbivore.

I shudder and wish I could glance at Naoise behind me in the saddle. His silence makes me wonder if he's forgotten I'm here. Or maybe he's busy plotting my demise. I readjust my numb hands and stare ahead at the black horizon.

The forest lining the pastures turned a while back, and a marshland took its place. Mist settles near the ground with a heaviness that fits my mood all too well. A bed of moss and scraggly grass creates a lumpy, uneven terrain.

Naoise leaps down from the horse. He is still solemn and contemplative, and I don't know whether I should feel relieved or not. Part of me prefers his brash fury to this silent torment. As least when he's screaming at me I have a better grasp on what he's thinking.

"This, my rose, is a beloved place." He looks out over the mist. "As a child, I was raised in the Western Moors, a land nearly identical to what you see here."

He turns to me, his clear eyes holding a level of sincerity I didn't think possible in someone like him.

"Do you know your parents?"

The question catches me off guard. He helps me down from the horse as I stumble over an answer. "It's complicated. I mean, no, I don't. They left when I was young."

His hand finds mine, and our fingers intertwine as he leads me along. The smallest touch from him electrifies my nerves, heightening every color, every sound. My already-fragile heart aches as I battle feelings I know I can't trust.

He threatened Darren. Remember that.

The squishy ground gives under my boots, and I hop from one knoll to the next. When I turn back, his demon horse is barely visible through the curtain of gray fog.

"My first memories are equally tragic," he says. "As you know, the only knowledge I have of my parents came from the faery who raised me. That, and the discoveries I made once I was old enough to return to the Shadowlands."

"So you're an orphan."

He looks at me, and his glowing eyes pierce the mist. "If *orphan* signifies someone who cannot forgive their abandonment, then aye, I am an orphan."

We circle back around the way we came. Or at least, that's what I'm hoping. There's something disorienting yet soothing about this place, and it gets me all turned around.

"And do you also consider yourself an orphan?"

The luminescent green grass of the pastures appears through the fog. Naoise slows to a stop on the edge of the moors, watching me intently. The security of his fingers around mine feels less like a cage somehow.

I can't invite enough air through my nose to stop the tingling burn behind my eyes. *Orphan: someone who cannot forgive their abandonment.*

"Yeah," I say. "I'm an orphan."

Everything beyond the moors seems too much to handle. I just want to curl up on the ground and sink into a bed of soft moss and a blanket of mist. I want to forget about the responsibilities and pressures that wait for me back at the castle.

Just seven more days until the competitions begin.

Before I know what's happening, Naoise pulls me to his chest, shielding me in his dark cloak. His hand cradles the back of my head, and the other wraps around my torso until his forearm rests against my lower back. The material of his shirt feels soft and velvety. It smells inviting, like a moonlit path in the woods leading to who knows where.

My arms rest stiffly against my sides. I don't dare embrace him, but I'm not willing to push him away.

His voice reminds me of a wolf, haunting me the way a distant howl pricks the hair on my neck.

"From the moment I looked into your eyes, I saw through the chainmail and armor and into the scared heart of a creature not unlike myself. Alone. Abandoned. Forgotten and underestimated."

Cocooned in his cloak, I hear his heartbeat pounding against my head.

Or is it my own heartbeat?

"You are more to me than a summer bride, Róisín. I would have you as my mate, to stand with me as I take this kingdom and many more hereafter."

Pulling back, he presses his mouth against mine.

He tastes just like I imaged he would. Smooth and dark, with the hint of a bitter aftertaste—like a bite of midnight chocolate.

Our lips part, and he cups my chin in his hand as he whispers, "Be mine forever, and you shall never feel alone again."

{ 23 }

These Tuatha were great necromancers, skilled in all magic, and excellent in all the arts as builders, poets, and musicians.

- Ancient Legends, Mystic Charms, and Superstitions of Ireland by Lady Francesca Speranza Wilde (1887)

More faeries than I've ever seen crowd the honey-colored marble halls. The buzz of voices fills the air. The rest of the competitors arrive today, and preparations for the festival bring new life to the castle.

Morning sunlight bathes the tapestries and paintings decorating every wall as I cross the familiar, high-ceilinged room that connects several smaller hallways. Faeries gather in groups throughout the great room, lining stairs that lead to balconies I thought were off limits.

I squeeze past a table piled with fruits, foreign dishes, and lots of summer wine. By now I recognize the golden drink that the fae seem to have on hand 24/7.

Before she disappeared, Hafwin warned me that—even if I decided at my own risk to try fae food—I should never taste the wine. She said my body couldn't handle the drink. With multiple lives depending on my ability to perform in the games, I don't need any more convincing to shy away from the sweet-smelling liquid.

Munching on the non-fae apple I brought from my room, I pick up on the conversation between two faeries beside me.

"Well, I heard Naoise of the Western Moors secured the throne during the last moon cycle," a female with curly brown hair says as she pops a cherry in her mouth.

"That's not what my source told me," her friend says, brushing his red braid across his shoulder as he reaches for more wine. "I heard Naoise will not be crowned until the council rules on the cause of the deaths."

The female laughs, the noise reminding me of birdsong. "Do not fool yourself. Humans caused the deaths and will continue to murder us all until every last one is hounded, captured, and offered as a sacrifice to appease the gods."

Unable to listen to any more of the sick gossip, I duck around the last of the faeries blocking my way and escape down the emptiest hallway.

I turn a corner and see Orla coming from the other direction. She meets my gaze with surprise that hardens into a keen interest that makes me nervous. I've managed to dodge her since I overheard her explanation beside the tent, and I was hoping to avoid crossing her path again.

Her charcoal-gray dress is paired with a light fur scarf that drapes around her neck and torso like a shawl. The color matches her steel eyes.

She stops in front of me, and when it's clear that she won't be the first to speak, I say, "I'm trying to find the storytelling lessons."

She scans my outlandish outfit—which is similar to the hot pirate but lacks the flowers in my hair. Two days have passed since Naoise reinstated me, and I still haven't seen the pastel-clad girls anywhere. While dressing myself feels liberating, wandering around the castle in search of food or the next lesson wastes precious time.

Orla gestures for me to follow her to her left. We stop in front of an open archway.

I peek over her shoulder, realizing how small she is up close despite her strong personality that makes her seem intimidating and larger than life.

Two faeries read scrolls near the back corner. In the center of the room stands a female older than Orla but just as stunning. Her auburn hair, streaked with white and gray, is gathered in a thick braid that tumbles around her shoulder. She has a tall forehead and the kind of wrinkles around her eyes and mouth that reflect a lifetime of talking and laughing.

She is focused on a blond girl in front of her who stands a few paces away. I recognize her long yellow ponytail from a spear fight in the courtyard the other day, which means that she's probably competing in two of the same categories that I am.

"Aye, Ethne," the elderly faery is saying. "Your dynamics have improved. Although I suggest a tale where the king is not eaten by kelpies. Perhaps a story where the hero and his hounds hunt a beast, or something equally satisfying. This is a burial festival, after all."

Ethne curtsies and exits. I move out of the way to let her through, and she keeps her head of blond hair held high as she hisses, "Vermin," in my ear and walks away. I imagine sticking out my boot and tripping her, and I smile to myself.

That smile melts away when I realize I'm next. Orla escorts me inside. She walks up to the instructor, and they share a respectful nod.

"Lady Aimsir."

"Lady Orla."

"This is the mortal chosen by Naoise to compete in the games."

Aimsir regards me with a neutral expression, not the typical response I get when someone realizes I'm human.

"Greetings. Your name?"

"Róisín," I say.

Orla continues in the same collected tone, "As she is indeed human, you cannot expect her skill level to compare to that of your other pupils. However, fulfill your duty. This decision was made for reasons that do not concern you."

Aimsir nods, and Orla leaves the room. I'm trying to grapple with what just went down. If Orla's condescending tone injured my ego, this sage storyteller had to feel the sting too.

"So, Róisín, tell me your story."

Her question takes me aback. I fumble with my hands, suddenly feeling like I don't know what to do with them.

"My story?"

"Yes. Every being has a story. It can include, but is not limited to, your past, present, and future. Who you were as a child. What journeys you have taken. Where you dream to be one-hundred sunsets from now."

Far away from here.

I clear my throat. "Okay, I guess it's obvious I'm not a local. I grew up in foster care, I have a little brother, and I'm only a few months away from being an 'adult' in human terms." I air quote *adult* and then feel silly.

"And what of your present? Is there a reason you are competing in these games?"

I glance around, not wanting to spew the truth carelessly. Something tells me that Aimsir doesn't have any ulterior motives, so I continue.

"If I win two events, my brother and I can go back home."

Her eyebrows lift to the center of her high forehead. "And if you lose?"

My gut clenches, and my hands start to tingle. "I-I can't lose," I stammer, injecting as much determination into the words as possible as I meet her gaze. "I'll do whatever it takes to win."

Her lips pull into a smile that doesn't show her teeth. "Good. Now tell me what experience you have with bards. What legends or stories have you memorized? And do you prefer singing to acting?"

No one ever said anything about singing or *acting.*

"Um, I know some stories from American history," I say, frantically digging through the dusty files of my mind where I store every history class I've endured. "The Civil War has some pretty intense stories."

"You will not win telling those histories." She reaches for a stack of thick books and scrolls on a table. "The fae are only interested in hearing about the fae. Perhaps you will recognize one of these legends from Celtic history."

She hands me a partially opened scroll, and I wrap my hands around the top and bottom handles in order to see the scrawled text. Strange lines group together to form a series of runes—impossible to read. The leathery paper rolls together as I hand it back.

"I can't read that."

Aimsir exhales in a huff. "If you do not know any Celtic legends by heart, assigning someone to translate the handwritten words for you will be breath wasted. The second best thing to fae legends is a story pulled from your own life tapestry."

"So that's it?" I say, frustration leaking into my tone. "I'm supposed to tell my own story and hope it's good enough?"

"Aye, that is what I recommend." Her tone is casual and dismissive, as if she's already moved on to her next order of business. She picks up another scroll, and her eyes dart over the unreadable words. "Return to me when you are prepared to recite your story. I will instruct you from there."

Her gaze flickers up from the page. "And do not underestimate a personal story. Who knows but that your own history could be crafted into a legend of its own."

Feeling more lost than ever, I leave Aimsir and her stuffy scrolls without another word. If I had known how stressful this storytelling task would be, I would have signed up for something else. Anything else.

All the time in the world can't transform my pathetic life story into an epic legend—and I only have a few days left.

{ 24 }

Shapeshifting is an integral part of Celtic . . . experience. Look first at . . . animal guises. [A selkie], a seal which can change into a [human].

- *Encyclopedia of Celtic Wisdom* by Caitlín and John Matthews (1994)

My bedroom smells like lavender and rain. Hafwin has come and gone, helping me bathe and dress in a silky night-gown. I tried to ask about the other girls, especially Lana, but Hafwin's clipped responses told me that she wasn't in the chatting mood.

I'm sitting in a nest of pillows and blankets where she left me on the bed. Some paper and a feather pen sit on the dresser, waiting for me to write my lame story that's supposed to be legendary enough to win over a crowd.

I imagine myself standing under a spotlight on a huge stage, holding my paper as my vision blurs.

What will I even say?

I let the paper wait a bit longer, scanning the rest of the room. It feels more comforting to me now than many of my previous bedrooms. The furniture is a strange blend of ancient and modern. The bed, for example, is nicer than anything I've ever slept in. But instead of electric bulbs, the only lighting comes from the low embers in the fireplace and the pink will-ó-the-wisp that has stayed in the room even after I tried to chase it out.

The tallest window is propped open, the source of the gentle scent of moisture. Rain clouds block out the evening sky, enveloping the sunset like a cold embrace.

I throw off the blanket and place my feet on the stone floor. I've never been alone with the window open before, and it tempts me closer. I'm like a wild bird, unable to ignore an unlocked cage door.

I pass the fireplace, feeling the warmth caress my legs, and move toward the tall window. After lifting myself onto the ledge, I still can't reach the opening even with my arms raised. Climbing the drapes is the next-best option.

A distinct knock on the door jars me back to reality. *Idiot. You can't run away without Darren.*

And even then, I know now that Naoise will go to extreme measures to find us. Would he kill Darren before dragging me back underground?

I leap down from the window ledge, leaving all thoughts of Naoise behind, and open the door just a crack. The firelight from my room cuts a line across Vera's shadowed face. Her large dark eyes blink at me.

Swallowing my shock, I just stare. Curiosity keeps me from slamming the door in her pretty face.

"I was summoned to escort you to the dungeons," she says. "The one who calls herself Markie of the Strong-arm wishes for an update on your training."

"Why can't you just bring them a message? You seem to be fond of passing notes."

Truth be told, I'm longing to visit Darren again, and this might be my only chance before the festival. But who knows how many chances I have left to contradict Vera, even with the dumbest of comebacks?

Her steady gaze doesn't waver. "Will you come or not?"

My fingers squeeze the door. "Fine. Just a sec."

I leave her standing in the hall and grab a shawl from the armoire, wrapping it around my shoulders as I shut the door behind me. We wordlessly travel down the aisle of doors and through the great hall. Torches flicker against the stone walls, their flames like fluttering wings.

After a pair of faeries passes us, whispering intimately with each other, I break the silence.

"If you're not human or faery, what are you?"

Vera's white hair gleams in the cloudy moonlight as we walk past a series of windows.

"I am a selkie."

She says it matter-of-factly, as if it's the most obvious thing in the world.

"What's that?"

Her doe-eyes flash at me in the torchlight. "What you see of me now is not my true form. I belong to the sea."

I match her graceful pace, wondering if her legs look as human as the rest of her or if she's hiding a fin underneath her dress.

"I was coaxed from my home beneath the waves by a faery who promised his heart to me."

My feet falter, and my chest tightens. I ask the question before I can stop myself. "Who's the faery?"

"Someone I never should have trusted," she says, her voice full of venom. "He told me I belonged to him, told me I would never return to the sea. I went to search for my selkie skin along the shore, where I shed it to become the human you see now. He followed, taunting me, telling me the skin was gone."

We round a familiar corner, nearing the stairwell that leads to the dungeon. Vera's words cling to me like a cold fog. I watch her strange white hair and grayish skin, waiting for the end of the story, not knowing how to feel until I know if this faery is Cináed.

"Once I realized he had taken the skin and refused to divulge its hiding place, I did what I had to do."

She pauses, and I see her hands trembling before she hides them by holding her skirt.

"I feigned forgiveness, telling my new lover that I would stay with him and forget about my old life. After several days, I asked if he and I could swim together like we had the day we met. He obliged, swimming with me far away from the shore. I began to sing, calling to my selkie kin. If my lover suspected anything, he discovered my plot too late. The selkie swarmed us and pulled him deep below the surface—into the water where I longed to be but could not go."

I swear I see a tear on her cheek, but when we pass into the glow of the next torch, her eyes are dry and her expression hard.

Only a handful of guards linger around the dungeon, each looking drunker than the last. I still keep my head lowered until we pass them. Vera leads the way down the stairs—from the look of twisted revenge on her beautiful face, I assume she's still lost in her own murderous daydream.

"Vera," I interrupt her thoughts with a question I can't ignore, "you don't owe me any more. What's in this for you?"

Stopping, she looks back at me. "I want you gone just as much as we both want to return home." She continues down the stairs. "The fewer annoying distractions wandering around the castle, the better."

The sooner I'm gone, the sooner she can wrap her fins—or whatever selkies have—all over Cináed.

I hide my anger, adopting the same expression of exaggerated inquisitiveness she used on me before.

"Curious." I pause. "Weren't you just saying that nothing exists between me and Cináed?"

Her eyes flash with warning. I smile and continue in the same drawling tone.

"But if that's the case, you wouldn't be calling me a distraction, now, would you?"

Even in the darkness, I see her smooth face contort. For a second I think she might lash out at me. Then she spins around and glides down the stairs, her veil of hair floating behind her.

I push past her once we reach the bottom, pressing my face into the metal gate in order to see through the shadows deepening the musky air.

"Darren?" I whisper.

Shuffling feet announce a large group of people, all of whom direct their haggard eyes at Vera and her basket of food.

My brother appears alongside Esperanza, who's hand-in-hand with Sterling. I call Darren over to me as Markie taps the gate with her knife.

"Hark, you on watch," she calls to the amiable guard I recognize from before. "Let Róisín in here with two staffs."

Markie shoots me a grin. "It's high time I showed her how to fight. And be warned." She looks pointedly at Es. "Everyone had better stand clear. I only stop fighting when the battle is won."

The guard unlocks the gate and hands two staffs through the bars. Vera, with her now-empty basket, nods to the guard and leaves without another word.

Good. I'd rather navigate the castle alone than with her perfect, obnoxious self there to mock me every step of the way. And now that I know her dark past—knowing what she's capable of—I don't think I'll ever look at her the same way again.

I pull Darren to my chest. "You okay?"

"By now Juliana and Howard probably think I'm dead."

The Robertses feel like a dream from years ago.

I imagine them forking out wads of cash to fund their search party. Private investigators. News reports. The whole shebang. Sue couldn't compete with that, even if she wanted to. Anyone looking for me is probably relying on Darren's search party to find both of us.

"They aren't the kind of people to give up on someone they care about." I pull away to study his dirt-stained face. "And hey, what did I tell you about us getting out of here?"

"I dunno." He wipes his button nose, glancing at the others huddled in the corner across from us. One girl in particular sends him a shy smile.

"Sure you do," I say, turning my attention away from his little crush as I give Markie and her two staffs the stink eye. She groans but backs off. "What did I promise you before we left Cináed's ship?"

He stares at his feet. "That you would learn how to protect us from faeries and then get us back home."

"And right now, I'm still learning how to protect you, okay? It's all part of the plan."

He nods and shuffles away to eat with the others.

Out of nowhere, Markie tosses a staff at my face. I slap it away before it hits me, and she snorts. I mumble that the lighting makes it impossible to see anything down here, already feeling my insides squirm as I remember my first failed lesson.

I can fight with my fists. It's this stupid stick that gets in the way.

My burly opponent takes her stance as I retrieve my staff from the ground. I mirror her position, and she lunges at me with a growl.

The sound of clashing wood echoes around the pit. We fight for nearly an hour, or at least that's my best guess without anything to tell time except my own building exhaustion. We pause several times so Markie can correct me or readjust my hold on the staff.

When she finally calls for us to stop, my wobbling knees give out, and I collapse in a heap on the ground. Most everyone stayed to watch from the other wall, and a handful of them offer small claps and cheers. Markie sinks the end of her staff into the soil and squats next to me, breathing heavily.

"You surprise me. I thought I would have to fight with only one-quarter of my usual strength just so I would not kill you by accident."

Sweat drips down my nose as I gasp in the dank air. "So, that was your full strength?"

"No. That was only half." She smacks my shoulder a little too hard and stands up. "But like I said, I underestimated you."

{ 25 }

All over Ireland the fairies have the reputation of being very beautiful, with long yellow hair sweeping the ground, and lithe light forms.

- Ancient Legends, Mystic Charms, and Superstitions of Ireland by Lady Francesca Speranza Wilde (1887)

The castle bustles with life as I make my way through the corridors in the direction of the horse pastures.

I've been putting off my riding lessons to avoid seeing Naoise. By now I've noticed he seems to steer clear of the main castle halls, either hiding in his lair or tearing up the pastures on his demon horse.

So when a group of faeries at the breakfast table mentioned they were going riding today, I decided to take advantage of the opportunity. Even if Naoise is out there, at least I won't be alone with him.

Not only do his powers and his threats against Darren make me sick, but sometimes what he says resonates with me in a way that terrifies me more than anything. That night on the moors told me how dangerous it is to spend time with him.

I should have hated him holding my hand or wrapping me in his arms. I should have spit in his face when he leaned in to kiss me.

But instead I balanced on the tightrope between loathing his existence and wanting to be a part of it. I entertained the idea of being queen and never answering to anyone again.

Which is why I have to avoid him at all costs during the games. He could use his influence over me to get his way in the end, even if I manage to win.

The clashing of spears and the subtle buzz of voices fades away. Golden marble floors turn into cobblestone paths as I near the outer wall. This part of the castle is a little too quiet. The silence, along with a clean breeze carrying the scent of garden flowers, should be a relief after the crowds. But any sudden stillness reminds me of a certain dark faery.

Out of nowhere, someone steps through the last archway. I almost have a heart attack before I recognize his face.

Cináed.

We both freeze. His eyes scan the hall behind me, no doubt checking to see if we're alone.

Last time I saw him, he was ordering me to stay locked up in the dungeons. For the last few days I've held my breath around every corner, both longing for and dreading this moment.

"I have been searching for you." He steps closer, and I can smell the outdoors on him.

"All you had to do is ask Vera where my room is," I snap, surprised by my coldness. "I thought by now she would have told you all about our little girls' night."

And how stupid I am for being into you when you could have someone like her. I can just imagine how *that* conversation went.

My guts squirm. I hate to admit it, but maybe I'd rather be caught alone unawares by Naoise than Cináed. This is way too painful, and Vera's right. I'm too fragile to handle this.

". . . your weak human disposition makes it easy to believe an illusion of the heart."

Cináed's eyebrows pinch together. "Vera and I are old acquaintances, yes. If I had known to ask her about your location, I would have. I only just returned from a journey north . . ."

His voice trails off. I notice he traded in his torn shorts for leather pants. Mud sprinkles his riding boots and the hem of his green cloak. The bright material complements his glowing neon eyes that make it hard to look away from him. That, and the fact that he's still as adorable as ever and won't stop staring at me.

"Well, I'm late for my lessons." My voice shakes, and I swallow hard. A vise tightens around my chest.

He locked you away in the dungeons because he doesn't think you're capable of anything more.

Vera runs his errands all day long. But I'm not Vera. I'm just a helpless human.

I move to step around him, but his arm wraps around my waist.

"Lessons? Róisín, you cannot step foot outside the castle walls. Naoise will—"

"Naoise knows I'm training to compete in the festival. I don't have time to explain myself to someone who expects me to hide till I'm rescued."

His eyes flicker between mine, fear and anger swirling in their green-and-blue depths. When he speaks, the strained words reveal his panic.

"I beg of you, do not go through with this. Whatever Naoise has told you, this madness is not worth your life."

Talking about Naoise adds to my growing discomfort. After the kiss on the moors, I feel weird wanting Cináed's attention. Like I betrayed a relationship with him that doesn't even exist.

"I tried to tell you earlier." I stare at his shoulder, emotion clogging my throat. "I had no other choice."

He shakes his head.

I resist my gut instinct that wants to comfort him. This has nothing to do with him. This is about me and Darren, and even the other humans trapped here.

"I will not let you compete. Whatever Naoise promised you means nothing in a game that you cannot win."

"Don't bring Naoise into this." I shrug and hold my ground. "At least he's letting me learn how to fight against faeries, which is the only reason I came here in the first place."

He cringes when I say Naoise's name, and his eyes blaze. "You are confusing graciousness with selfishness. He is playing you for a fool. And you naively agreed to his proposal without consulting me."

My laugh is joyless. "When did I suddenly need your permission?"

His jaw muscles flex, and he looks away. I've never seen him blush before.

He reaches for me, and I shove my hands into his chest. "No. I'm sick of this." I keep smacking him, ready to turn this into a brawl if I need to. "Unless you have a better plan, let me pass."

His arms lift me off the ground, and suddenly I'm up against the wall, his body pressed into me. His hands rest on each side of my head, and his hot, sweet breath tickles my cheeks.

He looks at me with a severity that grounds me. His lips part, and he leans in until our mouths collide in a tender kiss that drives every other thought from my mind.

When he pulls away, both of us are breathing hard. My hand has tangled itself in his hair, and I let it fall. He presses my palm to his mouth so my fingers cup the side of his face. My head rests against the cold stone.

Somehow the mess of emotions that sat like a ball of hot wires in my chest feels lighter and less pressing than before.

How long have I wanted to do that?

He lowers my hand and leans in again, this time pressing his mouth to my ear. "Never doubt my devotion to you, Róisín." A kiss as soft as a raindrop touches my cheek. "Regardless of the games you're playing or the deals you've made, I will do everything in my power to keep you safe."

"Like what? Why can't you just tell me what you're planning?"

Footsteps echo near us, and Cináed pulls me into the crevice between the castle and the garden walls. Sunshine and flowers perfume the limited air as Cináed uses his body to block me from view. When the stranger passes us, I continue, this time in a whisper.

"You went north for a specific reason. Tell me."

He continues, his voice low and eager. "There will be an uprising during the festival. I have gathered enough faeries and other creatures of the forest who are still loyal to King Rauri, who believe that the next ruler should be of the same bloodline, and not Naoise."

"I thought the king's only daughter married a fish."

"Aisling did marry the prince of the merfolk. If they have children, they cannot rule on land without complications. Perhaps in centuries past it would have been possible, but the fae magic is not what it once was."

He glances at me, as if remembering the point to all this. "But Rauri had a sister in the northernmost kingdom. If we can postpone the ruling on Naoise's ascension to the throne, I will travel even further to visit this sister and her two eligible children."

"And where does that leave me?" My boots sink into the grainy dirt as I lean against the wall. "I still have a deal to keep with Naoise, no matter how little you trust him."

He sighs, letting his hand linger over his face. "What exactly are the terms of this deal?"

I swallow hard, the question taking me aback. "Um, well, it's complicated."

His eyes flash. "Try me."

Turning away from his stare that could burn holes in my skin, I pick at a dried flower choked with finger-length thorns.

"If I win, all the humans go free."

"And if you lose?" His voice teeters. "What is his prize?"

Nervous laughter bubbles in my throat, and I try to cough it away. "This is ridiculous." I throw my hands in the air. "I don't have time for this. I should be training."

His hand rests on my collarbone, keeping me pinned to the wall. "Róisín."

I try to look anywhere but at his face. "I am."

"You are what?" It comes out as a growl.

"*I* am the prize. If I lose, I'll be his summer bride." I stop there, the look on his face warning me not to mention the part where I become Naoise's queen and eternal mate.

He stares at the ground, clenching his teeth and breathing deeply through his nose. "You have promised yourself to someone who will break you and cage you, as if he can manipulate your heart into submission."

He pauses, thick emotion weighing down his next words, as if he's talking more to himself than to me. "There is nowhere I could take you where he could not follow. Escape is futile."

Hearing him so defeated, as if I have no chance at all of winning, hurts more than I expected. I duck under his arm and start to walk away.

"Róisín, wait."

"I'm done with waiting," I call, not trusting myself to look back and still keep my own emotions in line. "You focus on your plan, and I'll deal with mine."

I crest the last hill, and the highlands stretch out in front of me as far as I can see. Horses graze near the golden tents. A chariot racer speeds across the horizon, and a fresh breeze catches at my bangs, trying to tug my braid loose.

When I don't find Sona's distinctive maroon coat among the others, I make my way to a building that looks like a barn, with a thatched roof and wide double doors.

Sure enough, the smell of manure and straw sits like a sour taste in the back of my mouth when I step inside. Stalls line each wall, leaving a wide aisle down the center where another set of doors exits into the pastures. Thankfully, I'm the only person around.

A low nicker followed by the appearance of a long red face tells me Sona didn't forget about me like I'd feared.

That, or he just wants to be fed.

He paws the ground and prances around his stall, and when I reach out my hand, he lowers his head so far that it's almost like he's bowing to me. I have to stand on the lip of the stall door and stretch out my fingers in order to touch his forehead.

"Hey, what's all this about?"

He peeks up at me, still refusing to lift his head.

"Look, I'm sorry too. Neither of us knew that would happen." *We didn't know just how crazy Naoise's mood swings can be.*

Sona snorts and knocks his head against my palm as he straightens his neck. I swear it sounds like he's chortling, making fun of how scared I was. My tight lips break into a small smile.

"You think it's funny now, but you're the one who ran to safety and left me stranded." I throw a handful of grain at Sona's head. He flinches and whinnies, prancing around like a total dork.

I climb up and swing a leg over the stall.

"Let's go for a ride. Only this time, how about we keep out of trouble instead of running off into the sunset?"

From the location of the sun in the semi-cloudy afternoon sky, I estimate a couple of hours have passed by the time Sona and I trot toward the stables. His coat is dark with sweat and carries a distinct, musty scent I know will take work to get out of my clothes.

My loose hair floats in a frizzy leftover braid around my glistening face. Every inch of me feels sticky, and I look forward to sinking into a bathtub full of flower petals tonight.

"We're due for a cleanup, huh, boy?"

He snorts, bobbing his head as he walks. We're passing the tents where several fierce-looking faeries are gathered. The one I saw racing his chariot looks up at me from where he stands beside his own gleaming horse. The blond named Ethne stops mid-sentence to sneer in my direction, and I return the favor, which makes chariot-guy grin.

I recognize several of them from this morning. Turns out that Naoise didn't show up today anyway, and I had the pastures to myself for the majority of the ride.

A small male rider with a pale blue horse shouts, "What do you call yourself?"

"Róisín."

"And are the rumors true, Róisín? You are, in fact, human?" Ethne asks coolly, flipping her long hair around her shoulder as she folds her toned arms.

Sona seems just as disinterested as I am in stopping to chat, so I let him keep walking as I turn to reply.

"I am, in fact, a human. Better watch out, or I might sneeze on you."

Her mouth pops open, and chariot-racer doubles over in laughter. The rider who asked my name looks like he's caught between a fearful cringe and a nervous smile. I wink at blondie, and as I turn around, the tent flap opens and none other than Naoise steps out.

Our gazes pass over each other like ships in the night, and I don't know if he does a double take or not because I turn my back to him and try not to kick Sona into a gallop. Panic grips my insides. I can almost feel Naoise's eyes locked on me.

"Halt."

I squeeze my eyes shut and pray he won't call for me again. *He'll let this go, thinking I didn't hear him.*

Sona's steady movement beneath me halts, and I know before I open my eyes that Naoise is standing beside us.

"Róisín." His clear eyes take me in, blinding me to everything else but him. "Your connection with your mount has improved, I see."

The other riders are slack-jawed and wide-eyed.

"You should have alerted me of your presence," he continues, his tone as smooth as black silk. "I might have joined you for a ride."

"I—" I clear my dry throat. "I didn't know you were here." Then I add with a pat on Sona's neck. "Besides, we're tired now, so maybe some other time."

His smile doesn't reach his eyes. I hold my breath as he kisses my hand, speaking loudly enough for the small crowd to hear.

"I look forward to that day, and to the endless days thereafter, that we shall spend together, my rose."

He lets me go, and I numbly urge Sona into a walk. Nausea burns the back of my throat, and I'm acutely aware of the eyes that follow me all the way to the stables.

{ 26 }

Do they die? Blake saw a fairy's funeral; but in Ireland we say they are immortal.

- *Irish Fairy and Folk Tales* by William Butler Yeats (1918)

Hafwin and Fodla twirl around me in a frenzied blur. I'm sitting on a stool in my room, trying to eat my dinner without much luck.

One of them tugs a little too hard on my hair, and I flinch.

"Ouch!" I cry around a mouthful of mashed potatoes. The girls ignore me, swirling around my head like birds. Hafwin opens the armoire, and I groan. "Can't I just use what I've been wearing the past few days?"

Tonight is the funeral party for King Rauri and Queen Finnabair. It's also the night that Lughnasa, along with the games, begins.

I've only been to one funeral, for a foster kid named Jason who got caught up in a gang. I didn't know him that well, but my foster parents convinced me that I should go. All I remember is that the man on the stand talked forever, and everyone cried their eyes out. It was the epitome of a solemn assembly.

Which is why all this talk of a funeral party—one that requires me to wear the fanciest gown Hafwin can find in that closet—is beyond my understanding. Maybe instead of crying, faeries prefer to celebrate the dead. I've always wondered why people say the deceased are in a better place but spend their lives mourning them.

Maybe they mourn for themselves, not the dead. *It's the ones who get left behind who hurt.*

I try not to make a face as Hafwin carries an enormous, fluffy gown over to me, beaming like it's my birthday.

No solemn assembly here, that's for certain.

Once my eyelids shimmer with silver glitter and my body is adorned in a blood-red dress that loops in an oval across my collarbone and around the edges of my shoulders, cascading down into waterfall sleeves that fade to charcoal black, I step into a pair of delicate leather shoes that tie around my calves with black ribbons.

My hair falls just below my shoulders except for two twisted braids that knot together at the back of my head. Fodla fusses over a series of little chains drooping over my hair, on which hangs a dark jewel that sits just above my eyes. She calls it a headdress.

"Bring me the case," Hafwin says. Fodla opens it and pulls out another black jewel connected to a set of silver chains.

"Your human ears will not be the focus tonight." She clasps the jewel at the top of my ear and lets the chains drape around it like its own little headdress. She clips the matching jewel on the opposite ear and then smiles at me in a way that I can only describe as adoring pride.

"Tonight, you are no longer a human child. Tonight, you are a rose of the fae," she says.

Fodla pipes up, "When Naoise requested that you wear this gown, I knew it must be because of your name."

I turn around to look at her. "Wait . . . Naoise requested this?"

She nods with a dreamy sigh. "A rose for my rose, he said."

Hafwin hushes her, and I follow them in silence down the hallway. My body feels torn, as if only half of me is wearing the dress and the other half is rejecting the unwanted gift.

Faeries clog the main entrance, each one wearing something more extravagant than the last. My gaze turns upwards as we walk through the gateway and across the stone bridge.

A handful of evening stars glitter in the cloudless sky. The sunset paints the high pastures a vibrant gold, and I see faeries flocking toward a hilltop. From here they look like a colorful bunch of ants, moving in serpentine fashion up the hill.

Fodla disappeared into the throng a while ago, but Hafwin still stands beside me, her feet barely touching the ground as her cream skirt floats around her ankles. Her rich auburn hair is pulled into an elegant knot at the back of her head, and I notice that her perfectly shaped lips are outlined in a red just darker than my dress.

"What's on top of the hill?" I ask.

Two lovers run between us, their hands interlocked as they race ahead of the others. The air smells like sweet grass and wildflowers, and all of the faeries are smiling and laughing with each other, carrying baskets of plants and pitchers of summer wine.

"It is tradition that at the commencement of the festival of Lughnasa, we journey to the peak of the tallest hillside. There we each place flowers in our hair, and someone tells a legend of a great ancestor or ruler from long ago."

"But I thought this was a funeral."

She glances at me with a flicker of sorrow in her eyes. "The king and queen are honored with the festival celebrations. We do not dwell on loss but instead choose to find joy in each moment. Change is inevitable. Any resistance will only prolong the suffering."

When I don't respond, she continues, this time lowering her voice. "Róisín, I feel there are more games to be played in these festivals than meet the eye. Be careful, and know that it is not in a faery's nature to offer a gift without expecting something in return."

She pointedly scans my dress, and I want to ask her why she put me in it if she knew it would come at a cost.

As if on cue, I see Naoise riding up beside us in a chariot. He's traded in his dark cloak for an indigo, high-collared, button-up shirt that reaches to the middle of his thigh, a pair of leather pants, and tall boots.

It's impossible to ignore his sudden appearance, especially when the driver veers the horse and cuts in front of me, the chariot wheels passing inches from my feet. I'm mid-yelp when Naoise reaches down and hoists me into the chariot beside him, and the driver peels out like we're in some archaic version of *The Fast and the Furious*.

Only a few faeries holler at nearly being run over, and the rest are too surprised to do more than stare as we tear up the hillside. Naoise's arm wraps around my middle, holding me against his hip. As my hair whips around my face, my hands clench the sides of the chariot. I bite back my first several cries, remembering Naoise's life-threatening mood swings.

I shout to be heard above the thundering hooves. "What are you doing?"

Naoise is staring out at the sea of faces we're rushing by. His model-status smile reminds me of a politician during an election. It isn't too far from the truth, seeing as he's running for the office of king.

Which makes me the first lady.

Without breaking his pose, he twists the back of my neck with his hand, turning my head away from him and toward the other faeries. He shouts back at me, maintaining his perfect smile.

"Look at them! Soon they will all bow to me, and to you, my rose. They may see you as an outsider, as a strange creature who cannot be trusted. But all of that will change once their kingdom is in our hands. Those that once controlled you will worship your every move."

We reach the top of the hill as the first of the crowd crests it. Naoise lifts me down from the chariot, and I slap his hands off me, feigning that I'm removing the dust from my dress.

He's distracted anyway and turns to mingle with some of the advisors. Cináed isn't among them, and I scan the scene, trying not to care too much whether I find him or not.

Another chariot stacked high with flowers stands nearby, and as faeries reach the hilltop, they start decorating each other's hair with bright blossoms and leaves.

As the sun continues to dip beneath the horizon, will-ó-the-wisps appear in bursts of light like multicolored stars. And the actual stars are even more glorious from up here, reminding me of the night on the ship when Cináed found me staring up at the sky.

My fingers itch to reach up and hold a star in my hand. They almost seem as attainable as one of the will-ó-the-wisps flying above.

Someone grabs my hand and pulls me toward the group of flower decorators. Surrounded by unfamiliar faces, I freeze, waiting for one of them to recognize me and call me a fraud, to tell me that human girls are not invited to the party.

But no one seems to notice or care. A young male faery who reminds me of Darren tugs on my sleeve and asks if I will bend down so he can place a large yellow flower in my hair. One by one, faeries take turns tucking blossoms and leaves in my hair and behind my ears. Not one of them notices that my ears are not pointed like theirs, and I'm glad Hafwin decided to cover them with jewels.

I'm trying to stick one more twig in a faery's already-bursting bouquet on top of her long red hair when I catch sight of some of the riders who are competing in the festival.

Ethne is watching me, draped in a revealing gown that sparkles in the sunset. The one with the blue horse nods, and the one who grinned at me waves me over. It's too late to pretend I didn't see them, so I warily approach the group. Other competitors that I've seen before, like the thick male with the red beard and the female with the battle-axe, are standing nearby.

The brown-haired faery who waved to me grins and holds out a red poppy. "May I?" He gestures to my head, which by now probably looks like a scraggly patch of wilted plants. I duck my head, and he gently places the flower with the others.

"That color is very becoming on you," he says shyly, glancing at my dress.

"You almost could be one of us," Blondie says. And then, sounding a little defeated, she adds, "It truly is a beautiful dress."

The noise starts to die down as one voice directs everyone's attention to the center of the hill where Orla stands in the back of a chariot. For once, her hair is down, and I'm surprised at how long it is as it tumbles down her back. Pieces of her silver hair are joined in a plaited braid, and a crystal headdress sits like a crown on her brow. She didn't stray from gray clothing, but the style of the gown is clearly extravagant, even for this setting.

"Here we gather on the tallest peak, as we have done since the great god Lugh first honored the death of his foster mother, Tailtiu," she says. "Decorating our brows with the gifts of summer, we remember the goodness of the gods for blessing us with plentiful rain and the promise of a bountiful harvest."

Voices cry out in agreement, and I can hear flutes and drums beginning to play a hypnotic rhythm. Orla finishes her speech, and the chariot moves, leaving a circle of grass at the center of the group. One faery stands. As he starts talking, I realize this must be the storyteller Hafwin mentioned.

Interested in watching the performance so that I know what's expected of me, I excuse myself from the group of contestants and meander through the crowd, trying to get a better look.

Naoise appears out of nowhere, taking my hand as if we're reuniting in this very location on purpose. He nods toward the front-row seats where Orla and the other advisors are standing to watch the performance. Again, I'm surprised that Cináed isn't with them.

Not wanting to make a scene, I follow Naoise's lead, ducking my head and hoping everyone is too busy watching the storyteller to see the dark faery flaunting our presumed relationship.

We step into the front line of the audience, and I can't wriggle my hand out of Naoise's grip fast enough. Folding my arms to prevent any further signs of affection, I direct my attention to the storyteller.

"On the eve of Lughnasa, we bards wish to gift you with a legend never before heard by a faery's ear."

Oohs and *ahhs* electrify the air.

"All we ask in return is that you participate in our little game. See, we are withholding the identity of these heroes and heroines alike, and we invite your assistance in revealing their names at the end of the performance." The narrator bows, and the crowd responds with laughter and applause.

He steps to the side of the ring, and Cináed leaps out of nowhere to take his place. My pulse races, and I find myself holding my breath as I watch his every move, not daring to even blink.

Cináed struts to the center of the circle, his face twisted in rage. "How could this happen?" He throws his hands in the air as he paces.

A female with long brown hair and an elegant purple dress approaches him. She and Cináed are both wearing ornate crowns on their heads.

"My love, would you not also run away if your father had betrothed you to a stranger?"

Cináed spins around to face the brunette. "She should be honored to marry in the name of peace, not take off in the night to try and escape her fate."

"A king and queen," Naoise murmurs beside me. "How intriguing."

The queen places her hands on her hips. "I do not excuse our daughter's actions. Above everything, I am concerned for her safety."

Cináed, the king, lowers his head, and the queen takes his hands.

"Make haste, and tell the warriors to search every corner of the kingdom—and further if need be."

The king nods. "Yes, my love. We shall retrieve our daughter before it is too late."

They both exit, and I hear several voices whispering ideas of what story this might be.

I look at Naoise, who's watching someone beside him. Peeking forward, I see Orla mouthing something before she sees me and goes silent. Her expression is more serious than usual—almost like she's in a panic.

Before I can try and make anything of it, another female runs into the circle, followed closely by a male. They both feign shortness of breath. The dark-haired female looks like a younger version of the queen.

"Come, we must not rest." She takes her companion's hand, but he doesn't move.

"We cannot outrun them forever." He looks over his shoulder, as if expecting someone to appear at any moment. "Your father surely sent his best hounds to hunt us down."

She pulls his hand, leading him across the circle. "I will not sit here and wait for that day."

The male, who I recognize as the faery who reminded me of an older Darren, takes his lover's face in his hands.

"My darling, let us forget about tomorrow. In this moment, we are eternal partners, bound by our love as two birds who mate for life."

The princess leans in to kiss him. When she pulls away, she adds, "I give you my heart, forever to hold. Come what may, you will always be the wings that carry my soul into eternity."

The audience seems moved by the young couple's forbidden love. I hear someone shout that they should forget about the betrothal because true love always prevails.

The narrator takes the stage with a stringed instrument similar to a banjo. He strums away and begins to sing about love and whatever.

Someone bumps my arm, and I turn to see Orla making her way through the crowd. Naoise is watching her too.

"Where's she going?" I ask.

He doesn't look at me when he says, "Nowhere of importance. Orla is not fond of gatherings."

Seems like she's not so fond of this particular play either.

Naoise pulls me close, and I stiffen against his side. "To think that someday the legend of King Naoise and Queen Róisín will be performed at such a festival as this."

His warm breath smells like summer wine mixed with the night. I look across the circle and see Cináed watching, looking at Naoise's arm around my waist. His mouth is pulled into a frown, and the fury in his eyes sends a shiver down my spine.

The actress playing the queen gets his attention, and Cináed looks away, his face hardening into calloused neutrality. They take the place of the singing narrator.

"Our daughter has been returned to us," the queen says.

Cináed glances at me again, and the queen takes his hand with an insistent look. Cináed clears his throat and faces the crowd.

"The gods are indeed sympathetic to our cause, as the betrothed prince has agreed to keep his agreements with us. The celebration of their union will be remembered forever."

"And if the fates allow, the knowledge of our daughter's brief absence will soon be forgotten."

They both bow and exit, and the narrator returns, this time without the instrument.

"This marks the end of our performance but the beginning of your own." He gestures to the performers standing on the side. "Who among you knows the identity of the king and queen, princess and forbidden lover?"

Names are shouted out left and right, and I catch a glimpse of two armored faeries weaving through the throng. Cináed steps in front of them before they breach the circular stage, and if the narrator notices what's going on, he doesn't pay it any attention.

"Yes, yes, come to the stage and announce your guesses." He waves others forward, and someone behind me is one of the first to approach the narrator.

My gaze is locked on Cináed, who is now arguing with the guards. One of them reaches for her sword. The faeries nearest them start to sense the tension, and a bubble of chaos erupts as everyone either tries to remove themselves from the scene or push in closer.

Naoise has noticed the commotion, and he tells me to stay put as he crosses the stage toward Cináed. The narrator tries his best to shout out the responses he's receiving, but no one is listening.

In a last-ditch effort to save the show, he starts yelling out the names, "King Rauri, Queen Finnabair, and Princess Aisling!"

The guards push through the last of the resisters, and Naoise plants himself in a prime location so that the guards have clear access to the stage.

The narrator can see what's coming for him, and his voice breaks into a strangled cry of desperation. "This is the true history of Princess Aisling! Her love child with the mysterious faery must be found! Their offspring is the rightful heir to the throne!"

I watch, unable to look away as one guard grabs a handful of the narrator's hair and shoves him to his knees. The other forcibly knocks the female playing the queen to the ground as she tries to intervene, and the first guard sinks her blade into the narrator's white neck, slicing his throat in one fluid motion.

I gag, holding my mouth as the narrator's body crumples to the ground. Everyone is screaming and pushing each other, trampling the forgotten flowers in the madness.

I squeeze through the terrified mosh pit. Somewhere, the clashing of metal slices the air, and a shrill scream freezes my blood. The crowd is torn between those pressing toward the fight and those fighting to escape it.

The faery who placed the poppy in my hair passes me by, a small dagger in his hand. Will-ó-the-wisps zoom around like trapped flies, illuminating everything in bright colors one second only to dash them into shadow the next.

As a large blue bulb races toward the forest, it highlights a head of blond curls. I start to move in that direction when I cross paths with someone who barrels me over, knocking me to the ground. Feet step on me like I'm nothing but a wilted flower, and I fight to get up until someone's boot kicks my head.

{ 27 }

And after a while the Druid of Teamhair that was with them said: "I am in dread . . . that there is some trouble near at hand, and look now at those dark clouds of blood," he said, "that are threatening us side by side overhead. And there is fear in me," he said, "that there is some destruction on [us]."

- *Gods and Fighting Men* by Lady Gregory (1904)

Low, lilting notes break against my eardrums like playful ocean waves. Each one brings me closer to the surface, closer to the memories.

Screams. Frantic mob. A white neck. Spurting blood. Pain. Darkness.

I sit up with a gasp, my eyelids flying open. My vision blurs and starts fading to black again, and I grip the sides of the bed as I gingerly lie back down.

"That's it." Cináed appears beside me, cradling the back of my head as I sink into the pillow. "You must rest, Róisín. You suffered a direct blow to the head, and the druid told me you are painted with bruises enough to compete with the stars in the sky."

"Where am I?" I croak, my eyes squinting to block out the throbbing pain in my skull.

The right side of my body sinks deeper into the mattress— I assume Cináed sits beside me.

"You are safe. If you must know the exact location, you are in my personal quarters."

I peek with one eye and focus on his smirking face. He's holding the same wooden flute I heard him playing on the ship, which explains the music that woke me up.

"I'm in your bedroom?"

He stands and walks out of view. "Aye. And here you shall remain until circumstances deem it safe for you to be moved anywhere else."

He returns with a small bundle that he presses against my forehead. It's warm and smells like peppermint and lavender. I close my eyes and breathe, feeling the pressure in my head subside a little.

"I can't hide in here," I say, my mind working to remember what I need to do today.

"The druid said the competitions are no longer an option for you—"

"The competitions!" I bolt up, this time fighting against the sharp pain and the subtle nausea that follows it. Cináed tries to hold me down, but I push him aside. "What time is it? Have I missed the horse race?"

"None of that matters. After last night's gruesome events, several competitors packed their things and left. I argued that we should cancel the games altogether, but my opinion is no longer of import to the advisors."

I can't make sense of the words. All I know is that I won't let a headache and some bruises stop me from competing. Not when everything that matters depends on it.

I see a red dress on a chair by the door. It's now that I realize I'm only wearing my nightgown, and the breeze from the window reminds me how thin the material is.

"You—why—how did you get this?" I grab the slick nightgown hugging my thighs and glare pointedly at Cináed, who hasn't moved from my side.

He raises both eyebrows. "I did not undress you, if that is what you mean."

"Then who did?"

He leaves the bed, giving me a wide berth as he reaches for the folded clothes next to the dress. "One of your attendants." He hands the clothes to me. It's my go-to outfit: tunic, vest, and leather pants. I see my boots underneath the chair.

"Hafwin?"

Cináed turns to the window, rubbing a hand over his face and through his hair. "I summoned her here along with the druid. They bandaged and dressed you while I negotiated with a courtroom of advisors for the lives of the remaining performers."

I take advantage of his turned back and pull the leggings on underneath the nightgown. He continues talking, his tone dark.

"When I returned with you from my last voyage, I should have been able to trust the decisions made in my absence. With Rauri and Finnabair taken in the same breath, the advisors should be a voice of unity in a time of chaos.

"But instead, I saw how some of the most virtuous, noble faeries had been corrupted by promises of power. None of them would listen when I argued for a kingdom-wide search for the rightful heir. Naoise has them all under his spell."

I pull the tunic over my bare torso, wincing when I bump my bandaged ribs, and I pause before reaching for the boots. He turns around, focusing on me with eyes the color of a storm.

The words sound fragile, broken. "Am I also right to believe that you have been captured by his charm?"

I stare at the ground as I pull my boots on, not trusting my expression to remain passive. "I made my deal with Naoise to learn what I could about fighting faeries and to get Darren and myself home."

And because he used his devilish charms on me.

I can feel Cináed judging my response to see if he can trust it. He looks away with a deep sigh.

"It only takes one rotted root to poison the entire tree." He rests a hand on the wall. "When good hearts are slain for speaking the truth, the darkness has already won. This kingdom will fall, and I cannot carry her weight on my own."

"You don't have to." I stand, using the bed for support until the room stops spinning. "No matter what happens in these games, I want to help you."

It's true. I haven't spoken the words out loud before, but I've known for some time that this fight is bigger than me. It always has been. And regardless of my incompetence as a human in a world of faeries, Cináed needs to know how I feel.

I start to close the distance between us. "For what it's worth, I'm on your side."

He watches me, eyeing my footing like I might fall over any second. What I wouldn't give to sink into his bed and sleep off this throbbing headache—to forget about the games and the life-altering promises tied to them.

But one glance out the window at the bubblegum-pink clouds tells me today will happen whether I'm ready for it or not.

Cináed gives me a brief, crooked smile. I can see the anguish in his eyes. This kind of grief terrifies me. I've never stopped long enough to face my own pain. I just keep running and pray it never catches up to me.

He takes my hand and pulls me close, grounding my wobbling knees. "And for what it's worth," he murmurs, tucking my bangs behind an ear, "*I* have been captured by *your* spell. You continue to amaze me, Róisín. If I've ever doubted you, know that it came from my own limiting beliefs."

Cradling my head with his hand, he pulls me even closer. "If anyone can defy Naoise of the Western Moors and come out the conqueror, it is you."

I press my lips to his warm mouth. He holds me, and for a moment everything dissolves to meaningless white noise. All that's left is our two beating hearts and our breath blending into one perfect sound.

Then I pull away. "I have to go," I say as he rests his forehead against mine.

"If only I could convince you otherwise." He kisses the spot between my eyebrows and looks at me. "But I know you will go, regardless, and I can no sooner stop this kingdom from falling than I can dream of standing in your way."

I kiss him again. He releases me, and I walk out the door without a second glance.

Cináed wasn't exaggerating when he said a lot of competitors ditched after last night. I rest my hand on Sona's maroon coat as I evaluate the remaining riders.

Blondie stands next to her chestnut horse, and I see the robin-egg-blue horse nearby, which means the shorter male is also racing.

I also see Irvin, the one who put the poppy in my hair, with a grey-speckled horse. He grins at me, then winces and holds the bandage taped across his face. I cringe, not wanting to think about how he managed to earn that wound during last night's mayhem.

Only a handful of advisors sit under the shaded platform near the tents. I spot Orla but no Naoise. A small crowd lines the racetrack marked with golden flags staked into the ground. The track circles around in a big loop and finishes where it starts.

Before last night, the event was going to start out with two heats. The top three from each group would then compete for the championship and some meaningless prize I don't care about. With nearly half the riders gone, however, there will just be one race.

Just one chance to do this right.

Sona snorts, and I jump, not realizing how lost I was in my thoughts. I look into his great brown eye, a similar color to my own, and wonder if he senses my fear. My gut says he does. But then again, my gut also says it wants to vomit all over my boots.

I mount, and we move toward the starting line.

". . . the first time since I can remember that it did not rain," says a female voice. The piece of conversation finds my ears, and I slow Sona to listen in.

Three faeries stand by their horses, talking under their breath. I recognize one of them as the faery with the long red braid that I'd seen at the breakfast table. He responds with a rough edge to his voice.

"This travesty reeks of one faery's doing, and one alone. Naoise should not be here. The gods made that clear when they didn't bless last night's festival with rain."

"But he will be crowned any day now," the third faery says. "Are you suggesting the advisors made a mistake?"

"You can't tell me you actually believe the rumors of Aisling's love child, the lost heir." The female almost laughs.

The redhead opens his mouth, then glances at me. I divert my gaze, pretending to adjust a stirrup, and continue to the track.

Ethne sidles up next to me, her blond hair pulled into a tight braid. She points at me and then pretends to slit her throat. The image of the narrator's head separating from his body flashes in my mind.

I turn away and bite down my growing nausea.

A hooded rider takes the lane on my other side, and Sona politely moves to make room. I roll my eyes.

Of course I'd pick the nice horse.

Sona, as if hearing my thoughts, turns and snorts at me. I apologize in my head, but he bends his neck even further, nipping at my leg.

"Hey!" I swat at him, and he jerks his face to dodge me.

"Riders, take your positions!"

While Blondie adjusts her hairdo, the hooded rider sinks low on his mount. I try to mimic the motion, internally pleading with my horse to work with me.

Everything depends on this, Sona. Everything.

The noise of the crowd and the other riders disappears. All I hear is Sona's exhale mirroring my own. He paws the ground as I grasp the reins in my palms.

"An rás a scaoileadh!"

It takes two seconds for me to realize that means *go*. By then, Sona has already leapt into a gallop along with the riders around us. The stampede churns up chunks of pasture, and loud drums echo the sound of the thundering hooves.

The noise of the drums and the roaring crowd fades as we reach the first turn. Sona surges ahead of the trailing riders, leaving four ahead of us. Ethne is in the lead, her yellow braid streaming behind her like the tail of her horse.

I can feel my legs and backside ache as they strain to match the horse's stride. The image of me slipping from the saddle and being trampled to death makes me cling to Sona like glue.

Then, as if moving with a mind of their own, my muscles release their tension. I can feel each of Sona's movements, and instead of bracing for every stride, I let go and ride the motion like a wave.

He must have sensed my shift because he kicks it into next gear and speeds ahead of Irvin as we take the final turn.

The hooded figure on the moss-green horse trails just behind the short rider and Blondie. When I reach the green horse, we ride neck-and-neck, and I realize I've been boxed in by the three of them without any room to cut ahead.

Then the green horse leaps between the two leads and veers into Ethne's chestnut horse. I can hear her scream as she tries to stay on the track.

As Sona matches the blue horse's stride, Ethne races back onto the track. The hooded rider got left behind after that reckless move, leaving me sandwiched between the last two riders.

Dirt fills my lungs, and I squint through the dust cloud at the finish line. Ethne's braid is so close I could almost reach over and pull her off her horse.

Wild cheers erupt. I catch sight of the finish line in the same moment we careen through it. Sona slows to a stop, his sides heaving in and out like a great balloon. I cough the dust from my throat, but the tangy smell of dirt and horse sweat sticks to my mouth.

The blue horse's rider raises his hands in the air, signaling that he won the race. Drums beat to the music, and the crowd goes wild as faeries toss flowers and blow kisses at their champion.

Naoise is standing on the platform, and I wonder if he watched the whole race.

He didn't need to see much to know that I didn't win.

Without any encouragement from me, Sona trots over to the stables, putting distance between us and the celebration that burns my ears with the hot sting of defeat.

{ 28 }

They also much desire the aid of a powerful mortal hand to assist them in their fairy wars, for they have often disputes and battles amongst themselves for the possession of some coveted rath or dancing ground.

- *Ancient Legends, Mystic Charms, and Superstitions of Ireland* by Lady Francesca Speranza Wilde (1887)

The sound of two staffs clashing fills the dungeon. I push against Markie's weapon, and we begin to circle each other, each one waiting for the perfect time to strike.

I know I have to pay close attention to every move she makes. The slightest misstep invites an attack, and if I'm not ready, I'll get a swift blow to the chest or stomach. And those parts of my body are already black and blue.

But no matter how hard I try to focus, I can't get Naoise's voice out of my head.

"If you win two out of three events . . ."

After losing the horse race, I have to win both sparring and storytelling, or I'm through.

Out of the three, I thought I stood the best chance in the horse race. Sona and I had bonded—or whatever you call a horse understanding your thoughts. Naoise had said that makes the most difference in a race.

"Almost had you that time," Markie says, her dark eyes dancing in the torchlight. "I get the feeling that you don't want this badly enough. You let your mind wander."

My teeth grind together. The other humans watch us from a safe distance, but I know they can hear everything Markie says. I don't think she could lower her voice below a near shout even if she wanted to.

And I know she doesn't want to. She loves any chance to berate me, especially in public.

I fake a blow toward her stomach, reroute once she's lowered her block, and aim for her exposed face.

She ducks just in time, and my arms swing through empty air. Her staff meets my forward momentum, and my lungs feel the blow. I fall to a knee.

She circles like a vulture. "I never thought you'd make it this far without getting yourself killed." She squats in front of me. "Then again, knowing all our lives depend on your pathetic willpower must be pretty inspiring."

"Don't patronize me."

"Don't tell me what to do," she snaps. "If you want something, you have to get your hands dirty. Faeries don't give a damn about words when they can use a weapon instead."

I leap forward, throwing her to the ground and shoving my staff beneath her neck. The toes of my boots hiss across the dark soil as I lean closer, nearly cutting off her airflow. I watch her eyes bulge, sweat glistening on her skin.

"Why don't you take your own advice then, Margarette?" I say through clenched teeth. "If you want to live to see a day outside of this pit, find your own way out. I'm through with you."

I walk away as she rolls over with a barking cough. Ignoring the mixed expressions of admiration and terror on the faces around me, I find Esperanza in the crowd.

"The scroll, Es," I say between breaths. "You said the kid would have it translated by now."

She nods and motions to a girl with two long braids, the one who made eyes at Darren the other night. Her hands shake as she offers the scroll and a piece of burlap.

"I was trained to never distort the histories by writing on the scrolls," she says. "So I had Vera bring something separate for me to write on."

Darren reaches for the scroll as I take the burlap and unfold it. Sure enough, there are small, delicate words—that I can actually understand—inked into the cloth. I hold in my sigh of relief when I see that the cloth is double-sided.

"I only wanted one translation. How many stories did you write on here?"

Es chimes in. "That *is* one history. The Tuatha De Danann were not known for their brevity."

My jaw clenches, and I fight to control the turmoil building in my core. I remember my lessons with Aimsir and her kind but unrelenting voice telling me to focus on my own story, not a memorized legend.

"If you cannot recount a fae legend without a script," she said, "you must tell your personal legend instead. You cannot hope to inspire a crowd otherwise."

But she refuses to understand that I don't have a personal legend. I even tried making up some stories that were way more interesting than the truth, but she called my bluff and kicked me out of her classroom.

I stare at the inked words in my hands. *If only I'd given up on listening to Aimsir sooner.* Memorizing this will be a beast, but at least I have a story to use.

Darren scans the scroll and hands it to me. "Were you there when that faery got killed?"

A lump sticks in my throat, and Es gives me a warning look before she goes to check on Markie, who's still nursing her injured pride in the corner.

I follow Darren's lead as he sits down. Everyone gathers on the floor in a loose circle, staring at me with the same empty eyes that I never want to see when I look at Darren.

The dungeon has already started to take a toll on him. I haven't heard him laugh or seen much of a smile in who knows how long.

I repeat what happened last night, leaving out the parts with Naoise, as well as the gorier details of the murder.

"So you actually watched it happen?" a boy just older than Darren asks when I'm finished. I think his name is Alex, the one who cheats at cards.

I nod, glad when Sterling diverts the subject.

"I'd heard rumor of Aisling's brief disappearance but never knew she had a secret lover."

"Do you think they'll find her baby?" Darren asks me.

The dirt crusted in his hair begs to be picked out. But I restrain myself, knowing that kind of thing would embarrass him in front of his lady friend. I wish I could bring him to my room where he could have a bath. And a proper meal. And a bed.

I respond, "It wouldn't be a baby anymore." I think of Cináed standing by his window, the weight of a kingdom on his shoulders. "But yes, I hope they find it."

"Can you imagine?" Esperanza's voice catches with excitement. "If Aisling's child is anything like her, we would all be freed."

Markie sits down in a huff, still brooding but clearly wanting to hear the conversation.

Sterling takes Es's hand as she nuzzles against him. "Surely her offspring would be half as sympathetic toward humans as she was. And half of her gracious heart would make a magnificent ruler indeed."

My curiosity gets the better of me. "Why was she married off to the mermaids?"

"King Rauri wished to keep peace with the merfolk," Sterling begins. "They rule the ocean west and south of Ireland. And they were sinking too many faerie vessels transporting human food and also children, nursemaids, and strong youth to be brought up as warriors."

"Skip to the part about the fish, Sterling," Markie says. Something Sterling said triggered her, and I get the feeling everyone knows why but me.

"Of course." Sterling nods. "Well, the merfolk would not be reasoned with, and so King Rauri promised his only daughter to the eldest son of the merfolk king. At the time, Rauri couldn't have known that his son, Prince Tiernan, would be struck with a terrible sickness and die before reaching his tenth year. By then, Aisling was married and they were left with no direct heir to the throne."

"Terrible sickness, my arse," Markie drawls. "Someone has been plotting this from the start. Killing them off one by one until the assassin can fill the empty throne."

Es shakes her head. "But why place the blame on the humans? Rumors of this sickness have been circling the castle since young Tiernan's death."

Markie shrugs. "Why not blame us? The easiest way to cover your tracks is to blame the ones at the bottom of the food chain."

"She's right," Sterling says, his voice tight. "We humans have always been a resource, pawns to be traded and used and eventually displaced when we can no longer fulfill our duties."

"Why didn't you guys leave when you had the chance?" I direct the question at all of them, and the girl with braids responds first.

"After a while I forgot about home," she begins, her voice as delicate as a feather. "And Gatha, the one who taught me how to translate runes, was kind to me. When the king's warriors came for me in the night, saying that I was going to poison her and the other scribes, she ran into the road after them . . ." She sniffs, and a tear drips from her chin. "She chased after their horses, crying my name."

A friend pulls her into her arms.

Then Esperanza begins speaking. "At first I tried desperately to find a doorway back to the mortal realm. I was taken from my home by a shadow faery who enslaved me, using my blood, my hair, even my nails for her potions. One day she left me stranded, alone in a world I knew nothing of." Sterling wraps an arm around her, but she continues, her voice distant.

"By the time I stumbled across another faery, I was nearly starved. That family took me in, and I helped care for their two children. Once they grew into adulthood, I was brought to the castle to assist Prince Tiernan's nursemaid."

Her eyes lock on mine. "I didn't stay for the creature who brought me here—it had everything to do with the faerie children I grew to love as my own."

One by one, they all tell their stories. Some surprise me more than others, like Markie, who was captured, stored on a ship to Ireland, and sold as a warrior before Rauri was even made king.

Sterling caught the attention of the fae because he worked as a history professor. They dragged him from his window one night, from the same room where his wife and son were sleeping. The faeries used his knowledge of ancient war strategies in the same battles that Markie was forced to fight.

"The War of Iarann eventually ended," Sterling says. "And while it would have been easy enough for me to find a way home, I knew stepping foot in the human realm would instantaneously age my body however many years I'd been gone. Returning would be a death sentence.

"I considered this form of suicide, knowing that both my wife and infant son had passed from old age." He looks at Es beside him with nothing short of complete devotion. "Soon after, I met Esperanza, who brought new purpose to my life. She is my home now."

She leans in to kiss him. I smile as Darren rests his head on my shoulder, his eyelashes touching his cheeks as he yawns.

"I've calculated the time change between realms," he says groggily. "If I'm right, we've only been gone a month."

"Then I'm sure you're right."

One month missing. It's strange to think school will be starting soon. I wonder if my handful of friends think I ran away. Or if they're too busy with summer jobs and camps to even notice I'm gone.

With Darren here, I don't have any valid reason to ever go back.

"I can't wait to see the look on Juliana's face when I show up like this," Darren mumbles. "She'll probably spray me down with the garden hose before I can even come inside."

His words center me, reminding me of our reality. Even if Cináed finds Aisling's child, even if the humans are released and Naoise exiled, I can't stay here. Darren's happiness is tied to the Robertses, and mine is tied to him.

{ 29 }

And so great was his love for her, he gave up his hunting and all the things he used to take pleasure in, and gave his mind to no other thing but herself.

- *Gods and Fighting Men* by Lady Gregory (1904)

Cináed's quarters take up the top section of one of the castle's main towers. His bedroom—with the window overlooking the castle grounds and his shelves decorated with leather books, large seashells, and other random knickknacks—leads upstairs to a gazebo-looking balcony and then downstairs to a lounge area.

We're in the lounge, having just come from a private sparring practice in the courtyard. Even though I managed to stay on my feet this time, I'm glad no one else but Cináed saw me stumbling around like a toddler with a stick.

If only I could ditch the staff and use my hands . . .

No. I shake my head, breathing in the subtle smell of sweat and grass clinging to my clothes. *Don't waste energy on the useless could-a-would-as.*

Attempting to distract my knotted stomach and whirring mind from thoughts of the fight tomorrow morning, I watch Cináed, squatting by the fireplace on the other side of the room.

I know he's just as uptight as I am. Naoise could become king any day now. And the scouts Cináed sent—Vera among them—to bring word from Rauri's sister haven't returned.

He also ordered his crew to start searching for Aisling's child. When I asked why he didn't go with them, he just looked at me, murmured something about too many responsibilities in the castle, and told me to change my fighting stance for the umpteenth time.

But as I watch him now, shoulders relaxed and hands busy making something over the burning embers, I would never guess the stress he's carrying. He catches me staring and smirks. My face flames, and I clear my throat, readjusting the navy-blue cushion supporting my lower back.

"Are you ever going to tell me what you're doing over there?"

He turns to the small pot, and I hear the faint bubbling of boiling water. "A blend of herbs I think you might like."

"It smells amazing."

His grin does little to calm my nerves. I swear, if my life weren't hanging in the balance because of these games, I'd have nothing distracting me from drooling all over the couch.

"This"—he nods toward the pot beside him—"is merely boiling water. I have yet to add the herbs for the tea."

More blushing. "Oh."

Duh.

"What you are smelling could be the potpourri." He points to a white dish full of dried orange-and-yellow flowers. "I created that blend primarily from Netherland tulips." He uses a cloth to remove the pot from the fireplace. "Or perhaps you smell the incense I traded for whilst traveling through India."

I take another deep breath through my nose, picking up on the floral and spice blend. "Are you trying to impress me?"

He ladles hot water into a rounded cup, still grinning. "More importantly," he pauses, sips from the cup with a wide straw, and looks at me beneath his brows, "is it working?"

I bite my lip and shake my head. It feels like embers are tap dancing across my skin.

How embarrassing.

"At least I tried." He shrugs and stands, bringing the steaming cup to me. "As you contemplate conceding to my charms, try this."

The smooth cup warms my hands, and I watch steam curl out from the blend of brownish-green herbs.

Like the purple mist that follows at Naoise's feet and obeys his command.

"Róisín?"

I blink and shudder. Cináed stares at me, his sea-green eyes pinched.

"Sorry," I say, a bit breathless, "just tired."

He plants a kiss on my forehead and walks past the fireplace and around the corner. I hear him fumbling around for something. "That is why I called for us to stop sparring when I did. You need your strength for tomorrow."

Settling into the plush couch, I force Naoise from my head.

He's not here. You're safe.

For now.

I blow on the cup and sip from the metal straw. My mouth holds the liquid, letting my tongue decipher its flavors. Grassy, floral, sweet, bitter, and . . . "Is there chocolate in this?"

"Very perceptive."

"What kind of tea is it?"

"Love potion."

I almost choke on the straw, panic closing my throat.

His head pops out from around the corner, a wicked gleam in his eye. "Only jesting."

I scowl and flip him off. He chuckles, sauntering to the couch with a stack of photographs in his hand.

He sits beside me, close enough that our legs and arms touch. "The tea contains bits of cocoa, dried rose, and lavender. But the base comes from South America. It's called Yerba mate. Natives drink it from chimarrãos." He taps the cup in my hand and shuffles through the photos.

"I saw your surname on the list of competitors and recognized Montes as having strong roots in Spain and South America, primarily Brazil."

"You took those pictures yourself?" I ask. It's weird to think of Cináed—in all his otherworldly perfection—doing something so . . . *human*.

He seems to ignore the question as he hands me a handful of photos. "These were taken in Brazil, Uruguay, and Argentina."

I'm captured by the images of clogged city streets, lush forests, and one of Cináed laughing, swarmed by bright, exotic birds.

Logan Miehl

My eyes linger on a photo of the ocean. "Who's that?" I ask, pointing at the profile of a girl's face as the sun sets behind her.

"Branna."

The way he says her name reminds me of my first foster mom, the one who taught me how to pray. She said God's name with the kind of reverence that sinks into your bones, like everything that mattered depended on one word alone.

That's how Cináed says *Branna*.

I set the photos down on the coffee table. As he stares ahead at nothing, a touch of severity threads through his voice.

"I wanted you to see these places, to experience a taste of what could be your heritage." He glances at me. "Although I know where I come from, in my own way I understand what it feels like to be homeless, with nothing to return to at the end of a voyage."

Hesitating, I take another sip of the drink. "Can you tell me about her?"

"You wish for me to talk about Branna?"

I don't know what hurts more: the brokenness in his voice or the jealous sting in my chest.

Don't be jealous of the dead, I scold myself. This isn't Vera we're talking about. This girl meant the world to him.

And he means so much to me.

"Yeah," I say, letting him wrap an arm around me, pulling me close and tucking my head underneath his chin.

So he talks, telling me about how he and Branna met during the War of Iarann, the battles Markie and Sterling lost everything for.

He tells me about the places they traveled, the adventures they shared together. The more he talks, the more he seems to relax.

When foster mom #4 lost a cat, she sat me down and told me the poor creature's entire life story. Thankfully, that life only consisted of five boring cat years. Lots of naps, meowing to be held, meowing to be let out, and more naps.

But I realized then that different people grieve in different ways.

That was also the day I realized I'd never properly grieved my parents. I still haven't.

"It took until we reached New England for me to realize the gravity of Branna's sickness," Cináed says. "We landed, and I searched for a druid, a witch, anyone who could heal her. But old magic is hard to find anymore, and by the time I located someone, Branna was gone."

He pauses, and I feel his chest waver as he breathes. "She asked me to stay with her, not to leave her side. Though I refused to admit it, she knew she would never return home with me again."

Shifting beneath me, he sits up and brushes the curls from his forehead. "This is why, although they are quite rare even in the Otherworld, I always travel with a druid. I was there, visiting her grave, the day that shadow faery tried to drown you."

So that wasn't just in my head.

"And you've been traveling ever since?" I ask, remembering what Vera had said.

"I've been avoiding the truth." He sighs. "And also trying to discover who I am without her."

My tone betrays my vulnerable desire. "And what have you found?"

"Pain," he says through a clenched jaw. "Pain like nothing I have ever known in my many years of existence."

He shakes his head. "I ran from it, and then I let it consume me, and finally I tried to bury my heart so I never had to feel again."

Then a light sparks in his eyes—a smile radiating from the inside out.

"And then, when I had given up on everything and told the gods to do with me what they would . . . I found you."

He wraps me in his arms, and I lean against his chest. Some internal piece of me readjusts, falling into place like a fragment of shattered glass in a window frame.

Cináed might not know it, but he's helping my screwed-up heart find itself again, one broken piece at a time.

{ 30 }

If we could love and hate with as good heart as the faeries do, we might grow to be long-lived like them.

- *The Celtic Twilight* by WB Yeats (1893, 1902)

Spectators line the courtyard, crowding the archways and straddling the glassless windowsills. I want to hate them for their eagerness. To judge them for their calloused lust for blood.

But as the drums echo off the stone walls and unseen voices chant a haunting melody that pounds in my veins, I can't help but lean closer, peering over the faeries in front of me as the first duo steps up to fight.

I recognize them both—the large, red-bearded faery with the fur vest and the female with a battle axe who seems to stick to his side.

But today they've shed their companionship, along with their thick clothing and bulky weapons. Tunics and leather pants complete their simple sparring outfits, and each grips a single spear. Sunlight peeks between the clouds and catches on the golden-tipped staffs.

I swallow hard, my stomach knotting.

I've known to expect these advanced weapons during the games. Practicing with a plain staff proved difficult enough. Adding a sharp blade ups the stakes.

The crowd shifts, blocking my view. When I manage to squeeze closer, it's just in time to watch battle-axe chick get launched through the air. Her head cracks against the ground with an audible *thud*.

I hiss through my teeth as the audience erupts.

Maybe she should have stuck with her axe instead of trying to fight with a staff.

Maybe they'll say the same thing about you when you lose in a few minutes, my mind retorts. *They'll say a human never should have tried to compete against faeries.*

Red-beard makes no move to help his supposed friend, who is still sprawled on the ground. Instead, he pumps his bulging arms in the air with an earth-shattering battle cry. The crowd cheers, and the female is half dragged from the courtyard.

Each duo is randomly paired, and only the winner moves on to the next round. I have to beat two contestants today in order to qualify for the second tier of the competition—the final event of the games.

For me to win, my opponent must stay on the ground for at least a few seconds—no one, not even Cináed, could give me a clear answer on the exact number of seconds—or my opponent must drop his or her spear. Cináed simply said that the faeries judging the event would decide when the fight had ended.

The announcer calls two more names over the soundtrack of drums, chants, and jeers. It takes me a moment to register that my name was called.

I push through the blockade in front of the archway, choosing a gold-pointed spear resting against the wall. My hands shake so badly I'm surprised I can grip the staff.

None other than Ethne waits for me at the center of the lawn. She tosses her blond ponytail to the side, cocking her hip as she watches me approach. Her malicious, calculating expression reminds me of a feral cat playing with its food.

Me.

My hands are sticky with sweat, and I readjust my hold on the staff as I take my position.

"Tosaigh!" the announcer calls.

"In case your human brain didn't understand," Blondie shouts above the noise, "that means you're about to die."

She takes a step to the left, and I move right. The circular dance begins, and straightaway I see she relies on her legs more than her torso and arms.

In order to keep up with Markie's brutal training sessions, I had to use her strengths against her. Markie also relies on her legs, so I learned to draw power from my upper body. This means that, while my blows might not carry the same weight, both my defensive and offensive movements are quicker.

Testing my theory, I let Ethne lunge first, raising my staff to meet hers inches before it hits my chin. I feel her breath on my face as a hint of surprise pinches the skin between her eyebrows.

I push against her, and she loses her footing just long enough for me to attack.

Digging my boots into the sod, I steamroll toward her with a yell, swinging my staff at her legs. She spins to my left, trying to stab my exposed side, but I dance out of her reach.

We both pause, breathing heavily. I watch her gaze flicker to my left a second before she moves. Blocking her blow to my still-bandaged ribs—a weak point she must have noticed—I scrape our staffs together and pinch her fingers.

She leaps back with a yelp, and I move to strike her chest. As planned, she lifts the spear to block me. At the last possible moment, I lower the blow and hit her right in the gut. I can feel the air on my face as she lets out a pained *woof.*

Not wanting her to regain her composure, I clash my spear against hers, pushing her backward. Now that her legs are stumbling behind her as she tries to keep herself from falling, I know she can't hold off my attack for long. Her feet move faster and faster until we nearly reach the outer wall.

Then her boot hits a rock, and we both tumble. I fall onto her, pinning her torso with my knee and her neck with my staff.

She squirms, trying to kick at me with her free legs. Every muscle in me trembles with exhaustion, and as her face turns an unnatural shade of red, I release the pressure on her throat, suddenly sick.

This isn't me. I'm not like them.

The announcer calls my name as the winner. I stay kneeling on Ethne, letting her breathe as hatred rages in her eyes.

"In case you didn't understand," I say between gasps, "that means I beat you."

The crowd roars as I stand and stride off the courtyard. Blondie exits on the other side, and I notice Cináed in that archway, his eyes trained on me.

I feel my already-flushed skin burn brighter. There's only one thing the look he gave me could mean.

Cináed thinks I'm hot when I fight.

I grab a water pouch on the table near a few other fighters waiting their turn. As I glance to see who's up next, I spew out my mouthful of water.

Red-beard stands at the center, and Cináed is walking over to him, his expression as cheerful as someone meeting a friend for lunch.

And by the looks of it, red-beard is thinking he's going to eat *Cináed* for lunch. The giant faery watches his opponent approach with a grin that speaks of excitement and concern. Like he's worried he might break him.

"No." I stand on the edge of the grass, shaking my head and murmuring over and over again, "No, no, no, no . . ."

What does he think he's doing?

If Cináed feels the smallest bit of fear, his crooked grin hides it. The announcer tells them to start, and red-beard lunges.

Cináed prances to the side with surprising speed. I remember how fast he moved the night he rescued Darren. Maybe not all faeries have that ability?

Red-beard continues his chase, and Cináed dances across the lawn, *laughing*.

"Catch me, you great oaf," he calls. "You bloated lion of a faery."

I hear gasps and laughter sprinkled throughout the audience. Cináed must be a crowd favorite. Already they're chanting his name to the beat of the drum.

I facepalm with a groan. *That's the guy you decided to crush on. That guy.*

Red-beard's face now matches the color of his wild hair. He pauses to catch his breath, having chased Cináed around the courtyard at least three times.

"Enough of this," red-beard pants. "Fight me like a warrior, face-to-face!"

The chanting transitions as the faeries shout, "Fight, fight, fight, fight!"

Cináed says something to his lumbering opponent, but I can't hear it above the crowd. Red-beard's leathered skin cracks into a wicked smile as he flexes his hands around his spear. I hold my breath, feeling like a boulder is sitting on my chest.

This time when red-beard lunges, Cináed rolls between his legs and pops up on the other side. Before his opponent can figure out what happened, Cináed leaps onto red-beard's back and uses the spear to choke his neck.

The bearded faery flails his arms, using his spear to stab at Cináed. He dodges the attack, and when the spear strikes again, Cináed reaches to swipe it from his hands and lands on his feet, waving two spears in the air.

It happens so fast I blink several times.

The crowd goes ham, screaming. After Cináed is announced the winner, he looks right at me and winks. I shake my head with an exasperated smile.

"Cináed the Wanderer and Róisín Montes!"

My smile dies. Cináed coaxes me toward him with a finger, as if he was planning for this all along.

Confusion fuddles my brain as I approach him, trying to use my expression to ask what my mouth can't.

Why?

He just smirks, and the audience eats it up, acting like wild animals.

My confusion turns sour as I realize what this means.

I have to beat him.

Before my mind can register my actions, I lunge at him, not even waiting for the announcer's signal.

My staff meets his exposed side, and he stumbles but spins around before I can make a second advance.

We circle each other once before he attacks. His movements are sluggish, and I block him without much effort. He stumbles back again as if I hit him when I didn't.

I hesitate. "What are you doing?" I mouth at him.

He just shakes his head and lunges again, this time so slowly that I send a blow to his stomach before his staff can reach me. Two more rounds of this bizarre routine, and I knock the staff from his hand. Defeated.

If the crowd notices the easy win, they don't show it. They even start chanting my name. I wipe the sweat from my face, and when I turn around, Cináed is gone.

Making my way off the lawn, I'm swarmed by nameless fans. Everyone pats me on the back, and someone hands me a water pouch. Despite having finally gained some favor with them, their praise doesn't fill the hollowness in my chest like I thought it would.

As soon as the next duo is called, the fanfare fades, and a pathway opens for me to escape. Drinking from the water pouch, I start down the quiet corridor, eager to leave that deafening, hostile environment behind.

If they believe in the sickness, I muse as I stride across the marble floor, *how could they forget I'm human that easily?*

Because they're faeries. Faeries aren't like humans. Remember how Naoise blew up when you tried to run away?

Faeries overreact. Faeries vacillate between extremes. Faeries either love you or hate you, no in between.

But they were chanting your *name,* an inner voice whispers. *Not Róisín the human, the infected, the vermin. Just Róisín—the girl who lived to compete another day.*

My confusing, back-and-forth dialogue goes quiet, and one resounding thought remains.

I made it to the final round.

"Hold there, champion!"

I turn to see Cináed running down the hall, his curls bouncing.

My pace slows only slightly. He catches up, breathless and beaming from ear to ear.

"I was searching everywhere for you," he says.

I can smell the sunshine on his tanned skin, and his eyes seem brighter than ever, capturing me in a sea of teal and neon green.

When I'm silent, he goes on, loping beside me like a care-free golden retriever. "Care to join me for a midday meal, my lady?"

"I have to practice for the storytelling event. I don't have the ending memorized."

That, and I can't pronounce half the names of the charac-ters.

We enter the main hall where a small crowd of faeries has gathered for lunch. Tables laden with food tempt my rumbling stomach.

"Not to worry." Cináed snatches a honey-colored fruit from a golden bowl. "Why not pace around the tables as you practice? Pacing seems to improve memorization. And that way I can place morsels in your beautiful mouth with each turn you take around the table."

"I have food in my room," I say, cutting across the hall. "*Human* food that won't mess me up."

"But of course!" Cináed says around a mouthful of apple. "At times I almost forget you are human. I trust someone told you about the consequences of fae food?"

Yeah, no thanks to you.

I spin around. "I know you're cheating to help me win."

We've stopped in the archway joining the food hall and the smaller corridor leading to my room. No one stands close enough to overhear us, but I keep my voice low as a precaution.

His smirk masks the fleeting concern glinting in his eyes. "Róisín, you are mistaken—"

"I know you competed in the horse race, hiding underneath that cloak. And today you somehow managed to pair up with me so you could let me win."

My words come fast but without venom. I want to be mad at him for not warning me about the food. For keeping his plans from me. But instead I feel relieved to have made it this far in the games. With his help—albeit dishonest—maybe I stand a chance.

He stares at me and sighs. "Yes. What you say is true."

Before I can respond, he continues, resting his hands on my arms. "But I could not stand by and watch you sacrifice everything when—when . . ."

He looks at the ground, biting his lip. When our eyes meet, emotion clouds his face. The pain I see in him splits me open, and it's all I can do not to pull him close and find a way to absorb his hurt.

At last, he murmurs, "When it is my fault you were brought here. The moment I learned of Rauri's death, I should have run with you, kept you safe."

His voice breaks, and I hold his jaw in my hand, brushing the curls from his forehead and around his pointed ear.

"Hey," I whisper, "it's no one's fault. You brought us here to keep us safe, remember?"

He kisses my palm, and his eyes turn a steely blue. "And I will keep my promise to you, Róisín. I will find a way to keep you safe from him."

The *him* he refers to needs no further explanation.

As if on cue, I glance behind Cináed and right into that piercing gaze I know all too well. Naoise watches us from the other side of the hallway, balancing a goblet in his hand as a dangerous scowl pulls on his lips.

My stomach drops to my feet. Cináed, noticing my body go rigid, turns around.

When their eyes meet, I feel as if the world will turn inside out, and everything that is will cease to exist. I can feel the air tingle with an electric heat. My mind tries to react, but my body freezes.

Before I know what's happening, Cináed is kissing me. He wraps an arm around my middle and the other behind my back, cradling my neck. His mouth works against mine, tasting like fierce summer winds and pulling me impossibly closer like the strongest ocean currents.

Kissing me like he's drowning in that ocean. And *I* am the air.

When he stops, I almost collapse, leaning on him for support. It takes one trembling breath for me to center myself and think about anything other than Cináed's touch burning my skin with gentle, fervent flames.

Then I remember the reason he kissed me.

Naoise.

The great hall bustles with faeries eating and talking at the tables. I scan their faces.

When I focus on the place I last saw him, I see the remains of the goblet on the floor, shattered into a thousand pieces.

[Faeries] are partly human and partly spiritual in their nature . . . Some of them are benevolent . . . Others are malevolent . . . abducting grown people, and bringing misfortune.

   - *The Folk-Lore of the Isle* of Man by A. W. Moore (1891)

"Róisín, wait!"

Cináed calls, chasing after me as I sprint through the castle. I take a turn too fast, boots slipping across the marble and sending me crashing into a wall.

I don't miss a beat, holding my now-pulsing shoulder as I continue my frantic pace.

Please, I plead. *Please still be there.*

The dungeon greets me with its usual odor of must and rot. I ignore the complaints from a guard, reaching the gate and rattling the bars.

"Darren! Darren, where are you?"

"Róisín." Sterling approaches carefully, holding out his hands in a peaceful gesture.

Or a gesture meant to comfort me.

My voice sounds like a frozen lake splitting open. "Where is he?"

Sterling hesitates, and that's when I see Esperanza, Markie, and a few others in the shadows. Es meets my gaze, her dark eyes spilling over with tears that glint off her tawny cheeks.

"Where is he?" I scream. My throat seizes up.

"Guards came, bringing hounds with them," Markie says in a deadpan tone. Then her eyes crease with what I guess to be sympathy lines. "They took him. There was nothing we could do."

A deep, guttural cry rips from my chest as I punch the metal.

I knew it. How *had I known it?*

Not pausing long enough to contemplate my astute intuition or register the pain in my bleeding knuckles, I tear up the stairs and collide with Cináed. He catches me before I tumble back down the darkened steps.

"Róisín!" He tries to look me in the eye as I blink through an onslaught of tears. "Róisín, tell me what the hell is going on."

I shove him, fighting to get free. "He took him! He took Darren!"

His hold tightens into an iron grasp, paralyzing my arms. The guards at the top of the stairs shoot sidelong glances in our direction. None of them are the guards I'm looking for.

I need to find the ones who wear leather clothes. And have human-sized hounds for pets.

"Naoise?" Cináed tries to brush the hair from my face, but I thrash my head out of reach. "I don't understand—"

"That's because you don't know him like I do!" I scream, and for once I think Cináed feels intimidated by me. "He took

Darren to punish me. He knows"—my throat snags on a sob—"he knows how to hurt me."

Cináed flexes his jaw, brow furrowed. "He wouldn't do such a thing," he says as if to convince himself. "With the council's decision so near, why waste effort he should be using to negotiate with the advisors?"

His hold softens, and I remove my arms from his grip, wiping my nose on my sleeve.

"You just don't get it," I murmur, my throat raw. "To him I'm more than a summer bride. I'm his queen. His"—my eyes flicker across his face—"mate."

The fury in his lucent eyes sends tingles down my spine. He turns, face cast in shadow, and I start inching up the stairs.

Cináed's voice changes, taking on an eagerness that sets my teeth on edge. "Then let us speak with the council. If they knew of his plans to crown a human as his consort, it would end his chance to become king."

A glimmer of hope rings in the words as he whispers, "This could change everything."

I'm standing in the archway, one foot in the hall.

His kiss set this in motion, put my brother's safety at risk. Bitterness settles over my heart like a mess of barbed wires that pinches my chest when I inhale.

He's not worried about Darren. And why would he be? Just because he claims to care for me doesn't mean he sees my brother as part of the deal.

I respond with my back to him, not caring to hear his answer.

"Do what you want, Cináed. I'm going after Darren."

Sona snorts, startling me in the bone-chilling silence, whisking his tail at a green will-ó-the-wisp that flies too close.

The mist hovering over the moors coats the earth in a gray cloud. We traverse the marshlands in the rapidly fading sunlight, and soon enough I'll be forced to leave Sona behind and continue on alone. I know better than to lead him through the uneven terrain in the dark.

After leaving Cináed, I ran straight for Naoise's lair. Just like before, part of me knew what I would find—an empty room but, more importantly, no Darren.

My uncanny knowledge of Naoise's next move—his intentions—but remaining one step behind him makes me feel like I'm spiraling out of control in a mad chase. After Cináed's kiss, it's almost like I can read Naoise better than ever before.

I just can't stop him.

Not till now, I correct myself with an intensity that radiates from my core. *No way is he hurting Darren.*

I tighten my hold on a spear I snagged from the courtyard. The weight steadies me, centering me in my purpose.

I'm about to show his sorry faerie ass what happens when you mess with the only family I've got.

Dismounting, I give Sona a final pat on the nose and breach the endless wall of fog. Besides my own breathing and the faint trickling of a stream, nothing disturbs the stillness.

An instinctual part of me—that I've been ignoring since the moment I decided to come after Naoise—forces its way into my mind once again. It screams through every muscle, begging me to stop before it's too late.

But what my body doesn't understand is that it's already too late. My life no longer matters.

Naoise launched these games to a whole new level when he decided to ignore our previous deal. Darren was off-limits unless I tried to run away again. Now Naoise is threatening my brother, using him as leverage or some form of twisted punishment to get to me. And it's my turn to match the offer.

Whatever it takes.

My foot sinks in ankle-deep mud, and the sucking sound of my boot popping back out nearly stops my heart. I freeze, scanning the lifeless scene for any sign of movement.

When nothing happens, I exhale through my nose and veer toward a small grove of trees veiled in vibrant moss, hoping the ground will be less muddy over there.

The fog thickens, and each of my steps is weighted with dread. At any moment, something could appear in front of me. A humid chill settles on me, and I start to regret all the horror movies I've ever watched. Images of monsters and ghosts flash in my mind, and I rest a hand on a tree just to have something tangible to hold onto.

If only it wasn't dark. I glare up at the moonless sky, betting that Naoise somehow convinced the sun to set faster and the moon to hide beneath layers of clouds. Just to freak me out even more.

Thinking about Darren, trapped out here with a real-life monster like Naoise, boils my blood. I surge ahead, refusing to give into my wild imaginations.

After what feels like hours of stumbling around blindly, I notice the mist beginning to change color.

Purple.

I drop into a squat, heart in my throat.

Unless I've gone insane from wandering through this unchanging, disorienting scenery for so long, this purple fog means Naoise must be close.

Like a police siren coming down the street, the sound of someone crying slices through the dense air, shocking my senses and injecting me with a fresh surge of adrenaline.

I leap into a sprint, barreling toward the sound. All thoughts of stealth and caution disappear in the mist swirling beneath my feet.

Darren.

Like a mother bear, I know his cry deep in my bones. It awakens the protective beast in me, blinding me to all reason.

Strange shapes appear ahead, looking like the outline of a giraffe. I slow as the shape solidifies into a knotted, leafless tree with one branch protruding from its side like a long neck.

The sight at the end of the branch punches my stomach, and I sink deeper into the mud.

Darren hangs by his bound hands from the branch. His feet dangle out of my reach.

He looks down, and his dull stare widens as he sees me.

"Raisin?"

I hold a finger to my lips, and he nods. It dawns on me that he hasn't been crying. Even from this distance, I see his face is pale but dry.

A cold sweat smothers me as panic clogs my airway.

Did Naoise mimic Darren's cry to lead me here?

With hot adrenaline battling my growing dread, I stick my spear into the softened bark, using the handhold to begin climbing the tree. If I can cut Darren down before Naoise returns, maybe we can get out of here.

"Róisín, look out!"

Something grabs my wrist and spins me around, suspending me in the air.

Naoise hovers a few feet away, tendrils of purple smoke curling around his feet like tentacles. One of the tentacles is wrapped around my wrist, and I claw at the intangible mist in vain.

"Enough, Naoise!" I holler, feeling like my arm will pop out of place. "You can't break our deal. Let my brother go."

"You knew to come to the moors." He gives a small smile. "The bond we share grows stronger."

He watches me, shifting in his black cloak. With a sickening clench in my gut, I realize Naoise never planned on using Darren as a pawn. He was the bait.

The bargaining speech I'd prepared on the way here dies on my lips. I decide instead to stall him while I formulate a new plan.

"I know why you're doing this," I say in the same coy tone he so often uses with me. I force myself to look only at Naoise and not at Darren, who listens from above.

He raises his dark brows, the swirling mist moving him closer. "Oh? Do enlighten me."

I try to swallow the now-constant lump in my throat. "You think you can force my loyalty to you, but you can't."

He stops, hovering in front of me. Darkness billows from him, overwhelming my senses. I push against the ring of black encroaching on my mind, beckoning me to surrender into the arms of unconsciousness.

"You have never been loyal to me—or to anyone else—my poisonous flower."

He reaches to caress my face, and my teeth snap at his fingers. He continues with a smile.

"No, what I am about tonight is of far greater importance than a traitorous kiss."

His fingers wave, and the tentacle around my wrist pulls me closer until our faces rest inches apart. An alluring scent of moonlight and honeysuckle fills my nose, and in an instant the desire to kiss him roars to life like an insatiable thirst.

I bite my lip hard and turn my face away. That magic won't work on me. *Not this time.*

His words brush my cheek, electrifying my skin. "You are incapable of loyalty until you first learn to be loyal to yourself. That is why I brought you here."

Although he doesn't touch me, his presence seems to absorb me, consuming me in shadow so thick I can barely breathe.

"I want you to see your true potential," he whispers. "The magnificent being I see in you, longing to be set free."

The mist lets my suspended arm fall, and I wince as sharp pain spikes through my pulsing shoulder. I stand on the billowing cloud beneath Naoise's feet. Our closeness is suffocating and almost impossible to bear.

How can I want to strangle him and be held by him at the same time?

Because he's a faery. And he's using his powers to make me feel things that aren't real.

A hiss of air, followed by a loud *thwunk*, cuts through my trance. A spear wobbles in Naoise's fist—he caught it mere inches before it would have entered his side. In one motion, Naoise pulls me behind him, snarling in the direction the spear came from.

The wall of fog hides the attacker, but I peer into the mist all the same.

When nothing stirs, Naoise calls, "Unless you possess another weapon and wish to try your luck a second time, I suggest you make yourself known."

A familiar head of curls breaks through the grayish-purple cloud. Cináed's glowing eyes rove across Naoise, over to Darren, and settle on me.

He came.

My chest nearly bursts at the sight of him. I hate myself for wanting him here with me.

You should have stayed away, I try to tell him with my eyes. *This isn't your fight.*

Cináed calls, "Release them, Naoise. I have spoken with the council, and your time as prospecting king has ended. You've lost."

Naoise flashes a smile. "Impossible."

Sensing a chance to escape, I judge the distance between the cloud and the ground below. When I try to move my leg, however, I realize I'm still locked in the mist's hold from the knee down.

Cináed responds, "Release the humans, and be gone before the court decides to punish you for the damage you've caused."

"If you lie, Wanderer, there is no ocean you could cross, no realm you could enter where I could not find you."

A fierce cold shivers down my spine but not from the night air. I stare at Cináed, trying to detect a lie. He said himself that the advisors had sold their souls to Naoise in exchange for power.

Would they give that up because of one human? Because they can't stand the idea of me being queen?

"Threaten my life all you like," Cináed says, grinning. "It will not change the truth. You do not belong here."

"A wanderer cannot profess to understand the word *belonging*." Naoise returns the cold smile. Then he continues, his sinister tone filling me with dread.

"Isn't it time you left on another voyage to visit the dead?" My breath catches at the look of horror on Cináed's face. "Your beloved mate, Branna of the Harp, was it not?" Naoise shakes his head in mock sympathy. "Truly unfortunate. I heard the duets you used to play were positively enchanting."

Seeing Cináed's blanched skin and tormented eyes fuels my growing rage.

Gripping Naoise's arm, I turn him toward me, swinging my fist around to punch him square in the jaw.

He grunts as his head rolls to the side, absorbing the blow. My knuckles, already cracked from hitting the prison bars, throb anew as a steady trail of blood drips from my fingers.

Instead of attacking me back, Naoise works his jaw and stares at me, a subtle line etched between his brows. Behind him, I see Cináed silently cross the distance to the tree and begin climbing.

Blood pounds in my ears and pulses in my bleeding fist. I think fast, wanting to distract Naoise long enough for Cináed and Darren to escape.

"No more games, Naoise," I say, my voice shaking. "Just let us go."

Cináed reaches the top of the tree and begins hoisting Darren up onto the branch. Anxiety threatens to suffocate me as I hope against hope that Naoise won't turn and notice them.

His candid response surprises me. "Without my intervention, you will never know your true potential."

"But I don't want to be queen!" Emotion clogs my throat. "I never wanted any of this."

"Desire can be suppressed." He reaches for my bleeding hand. I let him take it, playing along to buy more time. "But the longer we ignore that desire"—dark-blue sparks flicker from his fingers and settle on my skin. I gasp as the sinews of broken flesh pull together, healing my hand—"the more we wound ourselves in the process."

He rests his index finger and thumb on my forehead, and at his touch everything intensifies, heightening my senses with shocking clarity.

The cloak he wears isn't a plain black material but a cutout of the starry sky, glittering in an endless expanse of captured universe. The texture of the stubble tracing along his jaw, the fragments of icicles trapped in his eyes.

Even my mind feels clearer, less sluggish and weighed down.

"We are alike, you and I," he continues. "I want for you to understand how I came to be the faery standing before you. Perhaps then you will see what you must do to find your personal legend."

The moors, the mist floating between us, even the knowledge that Cináed is aiding Darren, begin to blur and fade.

My eyes close unbidden.

{ 32 }

[T]he visionary gift is seen as a two-edged sword, one which can bring great insight, but which can also cause trouble for the participants.

- *Encyclopedia of Celtic Wisdom* by Caitlín and John Matthews (1994)

When I open my eyes again, an unfamiliar scene appears in shadowed fragments. Like I've stepped into a dream.

I'm no longer hovering in front of Naoise. Instead, he appears beside me, holding my hand. Both of us wear gray cloaks that curl like tendrils of smoke.

Naoise gestures to the gray forms in front of us, and with a second glance, I realize they're people. Specifically, a fifteen-year-old version of Naoise and a short female with silver streaks in her blond hair and small crows feet branching from her large green eyes.

Without needing to ask, I know she's the faery who found Naoise and raised him from infancy.

"I forbid you to return to the Shadowlands," she says to teenage Naoise. "You do not know the danger—the sorrow—that this journey will bring."

Teenage Naoise moves to stand closer to his foster mom, eyes sparkling with intensity. "But I must know the truth of my past if I will ever amount to something greater than—"

He stops, looking at the ground. The female takes his hand, her voice understanding and gentle.

"Greater than a humble marshland faery? I know your opinions, Naoise, but I ask you to consider what your life would have been like if I had not found you."

"Why speculate on what might have been when I can know with surety?" he responds.

She sighs, mouth drawn in a deep frown. "Then go. But don't say I did not warn you when you return, haunted by truths you wish you could un-know."

The scene flashes white, and the shadows regroup to form a canopy of trees. Teenage Naoise wanders through the forest with a young black horse by his side, its head the same height as Naoise's shoulder.

Meall, the Pooka.

The shadows crumble and swirl into new shapes. An adult Naoise stands with another male, equally as handsome and formidable.

Naoise's dad.

The faery stands just taller than his son, his raven hair hanging in delicious, loose curls. His bright sapphire eyes glow in the shrouded forest.

Well, I know where Naoise gets his looks from.

I stifle a nervous hiccup, grateful this is just a memory. One Naoise is bad enough.

Naoise's father speaks, revealing a row of sharp teeth beneath his pale lips. "The time has come for you to seek after your personal legend. You were meant for much more than a life with the common fae-folk."

"But where will I go?" Naoise asks, not meeting his father's powerful stare. "My dual lineage sentences me to a life of reclusion, for I can be accepted in neither the Unseelie or Seelie Courts. I am born of both."

"Your mother was weak," his dad says coolly. "But while her fragility flows in your veins, you decide your own fate. I sense that a Seelie Kingdom will soon fall, and if you are ready, you may take it as your own."

The world fades white, and we stand with Naoise and his foster mother. She sits by a hearth, face in her hands, as Naoise storms through the small room.

"How could you?" he bellows, swinging his fist at a chair that goes flying across the floor. When it shatters against the wall, the female jumps in her seat.

Her voice trembles, "I—I did what I thought was best! Naoise, you must believe me. Your father is a monster. Do not listen to him!"

Naoise spins around, rage contorting his beauty. The words are low and drawn out, making them all the more terrifying. "How dare you speak of my father? You, who kept me from him, from discovering my potential."

She starts to stand, but he takes one step closer, and she sits back down, eyes shimmering.

"I acted out of love," she whispers, voice breaking. "You must know that."

He looks away, and a detached mask settles across his face.

"Your *love* nearly destroyed me, almost ruining my legend before it even began."

He looks at his foster mother the way someone looks at the world's vilest criminal. Cold hatred spills from every word as he says, "Now that I know you cannot keep my lineage a secret, I must silence the rumor you've spread before it reaches the Seelie Court."

She's shaking her head, lip trembling. "No, no please—"

Naoise snaps his finger, and outside the house the sound of horse hooves approaches, followed by the wailing of unseen people. The female begins to shout above the noise, pleading with him to stop.

But her son ignores her as he takes a piece of the broken chair, lights it in the hearth, and walks out the door with the flaming torch.

The scene begins to fade but not before I see a pillar of smoke in the doorway. The door slams shut, trapping his foster mother inside as her screams ring in my ears.

I come to in Naoise's arms, hovering on the cloud. Images of those green eyes pleading for deliverance churn my stomach, and I fight back the bile in my throat. Her screams reverberate in my mind.

Naoise killed his foster mom. He burned her alive.

Through blurred vision I see Cináed and Darren working their way down the tree in the exact location they were before.

As if no time has passed at all.

My words come out as a croak. "You killed them . . . *why?*"

The chaos outside the room. The look of panic in his foster mom's face. He'd slaughtered more than one innocent to keep his secrets hidden.

He answers, the words tinged with sorrow but not regret. "I did what I had to do. The creature who raised me feared what I could become. For as long as she lived, she would have prevented me from discovering my potential."

My hand itches to punch him again, to lash out at his cold barbarity.

"I am *nothing* like you, Naoise," I say, my voice breaking. "I could never be so cruel."

A small smile passes over his lips as he stares at the misted marsh of ground between us. "Perhaps not. But I doubt you'd care to take a journey with me into your darkest memories."

His words trigger a foreboding monster skulking in the deepest corner of my soul. As it ruffles inside me, I kick it back into its cage.

No way are we going there today.

I catch a glimpse of Cináed trying to get my attention. He has Darren on the ground, and aside from my brother's dazed expression, they're ready to run for it.

Go, I want to scream at them.

Instead, I face Naoise, my permanent glare giving me a headache. "You've lost, okay? Just leave while you can, and let us be."

The emphasis I place on the last sentence was meant more for Cináed than Naoise. I don't dare look again to see if he caught my clue.

Naoise's laugh begins low in his chest and builds until it rumbles like an avalanche.

"My foolish rose," he says, eyes shimmering, "how blind do you think I am?"

He lifts an arm in the air and snaps his fingers, never breaking eye contact with me. Fear paralyzes me as the distant sound of horse hooves pounds in my ears.

No!

I can't help myself now, and I turn to search for Cináed and Darren through the shadowy fog. A horse's sharp whinny slices through the night, piercing my chest.

Meall the Pooka appears, red eyes glowing as it steps toward us. Darren and Cináed sit on its back, seeming to be invisibly bound and gagged. Their eyes find me, Darren's revealing only fear while Cináed's scream in anger. Both fight against the hold that either the demon horse or Naoise has on them.

The cloud beneath us rotates so that we all face each other. Naoise *tsks*, still chuckling.

"You honestly believed I did not see you in that tree, Wanderer?" His grin flashes in the dark. "I expected more from Rauri's most trusted advisor. Then again, you *did* come here with just one spear."

Molten rage surges through my veins. With a roar, I lunge at Naoise, unable to move my legs but using my arms and hands to punch and claw at any part of him within reach.

In a matter of seconds, my arms zip behind me as a mist-tentacle holds them down. Naoise licks the blood trickling from a deep scratch I carved into his cheek.

His clear eyes burn my skin like frostbite, and for a moment I think he might kill me. Murder all three of us in one fell swoop.

Instead, he flicks his wrist, and Cináed flies into the air, a tentacle wrapped around his neck. Eyes bulging, his legs swing as he claws at his throat.

"No!"

I try to lunge again, fighting to break free. Already I can see his face turn a terrifying shade of purple as he tries in vain to breathe.

"Let him go! Please!"

Naoise stands with his hands outstretched by his sides, raven hair catching in the wind that rushes toward us.

"When I brought you here, I intended to remind you of the life you could have if you learned to let go of the things holding you back." Then, with a satisfied smirk at Cináed, he adds, "I knew the Wanderer would follow you. Killing him is merely a long-awaited prize, sweetening this moment."

I sob, watching Cináed in sickening agony as life fades from his body. With each spasm of his limbs, I feel as if my heart is being ripped to shreds.

The image of Cináed throwing my sneaker into the air flashes in my mind.

Faeries love making deals to the point of obsession.

"Wait!" I cry. "I'll make you a deal."

A pause. I hold my breath, pleading with fate.

The mist's hold on Cináed's throat must lessen because I hear the sweet sound of air filling his starved lungs.

"Another deal?" Naoise asks tentatively. "Choose your words wisely, Róisín, for there is little you could offer me now that will bring me more satisfaction than this."

My tongue feels like sandpaper as I wet my dry lips. "You want me to stay here. To be your queen."

Another hesitant pause. "Aye. You are more than the life you knew in the human realm."

I continue, words tumbling over each other in desperation. "Then I'll stay. I'll forfeit the games, and I'll stay."

Did I really just say that?

He quirks an eyebrow. "What of the boy?"

Glancing at Darren, my lungs expand and deflate in painful bursts. He's shaking his head, eyes frozen wide.

Darren.

I face Naoise. "He goes. He belongs back home."

Intrigue turns up the corners of his pale lips as he gauges my response. "And what of you? You will not be tempted to return to the human realm?"

I bite my lip, tears locked away where Darren can't see them.

He needs to think I want this. That I'll be happy here.

"As long as Darren gets home and you promise he'll be protected so no faery can hurt him again."

Naoise mulls over my words, turning to Cináed with a scowl curling his upper lip. "The Wanderer irks me. I cannot agree to any deal that means I will be forced to look upon him in the future."

The tentacle contracts again, choking Cináed.

"No!" I scream, but Naoise blocks me out, hatred darkening his features. Before I lose courage, I say, "He goes free but can't ever come back here."

Naoise's gaze flickers to me, his hand still flexed at his side. "Banished from the Otherworld?"

I nod, my bangs clinging to my damp eyelashes. "Yes. Let him go on the condition that he can't reenter this realm."

Like feathers floating to the earth, the mist eases us down until my feet rest on solid ground. Cináed is lowered onto the Pooka's back, still bound and silent but able to breathe.

I don't dare look at him, unable to face the consequences of my deal.

You banished a faery from his home.

Naoise takes a step forward and closes the gap between us, his eyes devouring me like a well-earned trophy. I wince as he kneels and takes my hand.

The dry blood on his cheek is symbolic of my own tears shriveled up inside me. I can't cry. Not when Darren and Cináed have been spared.

But as Naoise kisses my hand, whispering promises of our future together, I feel my heart start to decay. Its blackened edges wither like ash, and it's all I can do to keep from falling apart.

{ 33 }

And the chief among them . . . said: "Let us give a wife to every one . . . for it is from a wife that good or bad fortune comes.

- *Gods and Fighting Men* by Lady Gregory (1904)

I stare up at the dripping ceiling. A cold numbness has settled over me, leaving behind only a constant, dull ache in my chest.

Darren flinches beside me but doesn't wake. I hope he's not dreaming about last night. The prominent welts on his wrists remind me all too well of that waking nightmare.

After Naoise agreed to my deal, I made him promise that Darren and Cináed wouldn't be sent away until after the festival ended.

Then he set me behind Cináed on Meall's long back, and I felt a strange tingling as invisible binds wrapped around my body, paralyzing me so I could only breathe and blink.

Meall took the three of us to the castle in restrained silence.

When we reached the castle, the leather-clad thugs pulled us from the horse and led us to the dungeons.

It wasn't until they tossed Darren and me in with the humans—and coerced Cináed into a single cell, lined with jagged metal knives, under the stairs—that I could confront the unavoidable.

Naoise's thugs left, and a single golden-cloaked guard stood watch. Only one torch remained lit instead of the usual two, and in the deeper darkness, I couldn't decipher the guard's face to tell if he was someone loyal to Cináed or not. Keeping my voice low, I called to Cináed through the bars.

"You have every right to be upset, but I was just trying to keep you alive."

His whispered response might as well have been a shout. "You wrongfully assumed that my life would be worth living after watching everything I care about offered up to that demon."

I paused, glancing at Darren standing beside me. His empty stare belongs to someone who's seen too much too fast and is unable to process what's going on.

It's better that way. When the truth that he's going home without me fully registers, I need to be in a better place than I am now. I'll need to be strong for him, and right now I feel anything but strong.

Emotion caught in my sore throat. "Cináed, I couldn't let him kill you like that. Not when I had the chance to stop it. You ask too much if you expected me to just let you die."

Tears flooded my vision, but I could still see the hurt in Cináed's face. "And you ask too much if you expect me to walk away from all of this"—he gestures to Darren and me and the castle around us—"and still count myself lucky to be alive."

Remembering what it felt like to watch him use what little space he had in his cell to turn away from me, I'm forced to bite my raw cheek to keep from crying all over again.

For as long as I can remember, I didn't allow myself to care about anyone but Darren. Now I stand on the edge of everything I've known, falling headfirst into another life without either of them by my side.

The pain is unbearable. Denial offers some relief, sinking me into a state of desensitized nothingness.

Otherwise I'll completely lose it.

And I know once that happens, there's no picking myself back up again. Once I let reality settle in—bringing with it a heartache that might end me—I need both Darren and Cináed to be long gone. Especially Darren.

I kiss his hair, and he snuggles into my shoulder in his sleep.

He needs to believe I want this, that I'll be happy here. I know that's the only way he'll move on.

Thoughts of Naoise resurface from the foggy recesses of my mind. He has a knack for sweet-talking me into believing he knows best—that he knows me better than I know myself. A horrifying prospect, one that even now I refuse to admit.

Even though he saw right through you.

The inner monster that threatened to wake at Naoise's words catches me off guard. It moves from a place I haven't allowed myself to go for years. And when it expands, weighing on my lungs like a balloon, the memories hit me harder than a punch to the gut.

I'm eleven. Darren's four.

We were moved from a home where we'd lived for several years and into the foster house I hate most of all to this day. The one with the neighbor's greenhouse out back.

Because Darren was so young he could barely form a complete sentence, and all my friends were gone, I felt like I'd been stranded on an island.

When an orphan boy about my age told me of his plan to run away, I hardly gave it a second thought. We ran and didn't look back, joining up with some older foster kids who knew how to navigate the city, steal food, and break into rich people's vacant summer homes.

I felt like I had arrived. Instead of answering to the world, I was the master of my life.

That is, until I remembered Darren. Thinking of him, left in that awful house, I knew I had to go back.

My new friends told me to forget him.

"He's just a baby. He'll never remember you anyway."

I ignored the guilt for as long as I could. But eventually I caved, turning myself in.

What I didn't know then is that the foster-care authorities would decide to separate us "for Darren's safety." They labeled me a troubled kid who needed extra surveillance. Since then, my brother and I have lived apart.

At times I rebelled again, running from it all. But like a broken record, I couldn't get past the shame of what I'd done. If only I'd stayed with Darren, been the big sister he needed, maybe things would have turned out differently.

I let the tears fall silent and fast, trailing off my cheeks and down my neck. In the stillness of the dungeon, Naoise's voice replays in my ears, sinking me deeper into the cold embrace of loss, anger, and bitter grief.

"We are alike, you and I."

Hafwin comes for me as the first prisoners start to stir. Darren holds back tears during our temporary goodbye, and I promise to return as soon as possible.

Esperanza sits beside him, and I nod to her before stepping through the gate and following Hafwin up the stairs. I try to catch Cináed's eye on the way out, but he still sits facing the wall, his tense back and shoulder muscles visible through his shirt.

My chest gives another pitiful throb. *He'll never forgive me.*

But I'd never forgive myself if I'd let him die.

As we cross the quiet castle, not yet awake this early in the morning, Hafwin explains that I'm being moved into a new room and that I'm supposed to instruct her on my preferences before I move in.

"You will have a private room in the royal quarters," she says, "where the king and High Court dwell."

"But why am I being moved there?"

I stumble after her, sore from yesterday's wild ride to the moors and back. Then I remember I also sparred yesterday. Everything prior to my encounter with Naoise last night feels like it happened years ago.

Hafwin doesn't skip a beat as she says, "After Naoise was pronounced king late last night, he ordered the east wing to be redecorated and prepared to welcome his company."

My feet stop so fast it's like I've been cemented to the floor.

"What?"

Last night Cináed went to the council to try and disqualify Naoise as future king. Did he discover then that Naoise had already secured his victory?

And yet, he still came after me. Without any support from the council or hope of Naoise losing. He lied to try and save us.

And look how you repaid him.

Hafwin waits for me, her heart-shaped lips puckered in concern. "Aye, my lady. I thought you knew."

I shake my head. The numbness of denial, safeguarding me from a nervous breakdown, begins to crack.

Unbeknownst to me, I'd been holding out for a miracle. That Naoise's crown could be denied, voiding our deal. I didn't realize how strongly I was clinging to that last strand of hope until now.

Hafwin helps me the rest of the way to my new room, telling me how Naoise instructed her personally to arrange my living quarters and accommodations. She will be my head assistant, at my side whenever I need anything.

"Naoise also ordered me not to tell a single soul about your becoming queen." She links her arm with mine. Her touch steadies me, and I'm glad Naoise had the attentiveness to choose her.

"The bond we share grows stronger."

Ice creeps up my spine. *Can Naoise read my thoughts?*

I think of all the times I've caught myself daydreaming of his eyes, his voice, his scent. Despite my utter hatred of him, his power has sunk deep hooks into me. Breaking free from his orbit might be impossible, especially once . . .

Once we're married.

Hafwin continues, and I welcome the needed distraction.

Both her expression and tone are unreadable as she says, "Even Fodla and Lana do not yet know, although I assume they think you will be chosen as a summer bride.

"Naoise wishes to announce your union himself at the close of the festival, when everyone chooses a summer companion. He will be crowned that night at the Hill of Teamhair, and you will become queen."

Fodla and Lana are already in the new room, flying around the place in a blur of pastel skirts and flowing hair.

As Hafwin sits me down on a golden, high-backed chair trimmed in lace, I catch Lana's eye before she quickly returns to the window where her fingers work to hang a curtain. This is the first time I've really seen her since our run-in.

Just one more person I've managed to hurt.

Sensing my current lack of motor skills, Hafwin stands beside me, spoon-feeding me breakfast like the incompetent failure I am.

The porridge slides down my throat, and while I'm sure it's as delicious as before, all I taste is hot defeat. My swollen tongue and smarting cheek, both raw from all the times I bit them to keep my sanity, don't help the situation.

What a stellar queen you'll make, my cynical inner-critic drawls. *A helpless baby being spoon-fed and coddled.*

I imagine sitting beside Naoise on his throne, looking out at a sea of faces that despise me. I'll feel like such a fraud.

And somehow, despite all his back-alley dealings and cunning speeches, Naoise will most likely walk away unscathed. I was hell-bent on making him pay for all the hurt he's caused, and now he gets everything he wants.

The kingdom.

Cináed gone.

Me.

Fodla and Lana's conversation disrupts my thoughts.

"But I heard you danced beautifully," Fodla says, arranging clothes in the armoire. I notice this room has three of them, meaning three times the number of suffocating dresses.

Lana gives a small sigh, pausing to stare off with her large blue eyes. "I truly *felt* the music with me."

"Then you are sure to win." Fodla smiles. "At the ceremony, your name will be announced, and all the fae shall know the name of Lana of the Golden Feet."

Lana giggles and sighs again. Hafwin gives up on feeding me as I turn away, mind spinning.

"What's the prize for the events, anyway?"

Hafwin's mouth pulls to the side in a rueful smile. "Eternal glory is the only prize anyone cares for." Then she adds, "But the High Court also grants the champion of each event a single wish. As long as the wish does not harm or steal from another faery, it is usually granted."

Lana, clutching one of the gowns to her chest, twirls around dreamily. "I shall wish for a gown made of the finest blue satin and a day when all the Otherworld must dance until we cannot walk."

Fodla responds as I stand and start toward the door.

"Only one wish per event, Lana. I say choose the dress since I do not wish to dance for an entire day."

[The Sleagh Maith, or the Good People, are] terrified by nothing earthly so much as by cold Iron.

 - *The Secret Commonwealth* by Robert Kirk and Andrew Lang (1893)

My feet fly across the grass too quickly for me to feel the strange swelling sensation of the pasture rising up to carry me across the lawn.

I know from Aimsir's lessons that the storytelling event takes place out here, in front of the castle beneath the gray-blue sky. Sure enough, I can see the structure of a wooden stage—that must have been constructed overnight.

Golden tents and colorful flags flutter in the breeze. The wind catches my shirt, wafting the rich scent of B.O. up my nostrils.

In my rush out the door, I didn't even think to change out of my old sparring outfit. My tangled ponytail flops against my shoulders, and I don't even want to know how puffy and bloodshot my eyes have turned out after a night of crying.

Oh well, I groan, pushing my throbbing legs faster. *No time now.*

I reach the stage, noticing a reasonable crowd mingling on the lawn in front of the wooden structure. The beams support-ing the stage are wrapped in vines and a rainbow of vivacious flowers. Tables littered with fruit, cheese, and wine line the outer edges of the audience. I jump through them and sprint toward what looks like a group of competitors beside the stage.

Panting, I ask a random faery, "This is the storytelling competition, right?"

His eyes rove over me with a grimace, but he nods. "The last competitor just finished. The bards will announce the champion any moment now."

No.

Pushing past him, I see a shaded covering where the advisors sit chatting. Naoise is missing, but Orla makes eye contact with me. Part of me aches to see her smug expression wiped clean. I'll have to wait until Naoise announces our union. Sure, my life will be ruined. But I'll hold onto the satisfaction of watching her proven wrong. Maybe it'll lessen the sting.

Irvin, the male with the lopsided grin, waves to me. I meet him halfway.

"Irvin, has the event ended?"

"Aye." His smile falters as I draw closer, his furrowed brow crinkling the bandage on his face. "The bards are deciding now."

He motions to a table of elderly faeries, and I sprint toward them.

"Wait!" I holler, careening to a halt and slamming my hands on a table scattered with papers and scrolls. "I haven't competed."

The silver-bearded faery in front of me tilts so far back in his chair that another judge has to catch him before he falls.

"We are not accepting any more performances," says a female with soft wrinkles and loose, curly blond hair. She re-stacks a pile of papers.

"But my name's on the list." I begin digging through papers, ignoring their glares. "I swear my name is on there."

Silver-beard gathers his composure and peers at me with a frown, "No. More. Performers."

"But—"

"Let her compete."

All eyes turn toward Aimsir. She sits at the end, hands folded on the table and a firm glint in her eye.

"Aimsir, look at her," the blond female whispers, shooting a wary glance my way. "A human?"

"She is my pupil and deserves a chance to perform."

Aimsir meets my gaze, and we share a nod. My heart leaps as the rest of the judges consent.

Then Aimsir motions for me to go. "Take your place on the stage, child. Begin when you are ready."

I speed-walk toward the stage, muttering the last few lines of the memorized legend to myself. "Such is the tale of how Sétanta slew the Hound of Culain and became known as Cu-chulain, the Hound of Ulster."

How did the girl with braids pronounce that name again? "Couch-u-lane? Cow-chow-lin?"

I groan, my stomach rolling as I reach the stairs. Each step feels like an eternity. But when I stand in the center of the stage, I wish I'd had ten flights of stairs to climb.

You got this.

My vision zooms in and out of focus. My ears are ringing, and my hands clench into fists at my sides. Faeries begin to notice me, turning to watch expectantly. The harp playing in the background goes silent, and the sound of my breathing suddenly seems loud enough for everyone to hear.

A faery with a long braid stands out in the audience. Aimsir nods to me with a reassuring smile.

Tell my own story.

I think of Darren and Cináed in the dungeon. I think of the pain I've caused them both, the decisions I've made without their permission.

Hafwin's words echo back to me.

"The High Court grants the champion of each event a single wish."

If I win my last two events, I get two wishes. Something tells me they wouldn't grant a wish to kick Naoise off the throne. Hafwin said the wish can't take something from another faery. But as I ran from my room, I came up with the next best thing.

One wish to release all the humans, myself included.

And one wish to overturn Cináed's banishment from the Otherworld.

Tell my own story. That's the best chance I have at winning.

My mouth opens, and I start where I think a personal story might—with the first memory.

"There once was a young girl named Rose whose parents abandoned her in the night. When her baby brother wouldn't stop crying, she searched the cupboards, finding a box of Fruit

Loops. She fed her brother through the bars of his crib because she wasn't tall or strong enough to lift him out.

"When the food was gone, she left the house and wandered the neighborhood, looking for food but really just wanting to find her parents."

The words flow out of me like water from a faucet. I let them come, using my deeply rooted emotions to fuel the story. Saying the memories out loud feels as if I'm bulldozing into my heart, but as much as it hurts, I couldn't stop now even if I wanted to.

This has to come out.

"A neighbor called the authorities, and Rose and her brother were taken into foster care. A home for orphans.

"They were raised by more foster parents, and they lived in more foster homes than they could ever want to count. But Rose *does* count them. And she remembers every single face, every single bedroom. Except the ones that matter most."

I blink, and a fat tear jumps off my cheek. "No matter how hard she tries, she can't remember the face of her mother or the color of her father's hair. She doesn't remember if they had jobs or liked to watch the morning news. And the worst part is, even though she can't remember them, she can't make herself forget them."

The last word falls from my lips, and I exit the stage without another sound. Any reaction from the audience is lost on me. My eyes sting with unshed tears as I disappear behind the stage. If the crowd cheered, booed, or threw faerie tomatoes, I'll never know.

I toss a grape, and it drops into my cup of water with a satisfying *plink*. Fodla combs my wet hair as I pick at my food.

They still haven't chosen a winner for the storytelling competition. Apparently after I performed, the judges decided to postpone their announcement until tonight at the feast, saying they needed more time.

Waiting for this is worse than any test score I've ever agonized over. My grade on this test means everything.

I had spent the rest of the day in the dungeon with Darren. The golden-cloaked guards continue to let me come and go freely. I wish I could ask who they answer to, what side they're on.

Cináed would know, but last I saw, he hadn't budged from his slouched position all day. Es told me his cage is made of pure iron, a metal that draws strength from the fae, weakening even the strongest faeries.

Her dark eyes flickered to the cage, and she whispered, "Without iron, they would not be able to contain him like they could a lesser faery."

Markie told me later when someone brought food that the battles she fought were collectively called the War of Iarann for a reason.

"Iarann means iron," she said between bites of bread. "They learned how to use it on each other and became addicted to the bloodshed. Let's just say faeries don't die easy, and iron speeds up the process."

Sterling stared at nothing. A haunted look shadowed his features. He's grown a scraggly blond beard since the day I first saw him. It ages him in a way that scares me a little.

"Never before had the fae used steel or iron weapons," he said. "They knew the fatalities it would bring to a slowly dying race. But these wars turned gruesome, and faeries broke their own unspoken rule to achieve victory."

He wiped a hand across his face, and Es watched him with lines creasing her brow.

"That is why I was taken," Sterling said, wrapping his arms over his chest. "They knew I had studied ancient history, and they wanted my knowledge of human weapons of war."

"Swords, crossbows, battle axes," Markie drawled, then coughed into her fist. It sounded like gravel tearing up her throat.

"But those weapons were banned and destroyed," Es said, her tone ending the conversation. "Under King Rauri's rule, an era of peace began."

Sterling's response stuck with me, like a piece of unchewed food lodged in my chest.

"And under Naoise of the Western Moors, an era of shadow begins."

Fodla finishes drying my hair with a fresh towel. The heavenly floral smell of the Ura petals clings to my skin. I sit in a slip with a white fur blanket draped around my bare shoulders. A fire crackles in the hearth, filling the air with the warm scent of what Hafwin calls *turf*.

"Hardened bricks of marshland," she said as she coaxed the flames to life. "Fae of the moors gather and make the turf bricks that warm the hearths of every home."

I'd noted the distinct, earthy smell drifting around the castle before but never made an effort to find the source.

What else have I missed because I've been so focused on winning the games?

My gaze lingers on the orange flames licking across the turf. If the moors are harvesting grounds for these bricks, a misguided spark could light that place up in a second.

An image of Naoise's foster mom bursts into my mind. I see her running to the door as smoke billows around her. Her screams fill my ears.

"Róisín?"

I blink, returning to the room. All three girls are staring at me. Hafwin's amber eyes are anxious and calculating.

"Sorry." I shake my head to clear it.

Hafwin smiles, but it doesn't touch her eyes. "No, it is I who must apologize, my lady. You were unresponsive to your title, but I still should not have addressed you so informally."

"I don't want a title." I turn in the chair, facing each of them. "You can call me Róisín. Please."

Fodla smiles at me as she gathers petals from the empty tub. Lana averts her gaze, turning back to making the bed. Hafwin bites her lip but nods.

"As you wish, my la—" She stops, smiling at her near slip-up. "I mean, Róisín."

I clear my throat, feeling the need to say more. "I want you guys to know how grateful I am for all you've done for me."

An uncomfortable tension passes between them.

"No need to—" Hafwin begins.

I continue over her. "No, I'm serious. You took care of me because it was your job. But I doubt that required the level of kindness you've shown me."

Moving to one of the armoires, I throw the doors open. Ruffles explode in my face, and I spin around, looking each girl in the eye.

"I know faeries prefer actions to words." My stare falls on Lana last. Her butterfly lashes kiss her cheeks as she looks at the ground. "Take a dress. Heck, take as many dresses as you want. Wear them tonight at the feast."

Hafwin's mouth pops open in a perfect *o*. Fodla gasps, and Lana beams.

"Truly?" Lana says, excitement bubbling in her voice.

"Truly. Wear the bluest dress I have, Lana." Sobering, I add, "I don't blame you if you can't forgive me, but I hope to someday earn your trust again."

With a squeal, she kisses my cheek and throws her arms around my neck. "Oh, of course I forgive you!"

Then she falls back a step, eyes bulging. "I—I—"

A wry smile tugs on Hafwin's lips. "It seems Lana forgot you still might infect her with a *terrible sickness*."

Fodla covers her mouth to mask her snicker. Lana's skin burns, and she struggles to speak.

Quick as a flash, I lean in and plant a peck on her cheek. She inhales but doesn't retreat again as I say, "Might as well seal the deal!"

Hafwin and Fodla burst into fits of laughter. Slowly, like a small flower blooming, Lana's smile returns, and she dances around the room, giggling and kissing everyone's cheek in turn.

{ 35 }

[B]eware of eating the fairy food or drinking the fairy wine . . . [I]f a man is tempted to kiss a *Sighoge*, or young fairy spirit, in the dance, he is lost for ever—the madness of love will fall on him, and he will never again be able to return to earth or to leave the enchanted fairy palace. He is dead to his kindred and race for ever more.

- *Ancient Legends, Mystic Charms, and Superstitions of Ireland* by Lady Francesca Speranza Wilde (1887)

The chariot wheels glide across the tall grass. Two black horses with flaming orange manes and tails trot toward the distant sound of music and laughter. Crickets chirp, and a cloudless night sky twinkles with a million stars. I catch sight of glowing will-ó-the-wisps winking through the trees ahead.

I grip the chariot railing, regretting the moment I let the girls put a dress on me. My skin itches for a simple pair of leggings and a cotton tunic. At least Hafwin let me wear my boots instead of forcing me into slip-ons that pinch my toes.

Lana claimed I would regret the boots as soon as I started dancing. I was quick to inform her that while she can dance the night away if she wants, there will be zero dancing for this chick tonight.

Absolutely. Zero. Dancing.

Other than my mute driver, I ride in the chariot alone. I wanted the girls to join me. After our giggle-fest, we all helped each other get fancied up for the party. Lana found the perfect blue dress in my collection of gowns, and Fodla convinced Hafwin to let her auburn hair down from her standard updo.

But when it was time to go, they told me I had to ride alone.

"You must make an entrance," Hafwin said.

Fodla brushed glitter on my eyelids, and I tried not to sneeze. "What an entrance it will be!" she crooned. "Every faery will *long* to be you."

"Or *have* you," Lana giggled, twirling in circles.

For better or worse, I took Vera's advice and adapted parts of my party ensemble to better fit my tastes. I would say "style," but who am I kidding? Up until two weeks ago, my style consisted of hand-me-down jeans and T-shirts.

Fodla convinced me to let her trim my overgrown bangs, cropping them to the top of my eyebrows. She left the rest of my hair alone so it falls like a curtain to my shoulder blades. My hair grows crazy fast here for some reason.

Hafwin showed me drawers of sparkling tiaras and necklaces, and I chose a ringlet of gold-and-bronze leaves to match my eye shadow. When she offered me a pair of earrings to cover my unpointed ears, I shook my head.

Any faery who doesn't know I'm human by now can figure it out on their own time. I'm not hiding the obvious anymore.

Lana brought a gown from the armoire that stopped my heart. Not only was it ruffle-free, but the light, airy material felt like a cloud between my fingers. Black silk formed the base of the dress, hugging my torso and falling to my feet. Bronze-colored netting reached from the neckline, around my shoulders, and down my arms, and another slit trailed up my calf to my knee. Leaves and flowers decorated the netting in black embroidery.

Remembering the looks on their faces when I tried it on makes me feel a little less remorseful about wearing a dress. This one was *made* for me.

The horses step into the grove behind the castle, pulling the chariot into the shadows of a canopy of trees. The sounds of the feast meld with a warm aroma of nutty, flavorful foods. Fragments of colors and lights peek between the branches.

My stomach starts somersaulting, and I almost tell the driver to turn around.

What am I doing here? I hate fancy parties.

You've never been to a fancy party, wise-guy. I grip the railing tighter and brace myself for whatever's waiting on the other side of these trees.

The driver guides the horses through the last archway of mossy branches, and the scene unfolds before me. My jaw slackens, my eyes widen in disbelief, and my heart aches with wonder.

"Wow," I breathe.

The grove opens into a large meadow of clover and wild-flowers. Hanging lanterns dot the surrounding trees, casting the lawn in a soft, golden glow. Will-ó-the-wisps bob in and out of view, and the sweetest music I've ever heard caresses my ears, drifting over from a group of musicians near the tables of food.

And the *food*!

I thought the faeries went all out for every meal, but I was wrong. They saved the best for their feast.

Golden dishes glint in the light from the melting candles that line the center of the table. Each dish is piled high with roasted vegetables, potatoes, and meat. Bowls of blood-red cherries, golden apples, and fruits I don't recognize snuggle next to piping hot containers of various-colored soups.

The smell of cinnamon and nutmeg draws my eye to a steaming butternut squash. My mouth salivates.

Then I realize the chariot has stopped. I swallow and pull my eyes from the food, turning to face a crowd of gorgeous faeries. And they're all staring at me.

If the music wasn't still playing, I swear all I'd hear is crickets.

Then someone shouts, "Welcome, Róisín, to the feast of Lughnasa!"

Cheers erupt, and the musicians match the volume with a swell of music. I offer a small wave and a smile. In an instant, everyone resumes partying, and I take a deep breath as I climb down from the chariot.

I passed.

The chariot pulls away, and I'm left standing in the middle of the dance floor. Faeries twist and convulse in movements I didn't know were possible, their bodies flowing in an effort-less wave. If I try to focus on a single faery, I lose sight of them almost at once.

They act as one, like a pulsing vein. But each droplet, each individual dancer, could stand alone as the most awe-inspiring performer I've ever seen.

Without being trampled in the frenzy, I manage to cut across the meadow toward the food.

Classic wallflower tactic. Hide behind the food tables so no one asks me to dance.

Knowing I can't partake in the feast makes me wish I'd thought to pack a lunch. Of course Hafwin and the others assume I can eat fae food now that I'm living in the royal quarters. They probably can't imagine why on earth I could still want to return home.

I peer inside a pot of liquid and then wish I hadn't. The smell of spices had been coming from this hot cider. Cinnamon sticks float on the surface as I gaze at the drink. My throat dries up like a desert, tempting me to take a sip.

I rear back. *No.* No faerie food when there's a chance I can go home.

"Greetings, Róisín." Irvin sidles up beside me, wearing a pine-colored tunic. The bandage on his face was removed, revealing a prominent scar along his cheek and ending by his left eye. His light-brown hair is tucked behind a pointed ear, and he grins as he offers me a cup of the cider.

I shake my head. "No, thanks. Nice scar by the way."

He downs the cup, licking his lips for good measure. "If only you could see the warrior who gave it to me. He's far worse off."

"I saw you that night," I say. "What made you want to join the fight?"

His jovial expression grows somber. "I believe the future of this kingdom rests on those of us willing to sacrifice for a greater cause. If deceit clouds the sun, I wish to play my part in bringing the truth to light."

Then with a lopsided smile he adds, "You truly must have some wine, Róisín."

My brows rise. "*That's* wine?"

He reaches past me and ladles more into his cup. "White grapes, golden apples, and a bit of magic. The fae can make fruit wine with most anything." Leaning closer, he murmurs in my ear, "But it's the bit of magic that counts most of all."

I smile as he downs another cup. "You heard anything about the storytelling competition yet?"

"They announced the champion just before you arrived," he says, "but it's not someone I know."

My heart plummets.

I thought maybe, just maybe when they postponed the announcement, it meant I stood a chance.

Seeing my face fall, Irvin says, "Not to worry. There's always next year."

I lean into the table, lightheaded and a little nauseated. This means I have a shot at one wish. If, by some miracle, I win the sparring competitions, which will I choose?

You won't win, my logic cuts in. *It's time to face the facts.*

After losing both of the less-challenging events, maybe it makes sense to call it quits. Competing in the fights tomorrow will only sink the knife of defeat deeper.

I wince at the unintended pun and place a hand on my gut.

But my mind goes to Cináed, hunched in an iron cage that's sucking the life from his body. I imagine him wandering the globe for the rest of his existence—potentially hundreds of years. All this suffering connects back to me.

I owe it to him to at least try.

Besides, will life be worth living with Darren and Cináed gone forever? The chance to keep one of them here with me softens the ache in my chest.

If I win, I'll give my wish to Cináed. And when I'm queen, I'll make Naoise release the humans. Darren will be returned home and protected from harm. They will get their freedom back.

All but one.

Without thinking, I snatch the golden cup from Irvin's hand and ladle in some wine. The heat seeps into my hands as I breathe in the spices and take a sip.

My throat swallows, and I feel the warm liquid trickle down, down, down. Clarity explodes through my senses, just like when Naoise pressed his fingers to my head. The colors, sounds, smells that I thought I'd been experiencing were just the tip of the iceberg. I dive into the golden sea, beneath the constructs of reality, and witness the Otherworld for what it truly is.

Magical.

Irvin grins at me, taking my hand. "Here, try this too."

He leads me along the table, reaching for an apple. I bite into it, juice dripping down my chin. He hands me a spoonful of soup before my taste buds can recover from the edible gold.

Cherries. Potatoes. Lamb. Turnips. Three more cups of wine. I try it all.

As faces begin to blur, I pause, sitting on a bench. Irvin's lopsided smile appears to double. I snort into my cup. For some reason, everything is funnier after drinking faerie wine.

"I see you've been taking fine care of my bride-to-be."

That voice. It slithers down my spine, and my skin pimples with goose bumps.

Naoise places a hand on Irvin's shoulder, observing me with a small smile.

Irvin dismisses himself in a hurry. I wave to him and call, "Thanks for the wine!"

Naoise lifts me from the bench, steadying me in his arms. Why have I never let myself admire how defined his arms are?

Probably because he always wears a cloak.

At his touch, the fuzzy edges of wine settle into place again. I'm left with only the euphoria without the muddled thoughts. Hafwin told me the faerie wine would overwhelm my human senses, and I see now that she was right.

"Dance with me, my summer rose," Naoise says, clear eyes sparkling like the stars above.

A black crown rests on his head, blending in with his dark hair. A single sapphire glows at the center, bringing out the aqua hues in his eyes. He wears a satin tunic similar to Irvin's but in a blue so deep it looks black. His fitted sleeves reveal the muscles beneath the soft material.

A smile pulls on his lips at my dazed expression.

He swoops an arm around my waist, and we start to dance. Faeries move to make room, and soon we join the throng of god-like beings enraptured by the beat of the drums and the pull of the strings.

I catch sight of Hafwin and the others in the crowd, and my mouth falls open at the sight of Lana dancing. Her feet barely touch the ground as she floats and spins through the air. Her eyes are closed, yellow hair flying after her like a cape.

She really is Lana of the Golden Feet.

Wine tingles on my tongue, and I soak in every sight and sound. The gossamer gowns, the twirling hair, the sensation of weightlessness as Naoise carries us across the meadow.

I let the music hold my heart, cradling it from all obligation, worry, and expectation.

For tonight, at least, I'm free.

{ 36 }

The sound of distant drums accompanies my lonesome walk to the dungeons. It's the morning of the final sparring event and the closing ceremonies of the festival. Dawn inches over the windowsills and across the marble floors but doesn't reach my feet.

After a night reveling in the moonlight, images of glowing lights and the ghost of faerie wine on my tongue seem like far-off memories from another life. The dancing continued into the night, followed by a galloping chariot ride while faeries holding flaming branches and fists of long grass sprinted around the pasture in front of the castle.

I remember Naoise beside me, his constant presence like a shadow. He explained as we sped past these faeries that the ritual of burning branches symbolizes the end of summer. As the fire chases the sun and smoke spirals toward the heavens, we thank the gods for a blessed season and bountiful harvest.

When I heard the drums this morning, I bolted awake in my new bedroom. At first I thought the girls brought me there, but after I washed my face in a bowl of water left on the dresser, the truth came back to me.

Naoise carried me from the chariot, through the castle, and to my room. Clenching my eyes shut, I forced my bleary mind to retrace every step. My panic subsided when I remembered him setting me on my feet in front of the door, kissing my hand, and leaving without another word.

It's okay. Nothing happened.

That's not to say I didn't see plenty of other hookups taking place last night. Cináed was right when he said faeries are physical creatures. As the night wore on, the dancing mosh pit gave way to a conglomerate of make-out sessions that didn't seem to be anything but normal at the time.

Looking back now, I roll my eyes, glad Naoise knew not to go there with me. While it creeps me out even thinking it, maybe we do share some sort of . . . bond. He knew I probably would have punched him again if he tried to kiss me.

A guard nods to me as I cross into the darkened staircase and circle down to the dungeon. Blinking until my vision adjusts, I take in the familiar scene with an unexpected pang of sorrow.

For better or worse, this place has been my refuge. And since it's where Darren's been forced to lived, all of our memories from these past days are stored here.

The image of me standing in this pit weeks from today—when Darren and Cináed are gone and I've set every human free—fills me with an unbearable loneliness.

I never thought I'd say this, but I'll miss the dungeon.

Cináed's eyes meet mine. I can tell he wasn't expecting to see me down here this early. Before he can shift toward the wall again, I kneel beside the cage, my fingers longing to reach through the barbs and touch him.

"Wait," I plead. "Cináed, please."

He pauses, his brow shadowing his eyes. His sun-kissed skin seems duller, like he's losing some of his glow. My heart pulses in my throat, and my hands tremble. "I know words mean little, but I have to say that I'm sorry. For hurting you, for getting you banished, for not trusting you more. But most of all, I want to say that I'm *not* sorry I saved your life. Hate me if you want, but I'd do it again in an instant."

His gaze locks on me. Emotion thickens my voice as I rest a careful hand on the cage. "And I'll never give up until you can come back. I wanted you to know that in case—" I bite my lip, tears welling in my eyes.

I move to stand, and he says my name. The word trickles into my ears like the sweetest rainfall.

He said my name the way he says Branna's.

Holding my breath, I face him.

"Do not risk your safety. Not for me." Desperation colors his words.

His hand reaches for me, and he grits his teeth as he nears the iron. I sniff, working my hand into the cage to meet his. One of the barbs pricks my palm, but I ignore the pain.

Our hands brush, and he links our index fingers together. Resolution sets in his face, and his neon eyes glint.

"Do whatever it takes to gain your freedom, and leave the Otherworld," he says. "I will be waiting for you."

After a tearful goodbye, I wipe my face on my sleeve and step inside the large cell. Darren runs to me, wrapping his arms around me. The pressure of his head against my chest feels like home.

"Listen Darren," I say, a sob threatening to escape my throat. "Cináed will bring you back to Juliana and Howard. Tell them I made you run away with me. I'll make sure to have a constant watch on you and the house. It might get weird having invisible bodyguards only you can see, but as long as you're safe—"

"Raisin."

I look down at Darren's glistening face. His mouth is pressed in a tight line as he says, "Don't worry about me."

"I'm just sorry I couldn't find a way to come home with you."

He shakes his head, speaking with a maturity that surprises me. "Don't be sorry. You hated it there, remember? It's like the will-ó-the-wisp said—you look different here."

I brush his long locks from his forehead, thinking of all the hair and style changes he'll go through without me. All the teenage phases that I'll miss. Somehow I can't imagine him aging past adolescence. It hurts too much to think of Darren as a husband, a dad. My crumbling composure can only handle the thought of so much loss.

As I wave goodbye and the gate locks shut, Darren stands beside a crying Esperanza and a solemn Sterling. Markie and I share a mutual nod, and I turn to leave.

"I love you, Raisin," Darren calls, his voice catching.

My chest splits wide open as I say, "I love you more than anything in the world. I always will."

Darkness blankets me as I step into the stairwell. I make it to the hall before the sobs break free, wracking my body in uncontrollable waves of grief.

{ 37 }

[A]nd she felt the blood in her heart to be rising against him.

- *Gods and Fighting Men* by Lady Gregory (1904)

Faeries flock into the pastures in front of the castle. Folky music livens the atmosphere, and long tables laden with meats, roasted vegetables, and summer wine fill the air with scents of savory indulgence.

I don't let myself drool over the sight today. The constant throb of my heart calls louder than anything else. The pain centers me as I cross the lawn toward the sparring event.

Hafwin found me a pair of armored leggings and a vest to match. The extra padding helps to ease the thought of using—and defending myself from—a pointed staff again today.

Of the remaining contestants, red-beard is the only one I recognize. A female—who I heard won a wine-making com-petition—and two other males stand around sizing each other up.

All of them hold their spears with a familiarity still foreign to me, despite hours of practice. My pride beats on my will-power, begging me not to follow through with this and humil-iate myself into the next century.

Literally.

I think about Markie, who's lived here for decades—if not more—and still hasn't visibly aged past thirty. While I'm not prepared to embrace the hard facts of gaining a portion of immortality, the truth is that I've never remained in the same place long enough to put much weight on my reputation. If I messed up, I changed the scene.

Here, I won't only be outliving a normal human life, but I'll also be in the same place the entire time. Trapped in the Otherworld—a place where rumors spread faster than a marshland fire—my reputation will follow me wherever I go.

The drums beat louder, breaking through my reverie. I see Orla wrapped in a shawl of white foxtails, her curious gaze locked on me like a hawk. I ignore her mostly because of who sits beside her.

Naoise's attire today can only be described as kingly. His clothing catches the soft grays of early morning sunlight, glittering with silver threading and black jewels similar to the ones he gave me on the first night of the festival.

He leans forward when he sees me, and his crown glints as it's exposed to a ray of light that cuts across his marble skin. The harsh lighting only magnifies his flawless beauty. I swallow and extinguish the cool sparks threatening to ignite me.

Naoise might confront me before the fight begins. If he asks why I'm still competing, will he see through my lies? Is he reading my thoughts in this very moment?

Before panic takes complete control, I place iron walls around my mind and push through the gathering spectators to find the announcer.

When I return to the other competitors, they eye me like a fresh piece of meat. I hold my ground, my blood racing as I put my fists on my hips in a Wonder Woman stance. Each of them diverts their gaze in turn, last of all red-beard—whose corded arms flex as he twirls his spear around. The weapon looks like a toothpick in his meaty hands.

We stand along the fighting square marked with black lines burnt into the grass. Crossing a line carries the same penalty as dropping your spear or falling down for a few seconds.

An eager crowd presses closer to the lines, seemingly unafraid of being swung at in a fight as long as they don't miss the action. Naoise and the advisors have one of the lines to themselves, and they sit on a raised platform to get the best view.

Cold sweat gathers on my skin as my breath rushes in my ears. I stand on the black line and imagine stepping inside the ring when my name is called. My tongue feels swollen and thick in my dry mouth.

My gaze finds Irvin in the crowd. His genuine smile reminds me of his words at the feast.

"I believe the future of this kingdom rests on those of us willing to sacrifice for a greater cause. If deceit clouds the sun, I wish to play my part in bringing the truth to light."

My name is called. The announcer agreed to bump me to the top of the list. I wanted to make sure Naoise wouldn't get the chance to pull me aside before my turn arrived.

The cheering crowd and beating drums can't compete against the ringing in my ears. The defined edges of the scene fade, and I feel alone despite the throng pressing around me.

This is it.

No matter what I choose, the outcome is unknown. Either way I will likely gain and lose something.

My mind whirs. Brief moments in time replay like a sped-up slide show.

I remember all the sparring practices. The bruises on my skin whenever I took a bath. The hot shame of defeat and the sound of my name called as the winner.

I remember learning how to understand Sona. Moving with his stride. The tang of horse sweat in my nose and the gleam in his great brown eyes.

I remember rehearsing my memorized legend a million times over. The smile on Aimsir's face when I stood on the stage and started to tell my personal story. Releasing the memory festering inside me and—despite the defeat—feeling better for having spoken those words out loud.

Everything that's happened till now splays before me like a messy hand of cards. I sense the charged energy behind my next move—the pivotal card that will determine how this game ends.

I inhale through my nose. *Okay.*

As I enter the square, I see the wine-maker on the other side, pumping her shoulders and cracking her neck. I watch her movements, trying to detect the smallest weaknesses as she steps closer and takes her stance.

She heckles me as the drums fall quiet.

"What's a human doin' in these games, anyhow? You'd best give up now before you get hurt."

We circle each other once around the square as the audience laughs.

She grins, clearly enjoying the attention. "Follow me home to the countryside, wee one, and I'll trade that spear in your hands for cows' udders. Much softer a weapon, and I've been needin' a milkmaid since the last human was taken from me."

In an instant, she lunges. I reach up to block her at the last second, our spears forming an X across my face. She steps back and lunges again, and this time I meet her in the middle, using my back foot to push her closer to the line of burnt grass.

She does a duck-and-spin maneuver to get away, and we dance around the square. I can feel the audience picking up on the fact that I'm not going down easy.

Wine-maker grunts, sweat shining above her lip. I can tell she expected the fight to be over by now. I want to tell her that I wish it were over too.

I've spent too long traversing a tightrope more dangerous than the one on Cináed's boat or the black line marking the square. I'm tired of playing this endless game.

A splash of indigo in the crowd tells me that Naoise has stepped down from the advisors' seating and is standing on the edge of the square.

One glance is all it takes to see the confusion etched on his brow, the intrigue sparkling in his eyes.

He has no clue what I'm doing out here.

Wine-maker senses my distraction and swings wide, catching my sleeved arm with the point of her spear. I fall back with a cry as hot pain lances up my arm. I refuse to look at it, afraid if I see how bad the cut is I'll be tempted to favor it.

My opponent studies me, watching my arm. Warm liquid trickles down my skin, and I clench my jaw to keep from crying out again.

I take my stance, calling to her through my teeth. "Is that all you've got?"

Her nostrils flare. I move before she can position herself for my attack. Aiming for her right thigh, the one she's shielded from me in our dance around the square, I feel the spearhead catch something more dense than clothing.

My follow-through on the swing leaves me vulnerable to a blow from the side, and I dodge her blow just in time. She grunts as she tumbles forward. I shove my staff into her back, and she sinks to her knees.

The crowd erupts. I catch my breath as wine-maker pushes off the ground, facing me with rage trembling in her lips.

I sense Naoise's presence without needing to look again. He stands to my right at the edge of the line, casting a shadow onto the grass at my feet. I can almost smell his alluring scent from here.

A deep pressure builds up inside me, like a time bomb that can no longer be contained. Every second that ticks by rings in my head, fueling the wild embers about to catch fire.

Enough.

I step toward my opponent, targeting her right thigh again. As she reaches to block me, I alter my movement and come down on top of her staff, breaking it in two. Splinters litter the grass as I kick at wine-maker's gut, sending her tumbling onto her backside.

Before she even hits the ground, I spin to my right and thrust the sharp edge of my spear through Naoise's stomach.

His exhale is cool on my face, and his eyes widen. My fist presses against his gut where the spearhead stops, and hot liquid oozes onto my fingers.

"My rose—" he chokes, and before his hand can reach up to caress my face, he evaporates into a million particles of misty air and disappears like a faint purple cloud into the gray sky.

Thunder rumbles in my chest as the wind picks up in a sudden flurry. The once soft gray clouds swirl and darken, like an unseen finger is blending the day and night into one.

Eyes watch me from every direction. My hands and arms shake, reeking of blood.

My blood. Naoise's blood.

Naoise.

A cry of rage jostles me from my stupor, and I look up just in time to see a leather-clad guard swing a long knife toward my neck.

Another knife blocks the attack, and metal collides in a spray of sparks. Irvin shoves the guard backward with a roar and charges again.

I stumble into the square, and a fat raindrop hits my cheek. Thunder cracks, splitting the heavens. As fights break out in the throng around me, I see a sheet of rain move across the hills, blanketing the earth in a gray-blue curtain.

The moment it hits us, everything devolves into complete chaos.

Blinking against the downpour, I duck as a golden goblet flies over my head and hits the female behind me in the face.

Red-beard barrels past, spear raised. Irvin sinks his knife into the leather-clad guard's chest. My stomach heaves, and I vomit onto the grass.

Blood. So much blood.

As I right myself, strong hands wrap around my arm. A familiar face guides me through the frenzy, his golden cloak turned a dark sunflower yellow in the rain.

It's one of the guards loyal to Cináed.

I stumble beside him, letting him lead the way.

He stops and lifts me from the path of two screaming female faeries scratching each other's faces as they roll in the mud.

The fight dwindles the closer we get to the castle. More golden-cloaked guards glide across the pasture toward the battle, each with a tipped spear in hand.

That's when it registers that I'm still holding my spear with my good arm. I think about dropping it, not wanting to look at the thick blood darkening the wood. But I clutch it tighter, afraid of abandoning my defensive weapon when I don't know what's coming.

Cináed's guard takes us around to the side of the main gate. As we step inside the castle and leave the storm behind, the deafening silence presses on me like I'm being buried alive.

Rainwater pools around our feet as we travel down the empty hallway. One glance tells me the wound in my arm still bleeds, but not enough to leave a trail of blood. The black clouds cast everything in dark shadow, making the still-early morning feel like a heavy dusk.

The unlit hallway brings back memories. I walked down here with Cináed. This leads toward his tower.

Although he doesn't say it out loud, the caution in the guard's glowing eyes warns me not to speak.

We reach the door to Cináed's quarters, and the guard pulls a key from his cloak and unlocks it. He ushers me into the living room, closing the door behind him without making a sound.

As he turns to me, he says, "You have been here before?"

I nod.

"Then you know where Lord Cináed keeps his clothing, his various possessions." He glides to the darkened fireplace and takes a knee, his cloak hanging from his shoulders like a damp curtain. "You are to remain here for your own safety. I suggest you take what you need from Lord Cináed's belongings and pack for your journey."

I shift in the puddle forming beneath my muddy boots. The numbness in my arm is starting to fade. That, or my shock is giving way to the reality of the piercing pain.

"Journey?"

Blowing on the kindling, the guard coaxes an orange spark to life. "Aye. You are not safe in the castle. Those loyal to Naoise will seek revenge."

The face of the leather-clad guard, blood squirting from his mouth, flashes in my mind. I move to sit stiffly on the couch, my staff propped on my trembling knees.

I'm still not safe. Even with Naoise gone, I'm never safe as long as I'm in the Otherworld.

"I'm taking my brother from the dungeon, and we're going home," I say. "I know a portal to the human realm."

"Knowing where the portal is located is not the same as reaching it without being hunted down."

The guard stands. The warm scent of rich earth pulses in the fireplace, blending with the other smells in this room I've come to love.

I want to argue that I don't care if I die trying to escape. Better that than to die hiding in plain sight.

Instead I ask, "Where's Cináed?"

"I do not know. Last I saw he was imprisoned in the dungeons, but that was before you altered the playing field." The guard watches me steadily, hand resting on the golden sword on his hip. Something like respect tinges his next words.

"A human child challenging a powerful shadow faery. No seer could have prophesied such an act of courage. May the Tuatha not curse me for saying it, but Manannan, the god of trickery himself, could learn a thing or two from a cunning creature such as your ladyship."

My lips pull into a taut line.

The guard moves toward the door. "As I said, prepare to travel at a moment's notice. If Lord Cináed has not been freed from his prison by now, I would like nothing better than to do the honor myself."

"Wait." I move to stand but realize my mistake. My legs feel as useful as melted rubber. "Thanks for saving me back there. I hope I get the chance to show my gratitude someday."

He offers a small smile and reaches for the doorknob. In a somber tone, he says, "Siochan leat, my lady. You do not realize the gift of hope you have given us. May your legend live on in the histories of the fae forever."

The door closes, and I'm left alone.

Do not expect direct answers to direct questions. Do expect indirect answers to indirect questions.

- *The Shadowhunters Codex* by Cassandra Clare and Joshua Lewis. (2013)

I pace beside the glowing embers that remain in the fireplace. My drenched clothes are drip-drying across a chair, and I hug my loose tunic around my body. Cináed's scent—sunshine and ocean salt—clings to the soft material.

Hopefully my leggings can dry before someone comes for me. One glance at Cináed's armoire told me his svelte leggings wouldn't fit over my full hips.

After cleaning and bandaging my wound—a deep cut along my bicep, but nothing that won't heal—I found a leather pack in his bedroom upstairs and filled it with a few things we might need. As the painful minutes turn to excruciating hours, I come closer and closer to snatching the pack, finding Darren, and running for it.

But fear traps me. I've already tempted fate enough for one day. The guard said faeries will be searching for me. And who knows what kind of scene I could find downstairs.

Is the anti-Naoise faction strong enough to stage an uprising and take control of the castle? What will happen to the advisors loyal to Naoise? Is Cináed free? What about the humans?

The questions whirl around my head in a never-ending circle. Hours of waiting, and I've come to zero conclusions. How can I when I'm isolated up here—high enough above the main castle that I wouldn't know if a war waged beneath my feet.

The door behind me shuts with a *click.*

I spin around. Orla stands in the room, tucking a slender stick into the folds of her foxtail shawl.

My mouth works, but no words come. *I know I locked the door.* She wouldn't have a key, would she?

"Sit."

Her order knocks me back. She breaks in here without permission and still gets to call the shots?

Frowning, I plant my feet. "What are you doing here?"

"I will not have this conversation on foot." She smoothes a stray hair from her almost-frazzled updo. "Sit, girl."

Hesitating, I keep my distance as I choose a seat that allows me a clear shot to the door. She sinks into the couch across from me with a sigh that seems to emanate from deep in her chest.

"What mayhem," she says. "The kingdom lies in complete disarray. It will take weeks, nay, months to restore order."

Those words should sound more devastated than they do coming from her. I peer at her, not trusting the pleasure she's finding in all of this.

"Why are you here?

"You were selected as the champion of the sparring event. I have come to award you a single wish."

My mouth falls open. "I *what?*"

Another deep sigh. "I do not have time for this, Róisín. With everything going on, you are lucky I'm offering this at all."

Hearing her say my name startles me. I guess I assumed she didn't know it, or wouldn't care to remember it, anyway.

I want to ask why she's offering me anything but a death sentence. She should hate me even more than she did before.

She continues before I can respond. "I do warn you to choose your wish wisely. Word has spread of your deeds, and it is common knowledge that a human could not inflict such harm on a shadow faery."

I work through her words like I'm wading in mud. She just openly admitted that Naoise was a shadow faery.

Leaning forward slightly, she says, "You are a half-breed, as we call them. Born of both human and fae bloodlines. Now that you know, the threat you pose to our race increases tenfold. It would be wise of you to leave the Otherworld and never return."

A silent pause.

I suck in a steadying breath, glad I'm sitting down so I don't crumple like a piece of paper.

"You are a half-breed."

My throat constricts. I tuck my trembling hands beneath my thighs.

"So you're saying I should use my wish to get home?"

"I strongly advise that, yes." Her sharp gray eyes glint. Like a hawk about to strike. "There are those who would end your life if given the chance. Any moment now, perhaps."

Alarms go off in my head. I don't need to know rocket science to catch her foreboding warning.

Orla could kill me right now.

My tongue feels like lead. "Then I wish for all thirty-eight prisoners in the castle to be cleared of their charges, set free, and escorted to the nearest portal in safety."

She sits back, crossing her legs. "Thirty-eight?"

"Assuming Cináed is still locked up."

The way she lifts her eyebrows, her mouth twitching, sends heat to my cheeks.

I'd give most anything to read her thoughts—to see past the convoluted bull-crap. But I'd give everything to leave now and never have to see her face again.

"So?" I say. "We have a deal?"

She makes a noise to herself and meets my gaze. "Yes, we have a deal. An escort will bring you to the dungeons, where you can collect the prisoners and be gone. No one will touch you until you reach the doorway into the human realm."

Again with the underhanded warnings. I scowl. "Are you threatening to kill us once we reach the portal?"

Her smile doesn't reach her cold eyes. "I merely suggest that you, Róisín, depart this world as quickly as possible."

Okay. Maybe she *does* hate me even more than she used to.

Clenching my teeth, I stand and say, "Then there's no time to waste."

Orla makes me wait until dark, and an escort of five guards brings me to the dungeon.

We're forced to take the back route when we see that the hallway to the dungeon stairs is packed with guards. I recognize the thug who held a knife to my back standing with the others. A hound dozes on the floor beside him.

Instead, we access the pit from the trapdoor. Once I'm lowered inside, I call to the group, and we begin lifting people out.

Es told me Cináed was released hours ago by the guard who helped me. I grip Darren's hand like a vice and tell myself Cináed will be alright.

Orla only assigned five guards to protect thirty-seven humans. It's a loophole I should have caught, and it gets us into trouble before we reach the outer castle walls.

A handful of faeries see us coming and gather to block the path. With so many people, it's not like we have the gift of stealth on our side.

I shield Darren, moving toward the front of the group. Our escorts try reasoning with the blockade, but one of them points at me with a grin.

"That's her," she says, and I don't know why I didn't recognize Blondie sooner. Maybe because her hair is down instead of pulled into her typical braid. "That's the treacherous whore."

When the guards unsheathe their swords, the blockade moves enough for us to begin leading a few people through, I sense that Ethne and her cohorts won't be letting me get away so easy.

Esperanza takes Darren through, and I grip the spear, caked in Naoise's blood, and stare Ethne down.

"Let me through," I snarl.

"Not without a fair fight, vermin." She spits in my face. "You might have bested me once, but when I saw you stab the king, I realized that you win because you fight dirty."

Markie stands beside me. She and Sterling are the only ones who haven't passed through the archway and out of the castle.

In a motion almost too fast for a human, Markie grabs a handful of Blondie's hair and yanks her down, shoving a knife against her white throat.

"Listen here, you maggot," Markie breathes. "Let us pass, and I won't spill your blood with this iron blade."

Her blade is nothing more than the dull butter knife. But Ethne can't see it, and I don't doubt that, with enough force, Markie could turn it into a weapon. Especially if it really is made of iron.

Ethne concedes, shrieking for her friends to move aside and let us through. Markie drags her along until we're well out of range of the castle. When we reach the other humans, she dumps her on the grass.

"Run, little faery," Markie barks. Ethne scrambles up and sprints into the night. Markie turns to me with a satisfied gleam in her hooded eyes.

"Let's get the hell out of here."

{ 39 }

And Ciabhan got into the curragh, and his people said: "Is it to leave Ireland you have a mind[?]" "It is indeed," he said, "for in Ireland I get neither shelter nor protection." He bade farewell to his people then, and he left them very sorrowful after him, for to part with him was like the parting of life from the body.

- *Gods and Fighting Men* by Lady Gregory (1904)

Darren and I step onto the sidewalk. I wave to the nice lady who picked us up on the side of the road and drove us here. When I told her we were tourists who had just been camping for a couple weeks and needed a ride to the airport, I could tell she had strong doubts about my story.

And who could blame her?

It isn't every day you see two traumatized teenagers hitchhiking through the Irish countryside. It doesn't help that Darren hasn't bathed or seen daylight in weeks and that I'm wearing a grungy medieval outfit with blood seeping through the bandages on my arm.

But despite our frightening appearance, the lady took us along, saying she was already on her way to Dublin to visit her sister.

The airport bustles with activity. We pause in front of the automatic doors, and I reach for Darren with my good arm, taking his hand.

A crisp bite in the air reminds me we still need to figure out how much time has passed. I wanted to ask the lady who drove us here what today's date is, but I thought better of it.

I spent most of the car ride wracking my brain for a more believable story that we can tell the authorities. Saying we were kidnapped—which is the easiest way to describe what happened—would lead to a dumpster fire in a hurry. That's not the kind of thing you claim without any facts to prove it.

And I couldn't imagine trying to prove our story to a group of real-world adults.

I also considered not telling anyone anything, instead just calling the Robertses to buy our tickets and taking the rest in stride. Then I remembered that flying internationally requires a passport and who knows what else. I've never flown at all before. Navigating this mess is more than daunting.

Not as daunting as competing in a faerie festival.

I grip Darren's hand tighter. We made it this far, and that's all that matters.

We step inside, and a rush of stale air greets my nose. Being around so many average people—none of whom look like they'll either break your heart or eat you for breakfast—is more comforting than I'd expected.

Just average people, going about their average lives.

No weapons, no hidden agendas, no mind games.

How *refreshing.*

Darren has been on edge ever since we arrived in modern civilization again. A name is called over the intercom, and he leaps into the air.

"Hey there, big guy." I take his hand with a comforting smile. "You've gotten taller."

It's true. He grew at least an inch, if not more, in two weeks of faerie time.

He licks his lips, his eyes wide.

"What now?" he asks.

I don't respond because I'm still struggling to figure it out. An information desk catches my eye.

I step up, shielding my bandaged arm with my other hand, and offer a polite smile to the girl behind the counter. "I'm wondering if you can answer a few questions for me."

The spray-tanned brunette returns the smile, revealing a smudge of pink lipstick on her tooth. "I can indeed."

Glancing at Darren, I inhale and ask the safest question first. "When's the next available flight to Boston?"

The girl types on her computer. "There might be a couple of last-minute cancellations . . . yes, there's a flight at 1:15 from Dublin to Boston with two available seats."

I catch sight of a tiny calendar by the computer.

November.

We've been gone for four months.

The girl blinks at me above the computer, probably wondering how old I am. "Would you like to book them?"

Still reeling about the difference in faery and human time, I bite my lip.

About that . . .

I feel something slip into my hand and look down. Two small, blue booklets are pressed into my palm.

Turning around, my heart stops as a familiar pair of sea-green eyes meet mine.

Cináed's skin has an almost translucent glow. Being able to see both his visible and invisible forms at the same time reminds me of my encounter with the double-faced bus driver. Two versions of the same being meshed into one.

And only I can see both.

Why is Cináed here? And in disguise?

"Miss?"

I face the girl behind the counter and open one of the booklets. A shiny credit card winks at me.

"Y-yes," I stammer, handing her the card. "Yes we would like to purchase two tickets, please."

As the girl enters the information, I look at Darren, making sure he's seeing what I'm seeing. His bug-eyed stare confirms it.

Cináed is using his faerie glamour, and apparently his money, to get us home.

With two tickets in hand, we leave spray-tan girl and start toward security. As soon as we're out of earshot, I whip around. "How did you find us?"

Even through the faerie glamour, his dimpled grin melts me.

I'd started to miss him already.

"I have my ways," he says.

"Raisin," Darren mutters from the side of his mouth, "you look like a total weirdo."

Right. Cináed's invisible.

I drop my gaze and whisper to Cináed under my breath. "And the money . . . how did you pay for our flights?"

"Faeries have gold. Humans pay money for gold." He shrugs. "Believe me, the cost of the tickets did not scratch the surface of my resources."

I exhale, feeling like a bowling ball has been rolled off my chest.

Cináed came. He knows what to do. We're going to make it home.

The three of us cross through the airport toward the first security checkpoint. Cináed walks beside me, his hand brushing mine every now and then.

Before getting in line at security, Cináed tells us to enter a bookshop. The dude reading behind the counter doesn't look up as we step behind a shelf.

Cináed shrugs his jacket off and as he hands it to me, it turns visible in the blink of an eye.

"Cover your bandages," he says, eyeing my arm with a furrowed brow. "And Darren, turn your shirt inside out to hide the stains."

We obey as I ask, "What about passports? The ones you handed me are blank."

Darren tugs his shirt back on and Cináed motions for us to follow. He answers in my ear, "They are only blank unless made to appear otherwise."

Stepping in line, I open the booklets again. My fingers flip through blank page after blank page.

There's no way they'll let us through. *Right?*

I look up to see Cináed winking at Darren and nodding toward the man in line in front of us, before flicking the man's hat off his head. Darren snickers as the man fumbles for his hat, spinning around to spot the unseen culprit.

Once the man turns back around, I whisper to Cináed, "How will you use glamour if I'm the one holding the passports?"

"Oh, it will not be *me* using the glamour."

Dread drops like a deadweight and lands in my boots. My mouth dries up and I feel a flicker of panic in my gut.

"No," I shake my head, trying to hand the booklets to his invisible form, "no I can't do that."

Cináed's eyes sparkle as he focuses on me. "Róisín, you are capable of whatever you set your mind to." Then in an ominous tone that sends shivers down my arms he adds, "There is a reason you were blessed with the Sight. Do not underestimate that."

The man in front of us moves up the line and we follow. I catch a glimpse at his open passport in his hand. With surprising clarity, I take note of each detail. The placement of the words, the image of his face.

Cináed's voice seems to come from everywhere at once. Like an ocean breeze rushing around me. "Imagine what you wish it to be, and it will be."

One of the security workers motions us forward. I swallow hard and walk with Darren to the podium.

"Passports please," the lady says.

Shoot!

I glance at the passports, realizing she'll take them from me. How is the glamour supposed to work now?

I hand her the booklets, hoping she can't see me shaking. In my mind I picture the passports being filled out. One for Darren and one for me. Holding my breath, I stare at the first page she flips to.

There, in printed ink, is my passport information. Like it's been there all along.

She checks Darren's and waves us through. I walk in a daze, my mind working fast to replay memories.

All the times I've seen or heard unexplainable things that no one else could.

Orla's and my conversation in Cináed's room.

Acknowledging that I'd eaten fae food when I stepped through the portal and, to my complete amazement, having nothing happen.

As the list grows, I'm forced to see these memories for what they are. Clues leading me to my past—to Darren's and my parents.

To the fact that I could be half-fae.

We pass through several more checkpoints. All the while Cináed keeps a close watch on us, offering instruction when needed. And whenever someone asks for our passports, my confidence in manipulating the booklets' appearance increases a little more each time.

When we finally reach our gate number, Darren takes his turn in the restroom and I divert my gaze from Cináed, not ready for another goodbye.

"Róisín," he says.

I look up and see that he's dropped the invisibility guise. He keeps his subtle glow and neon eyes hidden in glamour, appearing as the adorable, curly haired, study abroad student that I fell for so long ago.

Before he can say something to make me cry, I say, "Thank you." My smile doesn't reach my eyes.

Too much has happened too fast, and a bone-deep exhaustion settles in my chest. Every time I think of the Otherworld, it seems to have slipped further away from me. Like I'm already forgetting. The thought scares me more than it should.

What if I am part faery?

Cináed quirks an eyebrow. "What did I tell you about verbal expressions of gratitude?"

"But I don't have anything of value," I protest, gesturing to my simple outfit. I left the pack of provisions with Markie and the others who stayed behind in the Otherworld—too old to step foot across the doorway without dying. "Unless you want your tunic and jacket back, I have no way to repay you."

A slow smile spreads across his face. I'm glad to see his sun-kissed skin no longer dulled by the iron cage.

"There *is* one way you could repay me," he drawls with a playful smirk.

I bite my lip, face flushing.

He leans closer, hands resting on my hips. The smell of clean, summer air floats around us. He rests a gentle hand against my face and I close my eyes, committing his touch to my memory.

His lips caress my mouth, tasting sweeter than faerie wine. For a moment, I let it all fade—the people walking past, wheeling their luggage behind them. The flight attendant on the intercom. The fear of never seeing Cináed again.

The time to board arrives. Darren gives Cináed a hug and moves toward the boarding line.

I wrap my arms around Cináed before he can see the tears in my eyes. Sniffing against his chest, I whisper, "Stay safe, and don't forget me."

"I will come for you, Róisín," he murmurs, his face tucked into my hair. "I promise."

Before I can ask what he means, he pulls away and fades into the crowd of people waiting to board. I stare after him before finding Darren.

At the end of the ramp, I feel someone's eyes trained on me. I turn and see him, hands in his pockets—invisible to all but me.

When Cináed knows that I've seen him, he tries to smile and wave, but emotion clouds his face and pulls on the corners of his mouth.

A fragment of my heart falls to my feet, and I know it will remain with him, belong to him, for as long as I'm still breathing.

Then I turn and follow Darren onto the plane.

ABOUT THE AUTHOR

Logan Miehl loves writing fantasy from the heart. When she's not writing, you can find her curled up with her cat and a good book, hiking in the mountains, or befriending a tree. She draws inspiration from nature, and her lasting belief that magic is real.

The Faerie Festival Series was inspired by her travels in Ireland and her studies of Celtic myth.

You can find her online at www.loganmiehl.com and on Instagram @loganmiehl.